Denny's blade leaped forward, into his foe's belly. Somehow he quelled the reflex to thrust and twist that would have strewn entrails on the sand. Even so the netman crumbled to the floor of the arena, bleeding heavily.

A roar from the crowd caused Denny to pause and look up.

The fallen netman held up his hand in the stylized plea for mercy. If it was awarded him, the ring attendants could probably get the man to the clinic in time to save his life. Denny found himself hoping desperately that mercy would be granted to his fallen foe.

But this was the final day of the games, and the bloodlust was on the crowd in full flood. They screamed, their thumbs jabbing down, or inward toward their own vitals, as though gesturing *here, here, give it to him here*.

MACK REYNOLDS
WITH MICHAEL BANKS

SWEET DREAMS,
SWEET PRINCES

BAEN BOOKS

SWEET DREAMS, SWEET PRINCES

Copyright © 1986 by The Literary Estate of Mack Reynolds

Portions of this volume appeared in substantially different form *Analog Science Fiction/Science Fact* © 1964 by The Cónde Nast Publications, Inc.

A Baen Books Original

Baen Publishing Enterprises
260 Fifth Avenue
New York, N.Y. 10001

First printing, October 1986

ISBN: 0-671-65595-7

Cover art by Vincent Di Fate

Printed in the United States of America

Distributed by
SIMON & SCHUSTER
TRADE PUBLISHING GROUP
1230 Avenue of the Americas
New York, N.Y. 10020

☐ CHAPTER ONE ☐

The amphitheater covered an area of some ten acres, slightly more than seven hundred by six hundred feet. The arena itself, the fighting arena, was two hundred eighty by one hundred seventy, surrounded by spacious and comfortable seating facilities for approximately fifty thousand persons. On an occasion such as this they packed in more than double that.

There were those who disgustedly contended that the place was just too big. A fan in the upper tiers of seats could hardly make out individuals in the fights below, and could certainly not follow the more delicate nuances of combat. But the arena never failed to play to a packed house—a packed and overpacked house. Ultimately, those who were allowed to buy seats were chosen by lottery. According to the oddsmakers there was one chance in a hundred of winning the right to an upper-tier seat, one in a thousand of actually getting one along the podium.

On this, the final day of the nation's ultimate gladiatorial contest, the arena was overflowing; more

1

than a hundred thousand fracas fanatics broiled in the hot Texas sun.

As Dennis Land looked up from the shade of a recess behind the Portal of Life, where he waited for the grand parade, he wondered briefly how many of those squeezed tightly in the aisles, sitting on steps, or jammed into the area supposedly reserved for the band had gotten in through bribery or trickery. He had heard of scalpers getting as much as a month's dividend for upper-tier seats. One brave entrepreneur had forged scores of tickets, all for the same choice seat located within a few yards of the Master of the Games. He had made himself a fortune before, by incredible coincidence, approaching the bearer of the real ticket.

Denny was less than happy about the situation confronting him. Today's scenario—the final battle of the National Games—was that of Secutores versus Retiarii, and he'd been unlucky enough to draw the equipment of a Secutor. He was fully aware of the low percentage of success among Secutores. The cognoscenti would offer odds of five to three in favor of a Retiarius against a Secutor, all other things being equal. And all other things were equal today.

Yet he'd survived the week—that meant a good deal. However, so had all the rest of the fighters lining up for the parade, half of them equipped as Retiarii, half as Secutores.

As a Secutor, his equipment consisted of a breastplate, helmet, and armor on his right arm and left leg. His left arm and right leg were left bare for the sake of agility. He carried a shield and a short sword, but was considerably less mobile than a

Retiarius, who was equipped solely with net and trident. And there lay the disadvantage—the weight of his armor hampered his mobility.

He cast his eyes back over the rest—twenty-four of the most excellent physical specimens in the land. Within the hour, at least half of them would be either dead or disabled as a result of the wounds.

And he was one of them. Dennis Land—quiet, unassuming history professor—was among the top professional killers in the land. As he had done too many times during the past week, he stopped to wonder at the events that had brought him here, to the national games. It had all started as a research project . . .

The Secutor next to him growled, "When's that damned band going to start playing? I'm getting worn out just carrying this tin shop."

A Retiarius behind them laughed. "In that case, I hope we stand here a couple more hours!"

Denny glanced at the Secutor, and recognized him by his short, stocky build. From time to time during the games they'd been thrown together. The day there had been a mock battle between the Macedonians and the Persians, they had stood side by side in the Macedonian phalanx. And the day of the chariot fights, the other had been his charioteer—and a good one, too; the casualties taken by both sides had been brutal, but they'd managed to survive. A bond had formed between the two, although they were strangers outside of the games.

Denny nodded in greeting. "Last day, Zero. Good luck. I hope you make it."

The other looked at him. It was hard to make out features through the helmet slits. He said, "Denny, eh? Same to you. But it's going to be rugged. The first day and the last day are the worst. That gong won't sound until half of us are sprawled out on the sand—a full half of us."

Just then the band struck up a lilting marching tune. One of the field crew, standing away from the group of combatants, called out, "All right, lads, let's go! Make this a good one. The crowd wants action."

"Care to join us, you fat funker?" Zero growled at him.

They swung across the sand-covered arena floor in close-order march, moving in perfect time to the music, and deployed before the judge's stand, facing the Master of the Games. He was flanked today by prominent citizens, both male and female, whose polite applause was drowned by the roar of the multitudes in the stands.

The Secutores lifted high their swords, and the Retiarii their tridents, as they chanted in unison.

"We who are about to die . . ."

The Master of the Games gestured with a modishly.limp hand, knowing his voice would never carry above the yelling, screaming fans. A trumpet sounded, and both band and crowd fell silent.

The games were opened.

The fighters scattered across the sand-covered arena floor at random, according to plan. Some took position near a wall, some out in the open, according to personal preference. Denny jogged over to the relatively empty area opposite the judges' stand and looked about.

A Retiarius Denny vaguely remembered seeing from time to time during the past week approached from his left flank. "All right, friend, let's go," his self-appointed opponent snapped. "It's going to be a long, long time before that gong sounds, and there's no use stalling."

Denny looked at him. "Nobody's stalling, fisherman. Let's see what you can do with that net."

All about them, netmen and Gauls—the popular idiom for Secutores—were squaring off. At the edge of his vision, Denny could make out a hapless Secutor already caught in the meshes of a net, struggling to extract himself before the net's owner could dispatch him with his sharp, three-pronged trident.

Denny shifted his shoulders within the breastplate and armor on his right side, then took stronger hold of his sword and shield. He carefully sized up his own opponent. The man's name was Philip something-or-other; or perhaps Philip was his last name. He'd won through to the last day of the games, which automatically rated him one of the most efficient fighters in the nation. But for that matter, it came to Denny again almost as a surprise, so had he. He, too, was one of the most efficient killers in the land.

Unfortunately, Denny had spent more time training as a Retiarius, with net and trident, than as a slower-moving Secutor. It was sheer bad luck for him to have been selected to take this part. But at least he knew all the tricks of the netman's trade and could watch out for them.

And now Philip was circling him slowly, net held for the cast. The net was made of heavy mesh and fringed with small lead weights, so that when thrown it would open up and settle quickly. While it looked innocent enough, as weapons go, it was anything but. The unsophisticated spectator in the stands, although there were few of those in the amphitheater today, might think the highly armored, sword-bearing Secutor was the more satisfactorily equipped of the two, but Denny knew otherwise—and so did Philip. Denny tracked the movements of the Retiarius carefully, angling so that his side, rather than his front or rear, was always presented to his foe.

Philip made a tentative cast, and Denny took a quick step backward, catching the edge of the net on his shield and tossing it off. Had there been time, he would have taken a slash at it with his sword; sometimes it was possible to cut up a net to the point that it became useless. But his opponent was too sharp to give Denny that kind of time— the net was cast and withdrawn with equal rapidity.

Philip growled, "Come on, fish. Let's get going. You heard what the man said—this crowd wants action!"

Denny was too old a hand to exhaust himself chasing his lightly clad opponent. Nor would he be baited. He grinned, shaking his head. "Come in and get me, fisherman. I'm—"

The other, seemingly rearranging his net, suddenly cast it, underhand. Denny was caught off guard by the move, and stumbled awkwardly, too late to avoid it. The cast was a perfect one, impossible to avoid. He lashed out wildly with both shield and sword, but the mesh was about him in a confusion that he knew from experience would take long, desperate moments to get out of.

The Retiarius was moving in fast, trident raised. Denny cut at the net again, slashing it in several places. Seconds were precious. If he could just . . .

The trident darted at him, struck his wrists sharply, and Denny dropped his sword. In an agony of realization that matched the sudden numbness in his wrists, Denny knew that he was lost. He stumbled back, dodging another thrust from the trident, freed himself from the net and tossed it away.

He looked desperately for his sword and spotted it, next to Philip's feet. The Retiarius smiled and gave the sword a kick which sent it spinning away.

Denny's eyes darted from his sword to his opponent as Philip moved in for the finish, stalking the unarmed fighter warily. Philip's lips were pulled back over his teeth in a killer's snarl as he muttered, "This is it."

The Retiarius lunged, and time slowed for Denny. During what seemed long minutes, he conceived and discarded several plans. Then, it came to him. In a fog, Denny stooped, grabbed up a handful of sand, and threw it even before he stood up. It hit Philip's eyes and the Retiarius made a quick double sidestep, clawing at his eyes with one hand while waving his trident with the other.

Denny was already lunging through the sand toward him. Philip slipped, fell to one knee, and shook his head as he rubbed his left arm frantically across his burning eyes.

Denny was on him a heartbeat later. He brought

the shield down on the other's neck with crushing force.

Without bothering to check whether his opponent was dead, Denny darted to his sword and scooped it up.

He took stock. Somewhere in the fight he'd taken two or three minor jabs from the trident. He couldn't remember when, now. In combat, wounds are seldom noticed. The pain comes later—if there is a later.

Of the twenty-four men who had marched into the arena a few minutes before, some four or five had already been eliminated from the fray. Ring attendants were hauling two of them out through the Portal of Death.

Most of the combatants were locked in individual fights, although in one case two Secutores had combined forces and were fighting back to back against the netmen who were tormenting them. Two or three fighters had, like Denny, dispatched their men and were standing momentarily alone and uncommitted. This wouldn't last long, Denny knew. In short order, the screaming mob in the stands would demand that they face one another.

As was to be expected, there were more Secutores eliminated than Retiarii. The slower-moving swordsmen were providing easy game for the netmen. And now, not far from where he had so shortly before terminated his own fight, Denny caught sight of a fellow Secutor at bay, trying to fight off a pair of netmen.

There was nothing against it in the rules; this was a fight of elimination. If the Retiarii eliminated all of the Secutores, they would be obliged to fight it out among themselves, if the gong had failed to sound by that time. Meanwhile, so long as the Secutores continued to survive at all, the Retiarii could devote their efforts to eliminating these easier opponents.

The single swordsman was in a hard way, trying to avoid two nets at once while dodging the two tridents continually darting at him. He had maneuvered to a spot fairly near the podium wall so that he could at least have his back secure, but it was only a matter of moments before he would be overwhelmed.

This was none of Denny's concern. It was each man for himself, and the sooner others were eliminated, the sooner the gong, the desperately longed-for gong, would sound.

But he found himself slogging through the sand to aid the hapless Secutor. The netmen, intent on their prey and on the immediate brink of success, failed to see him coming up from behind.

The Secutor thrashed wildly with shield and sword, entwined now in both nets. He hacked desperately, hopelessly, as he dodged the needle-point tridents again and yet again.

And then Denny was on them from behind. This was no time for niceties. Nor was there time to appreciate the show that he was putting on for the sweating masses in the stands. If the two netmen eliminated the Secutor, they would surely turn on Denny.

Guided perhaps by instinct, the Retiarius whirled at the shout. As he did, Denny's sword leaped forward, in jab rather than slash, and the blade slipped into his new foe's belly, ramming upward.

The netman crumbled to the sand floor of the arena, bleeding heavily.

His companion, aware now, wide-eyed and netless, hesitated, then retreated to the wall to reorganize.

A roar from the crowd caused Denny to pause and look up.

The fallen netman held up his hand in the stylized plea for mercy. If it was awarded him, the ring attendants could probably get the man to the arena clinic in time to save his life. Denny glanced at the wounded man, now curled in agony. He found himself hoping desperately that mercy would be granted to his fallen foe.

But this was the last of the games, and the bloodlust was on them in full flood. Was it because there would be no slaughter the following day, that they now must quaff the cup of death to its dregs? Was it because this fallen fighter had survived for the full week, had survived a hundred deaths, and had made it to the finals that he must die? Did the crowd find intensity of pleasure in the fact that he had found defeat so near success?

They screamed, their thumbs jabbing down, or inward toward their own vitals, as though gesturing *here, here, give it to him here*.

There was no doubt about their desire. Denny looked toward the judge's box. The Master of the Games gave the signal of death. There was no ignoring the command—he was liable for penalties up to and including death if he compromised the fray. Despite the emotions battling within him, he bent over and cut the netman's throat, as quickly and cleanly as possible.

His fellow Secutor, who had managed to untangle himself from the the two nets, turned to Denny and chuckled, "Thanks!"

It was Zero.

"Let's polish off this other one," Denny said, "before he finds his net." The Retiarius, apparently still confused by Denny's sudden attack, was edging toward them, eyeing the nets that Zero had tossed away.

Zero, leaning toward him as if to see behind the mask, said, "Oh, it's you, Denny. Well, thanks again!"

They set upon the remaining Retiarius mercilessly. He backed against the wall, glaring defiance at them. Equipped now with only the trident, he jabbed once, twice, three times, first toward Denny, then at Zero.

The jabs continued as they came in from opposite sides, bent forward and a bit low, their shields before them to take his thrusts.

He was almost within range of their short swords when he slipped and fell. The swordsmen dashed in for the kill.

As they closed in, the Retiarius thrust wildly and caught Denny in his unprotected right thigh. Denny jerked back, but not before the barbed prongs of the trident bit deep into his flesh. He found himself on one knee before he knew what had happened.

Zero finished the netman off, then turned quickly to Denny. "How bad did he get you?"

"Pretty bad," Denny grunted.

Zero's eyes darted quickly around the arena. There seemed to be more men on the sand than still standing. He grimaced. In the stands, the mob was still screaming frenzied instructions at them.

Denny struggled to his feet, despite the growing weight of his armor and the sharp pain in his leg. On this day, there would be no wound sufficient to allow a fighter to drop out of the fray, and if he went down, he would get the same treatment as the fallen netman moments ago. Thumbs down.

"Well, no gong so far," he muttered to Zero. "Let's get over there and see if we can find somebody in worse shape than we are." He tried to grin, but failed. "I'm about at the stage where a sixty-year-old dwarf could take me with a slingshot!"

Zero replied, his voice low. "No. Listen, Denny, you've had it. You can hardly walk. That gong is about to go, any minute now.

"Here's the plan: you and me—we'll fight right here. We can fake it until the gong sounds."

Denny could hear the crowd screaming for blood. He glanced up for a moment, and felt an urge to spring into the stands and give them what they wanted. Directly above him, a portly citizen was literally frothing at the mouth as he hoarsely exhorted Denny to kill the man whose life he'd just saved. A young woman at his side waved her hands in a gesture that was at once obscene and insulting. Their eyes were glazed over with a lust that was part drug-induced, part a result of the excitement, and part . . . something else.

Denny shook his head and looked away. Zero stood waiting, his sword and shield held ready. Denny wondered briefly if the other was setting him up for an easy victory. He'd saved Zero from the two netmen, but they were bound by the rules of the arena to fight any comer, and if they failed to do so the ring attendants themselves would finish them off.

But possibly Zero was right. It just might be that enough of their fellows had been eliminated that the Master of the Games would signal an end to the carnage. After all, the ultimate purpose here was to find the ten best combat men in the nation. The Master wouldn't let it continue until none at all survived.

Besides, he had nothing to lose now.

"Let's go," Denny said. He shifted his shoulders again in the heavy breastplate, grasped his sword, and advanced his shield and armored left leg. As he took the fighting stance, he felt the blood flowing from his thigh, and the weakness moving up from his leg to the rest of his body.

That portion of the crowd nearest them was still screaming hysterically. They had seen one Secutor rescued from a seemingly impossible situation by his fellow as the two combined to eliminate the two netmen. Now that team was at swordpoints, fighting it out.

Zero, even as he came in, whispered harshly, "Make it look good, or they'll see it. Then we'll both be sunk."

Denny nodded slightly, then swung at Zero. The sudden move revealed that his arm was weaker than he had thought, from both exhaustion and loss of blood. His sword clanged lightly against Zero's shield, and the crowd shrilled its contempt.

Zero whacked at him in turn, then moved closer,

so that their movements would be more difficult for the spectators to follow.

"Cover, damn it!" he growled. "Cover yourself. I could've got past your guard that time!"

The mob was howling for the kill now. It was obvious that Denny was faltering. They demanded that Zero strike the death blow.

"I . . ." Denny muttered weakly, "I'm blacking out . . . I . . ."

Zero cut at him twice more in a blur of motion, deliberately hitting on Denny's shield and breastplate. "Stall, Denny! Stall!" he rasped. "The gong will go any second now. Hang on!"

His sight had gone hazy, and he could no longer bear the weight of shield or sword. His left leg crumbled beneath him, and he was on the sand.

His eyes cleared for a moment. He stared up at Zero, who was looking at him in an agony of despair.

The crowd was roaring again—again? When had the roaring ceased for even a moment, since they had marched into the ring those long minutes ago?

In supreme effort he held up his right hand in the plea for mercy.

There was no mercy. A thousand, ten thousand thumbs jabbed down, down, down.

Zero shot his eyes to the judge's stand, his face working. A moment later, resigned despair spread over his features. He looked down at his fallen companion. "Sorry, Denny," he said. "I tried."

Then the sword began its descent, with a reluctant slowness that was no mercy for its victim.

Looking away from it, Denny chanced to focus on an excited telly reporter on the podium who was zeroing in on Denny's face even as the moment of truth, death, was on him. The tens of millions of viewers around the country who had not been lucky enough to win tickets to the final games could watch the final moments of his life.

The gong sounded.

Zero dropped his sword, swearing endlessly. He tried to pick Denny up, but failed. Some of the fighting buffs were still screaming for the kill, and Zero turned to glare at them. Either they hadn't heard the gong, or didn't care.

Zero snarled up at them, then yelled for the medics.

☐ CHAPTER TWO ☐

When Denny came out of the anesthetic, Zero was standing next to the bed, garbed in civilian wear. Denny had lost blood, but that was a simple matter. Only one of the wounds had been serious, and the arena clinic was more than able to handle any wound known to the games—at least any that left the victim among the living.

The short man grinned down at Denny, then put forth a hand.

"The name is Jesus Gonzales," he said, pronouncing it *hey-zeus*, Spanish style. "Zero to you."

Denny shook hands, wincing at the pain set off by the minor movement. "Land," he said. "Dennis Land. Denny to you. And thanks."

Zero shrugged. "No thanks called for. I was in the dill there, when you came galloping to the rescue." He pulled up a chair. "We're the only two Secutores who made it, along with six Retiarii. I'd like to get my hands on that Master of the Games, the bastard. Only eight of us allowed to come through! He could have made it twelve, easy."

He looked at Denny, who was staring blank-

17

faced. "You're not a pro, are you." He made it more a statement than a question.

"Me? Hell, no. And what's more, that's the last time I'll ever be in the arena, believe me."

Zero grunted. "You could make yourself a fistful of Variable common shares in exhibitions, you know."

Denny snorted contempt.

Zero looked at him oddly. "How'd you ever get sucked into the games, if you're so against them?"

"Sucked in is right. I'm an Etruscanologist, I guess you'd call it, and—"

"What in the name of Zen is a 'truscanologist?" Zero interrupted.

"An Etruscanologist," Denny repeated. "A historian and anthropologist who specializes in Etruscans. At any rate, I've always been fascinated by the *ludi*, as the Romans called the original games. The Romans got the idea from the Etruscans, you know, although the Etruscan version was much less rugged. Ancient arms and their use fascinate me, too—I've even written a book on the subject. Nobody bothered to read it, so far as I know. Now I'm working on another one."

"What's that got to do with you winding up in the national finals?"

Denny grinned ruefully. "Like a cloddy, I used to attend the local gladiatorial club's school to pick up material, since they use weapons that are identical to those the Romans used. I took the drill— I've always prided myself on staying in shape—and worked out three or four times a week with the club members. We studied Oriental and European martial arts, as well. Then we had mock combat—you know, where they have the electronic weapons and armor, and if you touch a man in a vital spot, a light goes on and he's eliminated?"

"I know," Zero replied flatly.

"Well, at any rate, when it came time this year for our club to name half a dozen members for the first elimination meets, the stupid"—Denny shot a quick look at the other before going on—"Upper who's the head of the club nominated me. I tried to back out and nearly got myself demoted to Low-Lower, not to speak of having my appropriation cut."

"Appropriation?"

"Yes, in support of my work as an Etruscanologist. It's nonproductive, so I have to get a special government grant pushed through for my expenses. At any rate, when my patriotism to the Westworld and the Welfare State was questioned, I reversed my engines in short order."

"Why didn't you take a dive in the early eliminations? The crowds aren't tough in those local meets, especially if you've got a lot of friends and relatives up there in the stands. You could have copped yourself a wound and dropped out."

Denny shook his head. "It didn't work that way. Everything went wrong—or right, I guess you could say, since I survived. My opponents evidently had the same idea; they were falling down all around me, before I could fall down in front of them!"

Zero was laughing.

"No joke," Denny protested. "By the time I realized what was going on and got to a point where I could have funked out, I probably would have had my throat slit, with the buffs giving me the thumbs down. I *had* to go on. How about you?"

"I guess I wanted the prestige," he said. "It'll mean a promotion for me. I might even get bounced a caste." His voice took on a slight tone of deference. "I'm only a Low-Middle. I suppose you're . . ."

Denny brushed it aside. "I'm only a Mid-Middle, myself."

"At that, we're probably the highest-ranking combatants to make the finals. Once in a while, you'll get some dilettante Upper who'll participate in the earlier eliminations, just for the glory of it—"

Denny chuckled.

"—but most of the poor bastards out there are Lowers," Zero continued, "and Low-Lowers at that. Making their fling for a bounce in caste and some extra common shares to make life more bearable."

The subject was getting a bit sticky for two strangers, no matter what they had just been through together. After a pause, Zero cleared his throat. "Well, at any rate, I suppose both of us can use the extra stock."

Denny shook his head. "Not for me, thanks. I'll donate my prize to whatever organization there might be that works for incapacitated gladiatorial vets, or their widows and children."

Zero's eyebrows went up. With his dark complexion, he must be Mexican, Denny decided. Mexican, or possibly Cuban. More Indian blood than Spanish, and stockier built than the average, but with the quick, lithe movements of the Latino. His face was open and friendly. Zero was basically a person of good will, Denny figured, and certainly a good man to have at your side in a tight spot.

Despite the feeling that he was striking a ridiculous pose in the eyes of the other, Denny continued, "It smells too much of blood money to me."

Gonzales considered him. "It's easier to have such feelings, I imagine, when you have the inalienable basic stock issued to you that a Mid-Middle rates."

"I don't deny that," Denny admitted. "Ideals come easier to those who can afford them. A growling stomach bows to few ethics."

Zero laughed suddenly. "For a couple of guys who were swinging ancient swords a few hours ago, we're waxing awfully philosophical. Look, the Category Medicine character outside said you needed rest. I'll take off. When'll I meet you again?"

Dennis Land hadn't been surprised that the short, dark man had dropped in to see him. After all, they owed their lives to one another. On the other hand, they undoubtedly had little in common beyond the arena. He wondered at the other's desire to continue their relationship. "Oh, around," he said evasively. "I do most of my work at the University."

Zero's face showed surprise. "You're Category Education?"

"That's right," Denny said, himself surprised at the other's reaction. "Category Education, Subdivision History, Branch Research, Rank Professor."

"Rank Professor!" Zero blurted, then laughed. "And a finalist in the national games! Zen! The first time in history." He rose to his feet and continued to chuckle.

Denny rankled at the laughter. To him there was nothing funny in the comedy of errors that had taken him from the security of his research and forced him into the blood, gore, terror, and desperation of the modern gladiatorial games.

Still chortling his amusement, Zero moved toward the door. "I'll be seeing you when you get out of that bed, Prof."

Dennis Land stared at the door after it had closed behind Zero. There was something about the dark man that didn't quite fit. On the face of it, they were indebted to each other—comrades in arms, so to speak, by right of blood shed in defense of one another's lives. But while he, Denny, had revealed his position in life, the nature and place of his work, and even his views on various subjects, Zero had said remarkably little about himself. He hadn't even mentioned his category. Perhaps it was Military, since he had hinted that he might achieve a bounce in caste as a result of being a finalist in the national games. But he didn't quite seem a soldier—he didn't have that soldier's stance. Besides, Denny knew enough about Category Military to know that an old pro wouldn't be foolish enough to participate in the national games. The percentages were too bad, and an old pro didn't become an old pro in the Category Military by failing to consider the percentages.

He shrugged. He wasn't really interested in the mystery of Jesus Gonzales. What he was interested in was getting out of this bed and back to his work. He suspected that his victory in the games was going to cut very little ice at the University. In fact, old man Updike, the Academician heading the history department, would undoubtedly take a dim view of the outcome of his research. Denny had just barely talked the man into allowing him this leave of absence for independent research, and he was certain that Updike hadn't expected the research to include taking part in the national games.

There was one thing he *was* sure of—Dennis Land was not going to jump a caste as a result of his foray into the gladiatorial meets. Not in Category Education, which was as frozen a field as could be found in the West-world. He had been born a Mid-Middle, in Category Education, and he had no doubt but that he would die a Mid-Middle. Theoretically, he could cross categories into one of the fields where a bounce in caste was possible, such as Military or Religion, but he had been raised in the atmosphere of the University, his father, grandfather, and great-grandfather all having been teachers before him. His abilities had been such that he had reached the rank of full professor sooner than any of his forebearers, it was true, but his chances of bouncing his caste to High-Middle were remote indeed.

He wondered, as he sat there, whether his refusal of the prizes due him as a survivor of the national games made sense. Dennis Land was no pacifist—his presence in the games proved that. If the cause was strong enough, he believed in fighting—to the death, if necessary—but he was no fracas buff. Fracas fans could have their sleazy entertainment. He had no yen to watch the telly coverage of small-scale wars between corporations, for example, in which hundreds or even thousands of mercenaries were killed. He found no pleasure in death—either in witnessing or dealing it. As a result, he was considered somewhat of a fuddy-duddy, even by University colleagues. All of this made his present situation all the more ironic—that, and the fact that he was a highly trained fighter by choice.

Although he was only marginally aware of it, Dennis Land was a survivor. Put him into any situation, and he *would* survive, or die trying. He had not created the institution of the national games and did not care for it, but placed in the middle of the fray, he did was what necessary to survive—up to and including killing others in the same position as himself.

He had been unable to avoid the situation; almost before he realized what was happening, it was either kill or be killed, but as long as it wasn't for money he could live with it.

Anyway, he had little need for extra income; in addition to his University pay, he had been issued the basic inalienable common shares that accrued a Mid-Middle upon birth. The income from those was sufficient to allow him to live in modest comfort, even modest luxury compared to the lot of, say, a High- or Mid-Lower, not to speak of the squalor of a Low-Lower.

It was the Welfare State, and there was security for all from cradle to grave, after a fashion. The most improvident fool had no manner in which to squander the inalienable basic common stock shares which were issued him, according to the caste into which he was born. Each month, dividends were deposited to his credit account, and that was that.

There was no way to steal common stock from an individual, or to gamble or con it away from him. Each citizen of the West-world was secure. Medical care, education, even entertainment was free. Lower castes might be at subsistence level, but no one starved, and nearly all were stuporously content.

The overwhelming majority of the population spent the greater part of their lives before their telly sets, sucking on their trank pills in drug-induced happiness, watching the telly screen for the excitement of the ultimate entertainment—violent death, as witnessed in the fracases and the gladiatorial games.

Such was the price paid by West-world citizens for security. The society was static in economic levels as well as social status. The average citizen had to accept what was given him—no more, no less. The automation that had begun in the mid-Twentieth Century had paved the way for this—the ultimate leisure-based society, one in which none wanted, and few worked. Robotics had become a fine art, practiced in large part by computers and robots, and had taken away not only the drudgery of mankind's existence, but also many of the reasons for it. The age-old dream of an economy that could support more than were required to operate it was reality in the West-world. The so-called utopia that many had foreseen as a result of the Industrial Revolutions and their successors, automation and robotics, had indeed come into being, but, like the imagined utopias before it, it was flawed.

The major flaw lay in the fact that, given a free

ride, the average citizen would not devote himself
to the goals of society. No, it was human nature
that the self be . . . selfish; it took an extra something to rise above that, and most didn't have that
extra something. So the government had developed tranks and the fracases—bread and circuses—
to keep the citizens happy and maintain the status
quo, because once the citizenry had become the
mob, it was the only alternative to revolt. It worked,
for awhile.

Of course, given ambition, and the good fortune
to be born into a category which still offered em-
ployment, it was possible to acquire additional
shares of common stock in the economy of the
West-world. Such shares could be bought and sold,
and an ambitious man could increase his basic
income considerably—if he was born into the right
category. However, it could prove difficult for one
who was born, say, in Category Food Preparation,
Subdivision Cooking, Rank Chef, since cooking
was no longer handled by individuals. Automation
had taken over with a vengeance in that field.
Given the option, it turned out that no one wanted
to eat food that had been handled, even after
AIDS was conquered and smallpox reconquered.

Dennis Land stirred in his bed. As a student of
history, he had studied the evolution and implications of the West-world state as few others could
or would. But he had accepted it throughout his
life; why was it coming back to him now? Was it,
perhaps, that the past couple of months, when he
had been face to face with death almost daily, had
brought him to the point of questioning some of
the aspects of his existence? Did the manner in

which he had been forced into the games make him resentful of authority now? Or was it something in Zero's manner, or his words?

He stayed awake long into the night, pondering these thoughts and the darker thoughts behind them.

The interview with Updike was considerably worse than he had expected.

Denny remained in the clinic for a week, after which he was pronounced fit. He felt that way, too. Zero had not returned during his stay, but there had been many other visitors—too many for Denny's tastes. It had started almost immediately—a steady stream of telly reporters seeking interviews, fracas buffs of both sexes seeking his autograph and attention, manufacturers' representatives offering endorsement contracts, and more. The staff finally barred all but workers, and legitimate friends and relatives of patients, from entering the clinic.

Even then, the buffs hadn't stopped trying. People climbed the wall to his window, and eventually a small detachment of Category Security types was placed around the clinic, after which Denny found some peace.

It was not until then that he realized that he had become a national celebrity. Odd, he didn't *feel* famous. Denny fleetingly wondered from time to time how Zero was handling it all.

Not that it meant anything to him. His position as a professor doing historical research was one that he valued considerably, and one which he had no wish to jeopardize.

Teaching, *per se*, held little charm for him. It

was seldom, these days, that one found a student in a class who was truly scholar material. Perhaps it was the fault of society, rather than of the individual student, although to have voiced such controversial opinion, even among his colleagues, would not have been wise. One simply didn't criticize the government, either directly or indirectly. Where was the need for the average student to buckle down and study, anyway? It was unlikely that academic achievement would improve his life. You were *born* secure, and you were born into a social niche into which you fitted for all of your days. What need was there for study, beyond the minimum education forced on all citizens of the Westworld?

Of course, there were occasional exceptions, like Dennis Land himself, who sought knowledge for the pleasure of finding it. He sometimes wondered why his kind were so few. Many of his fellow instructors actually resented having been chosen by the computers to fulfill the task for which they had been trained. Advanced education was one of the few fields in which the state stubbornly resisted automation. Certainly there was plenty of help in the form of telly lectures, computer tutors, and such, but for some reason the state felt that unsupervised higher learning was a bad thing. As a result, while a citizen born into Category Mining had less than one chance in a thousand of ever being called up to perform his function, a person born in Category Education had at least one chance in four. And yes, Dennis admitted, many of them resented the few years that they must devote to the Welfare of the State.

Most would have preferred to take their position alongside the Lowers, seated before their telly sets sucking their trank pills. Most would have preferred to live their lives away in a haze of happy satisfaction, untouched by reality.

Now, standing before Academician Ronald Updike, hereditary aristocrat, Upper by birth, and one of the few Academicians the University could boast, he felt all too close to reality. The interview had been scheduled for the afternoon of his return from the games, and Denny had not even had a chance to adjust to the time lag induced by the trip from the old Texas region. To him, it was already evening.

He stood like a schoolboy called on the carpet for too many violations of school rules. His superior gazed at him, head high and nostrils flaring. In the manner of aristocrats through the ages faced with a troublesome member of the lower orders who must be made to *feel* his place, he eyed Denny in a puzzled manner, as though wondering what made him tick.

Finally, he spoke. "I suppose, *Professor* Land, that you are unaware of the fact that during the past two weeks the campus has been literally flooded with gaping, gawking, drooling idiots."

Denny blushed. He was well aware that fans would have been hanging around the University. He had certainly seen enough of them at the clinic.

"Fracas buffs!" Updike exploded. "Gladiator fans, seeking a glimpse of their latest hero!

"Nor is that all," he continued in a calmer, more acid, tone. "Telly reporters. Fracas buff magazine columnists. Tri-Dee movie scouts. Even a moronic publicity man from some arms company or other, seeking *endorsement!*" Updike paused to glare at Denny, as if doing so would reveal the source of Denny's errant ways. "All of that, not to mention gangs of sex-happy groupies!"

Denny gestured with his hands in an attempt at placation. "Sir, this isn't of my doing. I had . . ."

"Not of your doing? You idiot cloddy! Do you think these cretins would be storming this campus if it had not been for your stupidity in participating, like a drivel-happy Lower, in those idiotic—" The Upper caught himself in midsentence. Even one in his position did not openly challenge an institution as firmly entrenched as the games. He switched topics, rapping his desk sharply with his knuckles. "I assume you have some sort of excuse for turning yourself into a public spectacle and deserting your duties as a research historian, Professor Land?"

Denny spoke quickly, hoping to get his say in before the Upper took off again. "Sir, it all began with that project I told you about some time ago— the book on ancient arms and their usage, which was to be published under both of our names."

"Are you attempting to lay this at *my* feet, Professor Land?"

"Sir, all I was saying was that the study would have been a unique one, and probably widely commented upon. For instance, the long-debated length of the pike used by Philip's Macedonians in the phalanx. For years, popular belief among historians was that the rear phalanx wielded an eighteen-foot pike. But my research, conducted on the spot and using actual drills with the ancient weapons, proved to me that the tradition is ridiculous. Such a spear would be absolutely unwieldy, and certainly would have caused more difficulty in the ranks than harm to the enemy. You could hardly carry one, much less run with it in a charge." Denny breathed a silent hope that displaying some of the results of his research would placate Updike.

"What has this got to do with your *antics?*" Updike spat.

"It was this very research that put me in a position where I couldn't refuse to participate. I had joined one of the more prominent clubs, a gladiator club, in which the members gather to fence, practice archery, and amuse themselves in learning to throw javelins." He went on to explain the process by which he had been drafted to represent the club in the local games, and why he was unable to refuse the "honor."

"By the way, sir," he interjected, absurdly caught up in his natural enthusiasm for the topic again, "I also learned that the alleged accuracy of the Roman and Etruscan spearthrower must have been greatly exaggerated."

"Land! You're a fool! A fool, you understand? You keep drifting away from the subject. The fact is, you have made this university notorious. A professor of history, winning in the national games. What sort of scholastic reputation does that create?"

It came to Denny, suddenly, that Updike was on mescaltranc. His eyes had that dull gleam. Mescaltranc, reserved for the use of Uppers, did not proportionately lower aggressive impulses as it lowered inhibitions. It was rumored that the drug made even the perception of pain a high pleasure.

Denny suddenly understood, too, the man's real motivation.

It was simply impossible for Ronald Updike, Low-Upper in caste, Academician in rank, to see another—Dennis Land, in this case—at the center of the stage. Denny was now a celebrity such as the school had never before produced. For the balance of this year, at least, he would be the focal point of hundreds of telly reporters and other media types seeking stories, and countless fans wanting autographs, souvenirs, sex.

No, it was beyond Updike to bear seeing another—someone of lower caste than he at that— the recipient of such adulation, no matter whether Denny wanted it or not. And this was not the first time that Denny had shown up his superiors. He was rapidly becoming *the* expert in his own field of research. He wondered now what the other was going to do about it.

The answer was not long in coming. "I've discussed this with my colleagues," Updike snapped. "We have decided it best that you take an indefinite leave of absence from the University."

"Indefinite?"

"At least a year, Professor. Possibly—just possibly—by the end of that time, we shall see fit to consider your return."

Denny protested. "But, sir, wouldn't it be possible for me to simply go abroad? To do some field work in central Italy, perhaps? My appropriation for Etruscan research is such that I could easily afford to spend a full year—"

"Professor Land, I am afraid that the staff has seen fit to reverse your appropriation. Frankly, I was never particularly impressed by the value of the subject you chose to pursue. No. I am afraid, Professor, that the funds involved here have already been diverted to other, more important work." Updike stood and pointed to the door. "Now, as you know, I am busy—more than busy."

Busy sitting here overtranking yourself, Denny thought bitterly. There wasn't a chance now. He knew that his department superior loathed him— and that the man was an ass. Academician he might be, but Denny knew who had done the actual work that resulted in that highest of university degrees. Well, what difference did that make? Ronald Updike was an Upper born, a gold spoon tucked carefully into the side of his mouth at birth.

Denny turned and left without further words.

The only thing in the world that he really wanted to do had been taken from him. He had no illusions; without the University's facilities, he was in no position to continue his work. This was the only place, this side of Rome, where the raw materials of his study were available.

A year. Ha! Updike's real meaning was clear. Dennis Land would not return to the University— not after a year, not after ten. He was persona non grata in the field to which he had devoted his life.

◻ CHAPTER THREE ◻

Colonel Yuri Malyshev had flown in late the day before on the shuttle from Alma-Ata. He could have reported to Chrezvychainaya Komissiya headquarters at that time, or any other time, for that matter; the ministry originally founded to combat counterrevolution, and which had now spread to deal with espionage and counterespionage as well, never slept. However, Yuri Malyshev was piqued. In a world where few devoted more than ten hours a week to their livelihood, he hadn't had a vacation in nearly a year.

So, instead of reporting in, he checked into the Hotel Gellert, there on Gellert Ter at the foot of the Buda hills and the edge of the Danube. The Gellert was one of the older hostelries of the capital of the Soviet Complex, but the colonel consistently used it. A former spa, it had an air of the less gaudy, less shiny, less raucous Budapest of long ago. Besides that, the well-situated terrace restaurant provided what in Yuri Malyshev's belief was the best *halaszle* fish soup and *rostelyos*—potted round steak in paprika sauce—in town, and Yuri considered himself a gourmet. For the food, the Tokay Aszu wine, and, of course, for the music, he could bear Budapest; for the rest he hated the bureaucratic capital city.

After a leisurely dinner, he strode across the Szabadsag-hid bridge, and then along the Corso where the night spots were clustered. He had to admit, despite his scorn for Budapest, that it offered considerably more in the way of nightlife than did, say, Moscow, which was still inclined to be on the stolid side. Yuri was seeking gypsy music, and he found it in the terrace club of the Duna hotel. Over a chilled bottle of Riesling, he sat and listened.

Of Cossack blood, the colonel was in his early thirties, tall for a Russian, and classically handsome. Though he was in mufti, his bearing was such that any observant person would have recognized him immediately as a soldier, one who had known war. Even without the faint scar running from temple to chin point, an observant person would have felt that the colonel had seen combat many times.

He had no doubts that he could easily find female companionship here at the Duna tonight—numerous open glances had assured him of that. But a lassitude had fallen on him. Damn it, he had a vacation coming to him, and here they'd put through a hurry call for him to report to the highest offices of the ministry. That meant an assignment of considerable import . . . and danger. Yuri sighed. He would have found less danger in life had he remained in the Pink Army, rather than going into counterespionage. Still, life in the Pink Army would have had little real meaning.

He dropped the line of thought, poured himself more of the slightly greenish, effervescent wine, and focused his attention on the violins. Before long, still vaguely disgruntled and on edge, he returned to his hotel and retired.

The next morning he had the hotel assign a hovercar to him—his priority being high enough to drive in the city—and drove leisurely over to the Pest side of the capital. He paralleled the river until he reached Margitsziget Island, then turned right on Szt. Istvankorut to Marx Square, which he crossed to emerge on Lenin.

He turned left off Lenin and onto the less busy Rudas Laszlo Utca, with its foreign embassies and governmental buildings. The building housing the offices of the Chrezvychainaya Komissiya was on the far end of the street, facing the park. From the entry, one could see the national museum and the colossal bronze monument to the Magyar warriors of antiquity.

He parked the car in the circular drive fronting the building and made his way up the steep steps to the entrance.

Colonel Yuri Malyshev had recently worked out of the ministry's offices in Alma-Ata, and occasionally Lhasa, Moscow, or Leningrad, but it had been years since he'd been in Budapest. Even so, he was well enough known that the two sentries snapped to attention at his approach. He marched through the foyer and to the corridor beyond, briefly admiring the marble flooring, the long rows of classical statuary, and the Hapsburg period tapestry. It came to him that the offices of the Komissiya had many aspects of a museum.

He stopped before the door to the offices that were his destination. "Colonel Yuri Malyshev," he snapped to the plainclothesman stationed there. "On appointment."

"Yes, Colonel." The guard opened the door for him and closed it behind him.

It was a reception room, bare of furnishings other than three chairs and a desk, behind which sat a receptionist in the uniform of an MVD.

Malyshev outranked the receptionist, but in these highest of echelons, rank meant less than elsewhere. Very possibly this captain was in a position, given reason, to pull the rug out from under such as Yuri Malyshev. Consequently, he made no attempt to pull rank. He said evenly, "Colonel Malyshev. My orders were to report immediately to Comrade Kodaly."

The captain looked him up and down, then said, "Very well, Comrade Colonel. If you'll just wait a moment." He gestured at the chairs.

Yuri sat down and crossed his legs. He wondered vaguely what it was this time. The nature of the ministry for which he worked had changed considerably in the long decades since the Revolution. He wondered whether Felix Dzerzhinsky, the Pole who had originated the Cheka back in Lenin's day, would recognize the organization it had become. The name had changed, down through the years. Cheka, GPU, OGPU, NKVD, MVD, and this department and that department within the Komissiya, the MGB and KGB, but the heart and soul of the organization remained the same.

The peasants who had once been purged in the millions were now tranquil, if indeed you could call them peasants any longer, and the military corelation of forces had stabilized after a fashion, but the ministry's function remained to repress dissent in Eastbloc and foment it elsewhere.

The colonel recrossed his legs. This was the way of bureaucracy. They hurried him all the way from Siberia as though the whole world was afire. Then he sat in an outer office, cooling his heels.

He cooled them for an hour, and began to wonder about his lunch. The captain at the desk ignored him, going about his business.

At last, the door to the inner sanctum opened, and a strikingly beautiful young comrade in the uniform of a sergeant of police emerged. Her uniform was not quite straight, nor was her walk. She smiled at the captain at the desk, straightened her blouse, shot Yuri Malyshev a roguish glance, then took her leave.

The captain said, without inflection, "You may enter now, Comrade Colonel."

Yuri came to his feet, his face set in the same expressionless cast as the captain's. He marched to the door that led to the office beyond, squared his shoulders, knocked once, and entered. It was the first time that he had actually met his ultimate superior, Ferencz Kodaly, who had only recently been given this post.

The man who was said to be Number One's closest companion sat behind his desk, eyeing a bottle of barack that was at least two-thirds empty. To his right was a serving cart covered with Hungarian *hors d'oeuvres*. It had been well but messily sampled. There was a couch on one side of the room, but the colonel's eyes avoided it.

He snapped to attention before the desk. "Colonel Malyshev, sir."

The other regarded him blearily. "Oh. Malyshev, eh? Heard a great deal about you, Comrade. Great deal. Have a drink."

One did not refuse to have a drink with Ferencz Kodaly. Besides that, Malyshev felt he could use one.

"With your permission, Comrade Commissar." He stepped forward to the open office bar which sat to one side, took up a three-ounce glass, and turned back to his superior. "For you, Comrade Commissar?"

The other mumbled something that ended in *barack*, which Yuri took for assent. He poured a stiff jolt of the apricot brandy, placed it before his chief, then poured another one for himself.

He held his glass up in toast. "The final goal, Comrade."

"Worl' revolution," Kodaly slurred, in the formula reply. Kodaly knocked the drink back in practiced, stiff-wristed style. Before putting his glass down, he filled it again from the bottle before him. Yuri took a drink from his own glass in a more moderate fashion. The liqueur was exceedingly dry, having been distilled to the point where it reminded him of vodka.

"Now then, eh, Colonel . . .?"

"Malyshev. Yuri Malyshev," Yuri prompted. He tried to mask the surprise and confusion that he knew were crossing his face.

"Um, yes. Of course. Well, what could I . . . I

do for you? Very busy, actually. Always busy, you know."

The man was drunk. There was no doubt of that. Yuri's eyes went to the window, as if to check the weather. It could be no later than eleven o'clock. At this time yesterday, he had been in Kazakhstan—in Alma-Ata, its capital. The orders he had received had been most definite. To report at once to Budapest, highest priority, for an immediate assignment. He had thought that he was being bold to the point of insubordination in not turning up at headquarters the evening before. But now . . .

He cleared his throat and said, "Colonel Yuri Malyshev, Comrade Commissar. Field Agent out of Alma-Ata. My orders were to drop everything and report immediately to your offices."

His ultimate commander stared at him.

Finally, he said, "Well, don't just stand there. Have another drink. Heard a great deal about your efforts. Imperialist spies, down in . . . Hanoi . . . wherever. Good job, Colonel Malyshev."

Malyshev had never been to Hanoi, nor anywhere else in the Viet region. A feeling of desperation began to manifest itself. What if this was all a mistake? Who would be blamed for his leaving his assignment? He covered by pouring the second drink his superior had offered him, although he hadn't quite finished the first.

The tiny screen on the desk's interoffice communicator lit up and Ferencz Kodaly stared glassily at it. He muttered something, then clicked it off with a curt gesture.

He looked up at Yuri Malyshev. "Assignment,

eh? Course, course. Very important project. Important. Details given to you by assistant. My assistant. Like another drink?" He half closed one eye, as though offering an indiscretion. "One for the road, as the British say, eh?"

Yuri came to attention again. "Thank you, Comrade Commissar, but if my wits are to remain sharp, I should avoid it."

Kodaly grunted at him as he eyed the brandy again.

Yuri stood there, not knowing if he was to leave. Finally, when the other said nothing, Yuri said, "With the Comrade Commissar's permission," and turned and left the room.

The captain's face was as expressionless as it had been when the girl sergeant had left earlier, but he stopped Yuri as he stepped from the office. "There was evidently a slight mistake in your appointment, Comrade Colonel," he said flatly. "You are to see Comrade Korda, rather than the Commissar. He has been trying to locate you."

"All right," Yuri replied, keeping testiness carefully from his voice. "Where do I find Comrade . . ."

"Korda," the captain supplied. "Zoltan Korda. One of the men in the corridor will take you to his office."

The office of Zoltan Korda contained neither bar, serving cart of dainties, nor couch. It contained very little besides Zoltan Korda, his desk, and two chairs. However, the outer office was jam-packed with desks, clerks, data terminals, communications equipment, and other office paraphernalia.

Malyshev was hurried on through, without pause or wait, and when the door of the small inner office was closed, the noise from outside was cut off completely.

Zoltan Korda eyed him up and down. Malyshev regarded him in turn, and saw a smallish, nervous man, inclined to bore his eyes into those of others.

Korda exploded. "Colonel, where have you been!"

Yuri Malyshev had heard of Korda. Kodaly had brought him along when assigned to this post—an office drudge to whom the Commissar handed over his routine, he had heard. It appeared that the Commissar handed over more than routine to Korda.

"My orders," he said wearily, "were to report to the offices of Commissar Kodaly immediately, for an important new assignment. I did."

"To the *offices* of the Commissar—not to the Commissar himself. You should have . . . well, never mind. Sit down. I have just been reading your dossier. It is an impressive one."

"Thank you, Comrade."

Korda suddenly fixed his sharp gaze on Malyshev. "You've been drinking! At this hour of the morning?"

Malyshev cleared his throat and ran a finger down the scar of his face. "The Commissar . . ." he began, ruefully.

Korda nodded. "I see. Well. Have you ever been to the West?"

There was a stir of excitement within him. "To the Americas?"

"Possibly, eventually. But actually, no farther than Common Europe, for now."

"On various assignments, Comrade. And on vacation. To Paris, Rome, once to Nice."

"This time you're on assignment, Colonel Malyshev. Probably the most important of your career." Korda paused to light another cigarette off the one he was smoking. "Colonel, I'm going to refresh your memory with some background, much of which you may already know. However, by way of preliminary, what does the term 'frigid fracas' mean to you?"

"Frigid fracas? Why, it's West-world idiom. In the early days following the Great Patriotic War—World War Two, as the Westerners say—they called the relationship between the Soviet Complex and the Imperialist nations a Cold War. As their slang shifted, the term fracas became popular, and cold war evolved to frigid fracas."

"Quite correct. Now, at what stage would you place the frigid fracas currently?"

Yuri Malyshev shifted in his chair, not having the faintest idea of what the man was leading to. "I'd say that it's truly frozen now. With the Universal Disarmament Pact, and complete inspection, the earlier dangers have been eliminated, Comrade."

The other nodded. "By the way, are you a Party member? Your dossier doesn't tell me."

He shook his head in response. "I didn't have the fortune to be born into the Party."

"Neither am I. Do you know the derivation of the salutation 'Comrade'?"

He shook his head again. Zoltan Korda, he found, was a confusing man. But then, Yuri Malyshev had found nearly all Hungarians confusing people.

"In the early days, the very early days of such pioneer socialists as Marx, Engels, and DeLeon, the term was used to designate fellow fighters for the cause. Their fight is no longer being fought. I find the term somewhat ridiculous, particularly when not being used by Party members."

Malyshev was inwardly surprised. This was not the way one talked—at least, not in the echelons with which he was familiar. Blankly, he said, "Yes, Com—sir."

Korda tapped the dossier on the desk before him. "I am somewhat surprised that you are not a Party member. I note that your illustrious great-great-grandfather, Vladimir Malyshev, was one of the earliest companions of Lenin, and a founder of the Bolsheviks."

"He was executed in 1938 as a Bukharinist Rightist Deviationist," Malyshev replied.

The bureaucrat shot another glance at the papers before him. "Whatever that means," he said wryly. "But he was rehabilitated more than a decade ago, his body exhumed and reburied in the Kremlin wall, beside those of his old comrades."

"However," Malyshev said, his voice still even, "my father was not a Party member, and, as a result . . ."

"Yes. Of course. By the way, what does the term 'Trotsky lives' mean to you?"

Malyshev looked at him. He quickly ran some facts through his mind, regarded Korda for a moment longer. Finally, he made a decision, and shook his head. "Why, nothing."

"Well," Korda said dryly, "if you ever hear it,

make note of the speaker and report him to this office."

Korda returned to the subject at hand, after inhaling deeply and expelling clouds of heavy smoke through his nostrils. From the smell, he was probably smoking dark Bulgarian tobacco, Malyshev decided, wondering how anyone's lungs could take the punishment.

"In the early days of the, ah, frigid fracas, the situation was a fairly simple one. We had our two great powers, the West, which consisted of the United States and her satellites, and Russia and hers. There were a sizable number of neutrals, which were at that time poorly organized and carried little weight in world affairs."

Thus far, Korda had said nothing unfamiliar to the most dullard schoolboy. But Yuri Malyshev held his peace.

Ash dropped unheeded onto the other's suit as he continued. "But times have changed. While the Soviet complex has, after various difficulties, amalgamated into a cohesive unit, most of the satellites of the United States finally broke away and joined into the state we now know as Common Europe, complete with satellites of its own, largely in Africa. The Americas, of course, slowly amalgamated so that they are now a true United States of the Americas—in short, the West-world."

There was still nothing new.

"And the neutrals, forced by necessity, if their voice was to be heard at all, strengthened their ties considerably and now operate as a strong block. Colonel Malyshev, instead of the two great powers confronting each other, as in the early days of the Cold War, the world is currently divided in four."

"The Neut-world hardly counts," Malyshev responded. "They never developed nuclear arms, although they did, at one point, have them provided in a roundabout way. And their rocketry technology precludes their being able to deliver a nuclear warhead to an important target. Cities, yes, but not to military installations. Of course, since the Disarmament Pact, neither we nor the West-world have strategic weapons systems, ostensibly. However, as everyone is aware, we can rebuild and reactivate quickly . . ."

It was his superior's turn to nod in agreement. "Yes. And who is so foolish to doubt that if war broke out between any, or all, of the great powers, that the race would be on to get into production. Fission devices, small and large, fusion and neutron bombs, missiles to carry them. Virtually none exist, though all exist in blueprint, as do plans for crash production programs."

Malyshev shifted again. This was still very elementary. Did the other think him ignorant of world affairs?

The Hungarian ground out his cigarette, and his eyes bore into those of his subordinate. "Colonel, what would you say if I told you that there is a present danger that the frigid fracas, the cold war, will get hot?"

Malyshev stared at him.

"No. No, sir," he said, after some thought. "We've reached a static status quo. The Soviet Complex is self-sufficient, and we are now conquering our problems and meeting the goals that we set so long ago. We were handicapped, compared with the West-world, by the requirements of ideological purity, and by having such a mass of population on our hands, particularly after the absorption of the Chinese state. But the bad days are gone. We're self-sufficient now, and neither want nor need war.

"And the West-world?" he shook his head again. "They have their Welfare State, as they call it. They've stratified into a society that wants no change. They, too, are self-sufficient, and their government has become so xenophobic that it discourages trade and other contact, not only with us, but with Common Europe and the Neut-world, as well. What reasons could they have for allowing their own position to be threatened—by taking the chance of precipitating war?"

Zoltan Korda nervously lit another cigarette. "You haven't mentioned Common Europe."

They had obviously come to the point.

Korda pointed with the cigarette. "Both the Sov-world and the West-world are self-sufficient. Neither needs raw materials from abroad, nor markets to sell surplus production, and space research and development is carried out in a limited and completely independent manner. We can each go it alone.

"But Common Europe is another matter. As you'll remember, Japan debouched into the second Industrial Revolution after the Great Patriotic War with an elan far and beyond anything seen throughout the rest of the world. With their industries largely demolished by bombing, they could only build anew and, obviously, built the most ultra-modern, automated plants that their scientists and engineers could devise.

"This was consciously repeated by the Europeans following the Little War of 1997 and the accompanying economic debacle. They were so far down that they had to reinvent their economies."

He seemed to switch topics. "Colonel, why did the United States and Japan fight during the Great Patriotic War?"

Malyshev scowled at him "Why . . . why the treacherous Japanese navy attacked the Imperialist American base at Pearl Harbor!"

His superior had raised his hand. "No. That was the immediate spark that set off the war. Perhaps I should have asked you why the Japanese attacked Pearl Harbor. Pearl Harbor was no more the reason the war started than the kidnaping of Helen brought on the Trojan war."

Yuri Malyshev was based firmly enough in the Materialist Conception of History to know what the other was driving at. "You mean what were the basic economic reasons behind the conflict."

"Of course. They were fairly similar to the ones that brought on the conflict between the Hellenes and the Trojans. The Trojans dominated the Hellespont, the straits through which the Greek merchants' ships had to pass to get to the Black Sea and the profitable trade there. It was intolerable to the Greeks that they be forbidden this passage, or overly taxed for it. The Hellenic government thus bowed to the pressure, and the war was on. In more modern times, the Japanese were attempting to unite all the Far East so that they could take it out as their own private domain, milking mainland China, Indonesia, and all the rest for their raw materials, and utilizing them as a dumping ground for Japanese production."

Korda leaned back in his chair and exhaled a cloud of smoke. "At least, that's the currently accepted version."

Malyshev refrained from stating his true feelings about the theory. Instead, he said slowly, "Sir, what has this got to do with our situation?"

Korda twisted his mouth. "You find me long-winded, perhaps. Believe me, the matter is most pressing, and you will, I hope, allow me time to present the whole picture. The thing is that neither the West-world nor the Soviet Complex, with our present socio-economic systems, are pressed for sources of raw materials or markets for manufactured surpluses.

"But that does not apply to Common Europe. The necessity for them to begin their economy anew has left them in a state far behind our enlightenment, and less stable than the West-world. For some years now, their long-term boom has been slackening. That area once known as Germany currently produces as many hovercars and trucks, among other products, as can be used by all of Common Europe. The same is true of the areas once known as Italy and France. They've gone into what was once called a recession by economists, and are heading into a full depression.

"This has resulted in a business panic. They *must* have more outlets, more sources of raw materials. The European Premier knows this very well, and would seem to be making plans."

Malyshev stirred. "Obviously, the Premier of

Europe is not so mad as to contemplate attacking either the Soviet Complex or the West-world!"

"Dictators, whether or not they are considered benevolent, are unpredictable," his superior stated. "However, I am inclined to agree with you. No, there is just one outlet for him and his Common Europe—the Neut-world, with its teeming population and its underdevelopment."

Malyshev was shaking his head, even as he scowled in thought. "There is just one difficulty with that. The Soviet Complex, the West-world, and the World Court would not permit a descent of the Common Europe armies on the largely defenseless Neut-world countries."

His superior had let his cigarette go out. Now he lit another. "We get to the point, and the reason for your being here. Earlier we mentioned the fact that although the West-world, Common Europe, and the Soviet Complex don't actually possess nuclear weapons, missiles to deliver them, or defense systems to shoot them down, we have them in blueprint and could hasten into production, given a breakdown of the World Court and the Universal Disarmament Pact.

"As it is, we are balanced, all in the same position, and hence safe—a balanced nuclear threat is enough. But suppose that any one of the three should come up with a practical defense against ICBMs and orbital launchers?"

Yuri Malyshev's face was blank, belying his inner excitement,

Zoltan Korda leaned forward. "The theory in nuclear missile warfare is that the attacker fires his nuclear warhead at his foe. The foe protects himself by attempting to intercept it with a system that will destroy the missile, or throw it off course, at the very least. There are, however, no defense systems that are completely effective. Anti-missile missiles can be confused, knocked out by other missiles, or overwhelmed by the sheer number of multiple warheads that can be delivered by one MIRV. And, like any ground-based defense system, anti-missiles are vulnerable to a first strike. High-energy laser and particle beam systems, working in concert from the ground and space, would seem to be the answer. Such a system could respond almost instantaneously and with great accuracy.

"But such a system has its flaws. For one, even high-energy lasers disperse in the atmosphere, and their accuracy drops off when trying to reach targets through cloud cover, from space or from the ground.

"More important, the complexity of a 'Star Wars' system—to use the sobriquet applied by the Western media and anti-nuclear factions during the 1980s—is such that controlling it is an almost impossible proposition." Korda stood and began pacing, his steps short and precise. "More than ten million lines of computer code were required to support the system proposed by then-President Reagan, and it was deadly certain that somewhere in that massive software system would be an error."

He grinned suddenly. "And there was no testing such a system. Thus, Colonel, while the most desirable anti-missile defense combines ground- and space-based elements utilizing high-energy lasers and particle beams, this system would be impossibly complex."

Yuri found himself warming to the subject. Space-based defense systems were a favorite topic of his; he had once aspired to the cosmonaut service, had even spent some time attached to the Baykonur Cosmodrome. "Certainly, what you have said is obvious. And the delivery of even one nuclear warhead to an industrial or population center is not to be tolerated. This is the basis for the current standoff. But the capability to knock out ICBMs in space or the upper atmosphere would make a difference in the balance of power."

Korda nodded. "At present, the theoretical prospect of mutual assured destruction is enough of a deterrent. Even postulating a massive first- or pre-emptive strike capability, neither side wants to risk losing more than the other."

"Then what of this defense, sir?"

Korda smiled.

"This original concept was to have everything tied in with a master control system, which proved impossible to bring to a failsafe level. In addition, it was found that a practical beam-guided laser had a ridiculously small range, measured in meters. You are aware of the theory?"

"Yes. A high energy, X-ray pumped laser is a more appealing weapon than a particle beam, due to the energy that it can deliver. And there is the fact that a particle beam, unfortunately, disperses in a vacuum. Since the problem has always been that the laser is flawed by its atmospheric dispersion—which meant, among other things, that it could not, figuratively or literally speaking, 'punch' through cloud cover—the idea of something to

serve as a guide for the laser and to punch a hole
through the atmosphere, in effect, has merit."

Korda nodded. "Well, it would seem that one of
the more brilliant minds of Common Europe has
devised a workable beam-guided laser of infinite
range. Ground and space-based defenses based on
this innovation would, as I'm sure you realize,
render its owners almost invulnerable to ICBMs."

"I see . . ." Malyshev mumbled. "But there
remains the problem of unifying and guiding such
a system."

"That same mind has happened upon a leftover
bit of West-world research, hidden away since the
last century—a rather unusual approach to artificial intelligence." He glanced at Malyshev, frowning in puzzlement. "An electronic entity, if you
will—a simulacrum, in the form of an array of
computer programs, which is capable of generat-
ing the programming code to control a complex
defense such as we have been discussing, and to
test it and self-correct any errors . . . instantly."

"So, the Europeans have their defense against
nuclear threat."

"Correct," Korda agreed. "But there is more.
Incidental to all of this, the particle beam/laser has
been developed as a weapon in its own right—a
weapon of near-infinite range, with no dispersal in
vacuum or atmosphere. This means that those using this system can not only knock out incoming
ICBMs, but spacecraft, aircraft, and such as our
salyuts, as well."

"Worse," Korda's eyes bored into Malyshev's,
"the hardware is almost all in place. The European
Hermes shuttles have been ferrying focusing re-

flectors into orbit for the past two years, and ground installations disguised as radio telescopes and microwave antennae are already in place. Unfortunately, our intelligence was a bit slow on that end of things."

"And the World Court does not protest?" Malyshev asked.

"No. It is feared that the repercussions would initiate an escalation; faced with no other alternative, Common Europe would move prematurely. It would appear that the situation is all or nothing with them. At the very least, there might be delaying actions, small wars fought, but the Europeans would eventually get their systems in place."

"Or," Malyshev said, "there could be all-out war."

"Precisely. If you like listing possibilities, the threat of the defense and beam weapon alone could win the Europeans their victory, should no one wish to test the system's viability. If cooler heads prevail among the world's leaders, and the nuclear threat is not reactivated, we may see Common Europe gobble up the Neut-world, after which . . ." he let the implication hang.

Malyshev remained silent, considering the possibilities. Finally, he said, "I suppose, then, that it is left to us to act?"

"Your task . . ." his superior began.

☐ CHAPTER FOUR ☐

Dennis Land, late a university professor, late an Etruscanologist of growing repute, stood in the middle of his apartment, hands thrust deep in his pockets. He gazed around him at the shelves of books, memory cubes, and holo-tapes; the desk, still littered with his work; the disorderly piles of notes and stacks of printout that comprised the current chapter of his book, *The Tarquin Gens and Its Origin*. This work was to have made him the world's leading authority on the subject—he and Updike, of course. Both of their names would have been on the volume. Ronald Updike's first, of course—Updike, who didn't know an Etruscan from a Trojan.

For a long moment he stared at the contents of a small, glassed-enclosed museum. He looked over the dozen or so shards of pottery he had picked up personally at Etruscan tomb digs. The small black vase which had been presented to him by Professor Uccello, curator of the Etruscan museum in the Villa Borghese in Rome. The tiny, corroded bronze statue of an Etruscan warrior he had bought at a fabulous price from one of the shady dealers in antiquities along the Via Condotti. In spite of the cost, he sometimes had his doubts about the warrior, but it made his little museum.

He turned abruptly to the auto-bar in the corner. A practicing athlete, Denny kept the auto-bar more for social occasions than solitary drinking—particularly serious solitary drinking. But now he extracted his credit card, put it into the slot on the bar's face, and dialed himself a John Brown's Body. The foot-square serving slot sank into the bar for a minute, then arose, capped with mint and a half slice of orange.

"The fruit salad," Denny muttered, "will be unnecessary." He fished the mint and orange out of the glass and threw them to the floor, then tilted the glass back and half emptied it.

But that ended the gesture. The desire to drown his sorrows in alcohol left him; he was too much of a realist not to know that they didn't drown, but were pickled. Nor did trank appeal; he liked to experience life straight, good or bad. He put the glass down, picked up his credit card, and took it to the computer terminal. After placing the card in the slot, he entered his personal access code and said, "Balance check."

A moment later the screen flickered and a synthesized voice reported, "Twenty shares of Inalienable common. Six shares of Variable common, current market value thirty thousand, three hundred and forty-four newDollars. Current cash credit, three hundred and forty-five point three zero newDollars." The screen died.

So. He had his Inalienable common stock, which guaranteed him an income sufficient to maintain himself decently as a Mid-Middle for the rest of his life. In addition, he had his life savings of six shares of Variable common stock, the income from which was enough for emergencies—even marriage—and for those little things that counted so much: rare books, vacation trips, an art object or two, an occasional descent on the flesh pots of the town.

But was there enough to sponsor his research to the point of a year or so in Tuscany, and then to publish the heavy tome he had in mind? No.

Face reality, he told himself. As a scholar, you've had it. Sure, you could have fought. Updike wasn't the final word. He could take it to the highest echelons of Category Education. But where would it get him? You can't fight the establishment. Suppose the higher echelons reinstated him and re-established his appropriation. Could he operate in open defiance of his department head? No. Updike, enraged, would put obstacles in his way which would make work impossible, and ultimately find some other reason for dismissing him.

The phone buzzed. Denny sighed and answered it. The screen lit up, showing a middle-aged woman. He didn't recognize the face, but the background was obviously that of an office. The woman said briskly, "Professor Land?"

"That's right."

"This is the Bureau of Investigation. You are requested to appear in Mr. Hodgson's office at your earliest convenience, today."

"Bureau of Investigation?" Denny blurted.

"In the Octagon, of course."

"But . . . but, what's the charge?"

"There is no charge, professor," she said, and broke the connection.

Octagon Building? Bureau of Investigation? He? Dennis stared at the screen and shook his head, mystified. Well, this Hodgson, whoever he was, was evidently in a hurry, and who wanted to irritate an official of the Bureau of Investigation?

He shrugged into his jacket and opened the narrow door leading to the outer hallway. Five minutes later he stepped out of an elevator at street level and into a typically overcast Seattle day.

The tube transit station was only two blocks away, and Denny jogged the distance, head bent. He had learned to be ever mindful of his status as a celebrity, necessary lest he find himself ambushed by gangs of overly zealous fans. He noted flashes of recognition on the faces of more than a few passers-by, but they were apparently too surprised to stop him.

The terminal building was old—the shell of a former factory that had been converted to accommodate the heavy flow of people. Slipping through the crowds with practiced ease, he walked past the terminal's local and regional staging areas until he reached the transcontinental departure concourse. Here he found a row of perhaps fifty massive booths arranged in a semi-circle, a terminal mounted on each. He chose the nearest and slipped his credit card into a slot above an old-style keyboard. The screen came to life immediately.

At the prompt, Denny typed his access code. The display echoed his input and, after a millisecond's pause, prompted him to enter his destination. He consulted a directory posted above the terminal, then entered the code for the Greater Washington corridor. This code would summon a shuttle car for him and place it in the slot for his basic destination; once he was in the car, he would be asked for his final destination.

He leaned casually against the wall until a rumbling noise announced the shuttle car's arrival. A green light above the hatchway glowed, and the door opened with a swooshing sound.

Behind him, someone said, "Hey, aren't you—," but Denny ignored it. A small vacuum tube two-seater waited, its side flush against the door seals. He climbed in, dropping the canopy over him and seating the pressurizer in one deft motion. The crash webbing unfolded itself around him automatically. He was now sealed off from the outside world. He hadn't the slightest idea what to dial, but the car had newer, voice-actuated controls as well as a keyboard, so he simply stated, "The Octagon, Bureau of Investigation."

There was a sinking-elevator sensation, which meant his car was dropping to the main grid level to be caught up by computer controls. Then more drops, and sudden shifts in direction, as the car was shuttled back and forth through the maze of the vacuum-tube transport network, preparatory to being shot to its basic destination.

After a few moments the car came to a halt. The air pressure in the cabin dropped slightly, and Denny closed his eyes in anticipation. He might be one of only eight survivors of the national games, but he hated that initial thrust and sudden feeling of free fall as much as the next man. No hero he, when it came to rappeling down a mountainside, parachuting from an aircraft, or facing the sudden nausea of vacuum-tube transport. He wondered if anybody ever got used to it.

An invisible force pushed him back into the pressure seat, and he knew that he was off, accelerating through one of the major transcon tubes. After several minutes, the acceleration eased off, and he felt the familiar falling sensation as the car glided along the nearly frictionless surface inside the tube. Except for occasional pushes as the car's speed was touched up, he felt no other sensations for more than an hour. He amused himself by scanning the car's selection of canned video programs on the small screen in the center of the dash.

At last, there was a jolt and he was pushed slowly forward, straining against the crash webbing. Greater Washington.

The shuttling started up again, and he had to go through a few traversing shots, which meant nothing. At last a green light flashed on the dash, and he undid the webbing, killed the pressurizer, slid the canopy back, and emerged into the king-size reception hall of the Bureau of Investigation.

A bright-eyed, nattily attired stereotype stepped up to him. "Professor Land?" he said.

Denny hadn't expected such immediate recognition. In fact, he had steeled himself to being hustled from one desk to another before reaching his destination. Evidently, there was to be none of that. This Hodgson was in a hurry to see him. He still couldn't imagine why.

He followed the young man—a Bureau of Investigation agent, Denny decided—across the reception hall to a heavy plasteel door beyond, then through it and down a lengthy corridor. Oh, it was the Octagon, all right. He idly wondered if considerable time wouldn't be saved by having some sort of vehicles in these halls.

He glanced at his guide. He'd heard about these highly trained BI agents. In fact, he'd seen telly shows based on their activities and, as was not the case with most other shows, the exploits and abilities credited them weren't far from the truth. BI agents, he knew, were fanatical about staying in shape, and followed a training regimen that would have made Denny's own training look like a walk in the park.

Thus it surprised him when the other said, "Just thought I'd tell you I wasn't able to get a seat at the amphitheater, but I followed the games on the telly. That was some fight you had with the Dimachaeri on the third day! For a while there, you were really in the dill."

Denny could hardly fail to remember what the agent was talking about. Dimachaeri fought with daggers in both hands, a form of gladiatorial combat with which he hadn't been very familiar. He'd won out by the skin of his teeth.

He was inwardly amused. At the same time he had been in awe of the other's training as an agent, the agent was awed by his skill with weapons of antiquity.

"It's more luck than anything else," he said now. "Lots of men better than me went down in that arena."

"Luck you can always use," the other said, admiration still in his voice. "But luck alone doesn't get you through the finals of the national games. It won't even get you *into* the finals."

Denny grunted in sour amusement. "I had another ace up my sleeve, I'm afraid. You see, I had access to the greatest library on primitive, ancient, and medieval arms and their usage in the world. Books on Roman military drill, scrolls on actual gladiatorial fights which became classics due to some tactic or other on the part of the participants. I studied them all, and practiced. When I went into that arena I knew more about the weapons we were carrying than any other man present."

Denny smiled, then added, "But I still needed the luck."

They had pulled up before a heavy door. His guide knocked, then opened the door and stood aside for Denny to enter. He didn't follow.

It was a small anteroom, and the woman who had phoned him earlier was at a desk in the center of the room. She was, to Denny's surprise, evidently a receptionist—a live receptionist. Offhand, he couldn't think of any task that a robot couldn't fulfill that a live . . . well, ostentation could be taken just so far. He wondered who this Hodgson could be.

She looked up, her features birdlike. "I'm Miss Mikhail," she said. "Mr. Hodgson is awaiting you, professor. Right through that door, there."

Denny said, "Thank you," but the words seemed inane. Thus far, he knew of no reason to thank anybody involved in this. He had been brought across the continent, at his own expense, for something he knew nothing about. In fact, as a citizen in good standing of the West-world and the Welfare State, he wondered if he shouldn't be getting indignant in here somewhere.

He opened the inner door, closed it behind him.

Jesus Gonzales said, "Hi, Denny."

Dennis Land gaped at him. "Zero! Are you . . .?"

"Am I Hodgson? Me?" Zero laughed. "Mr. Hodgson, may I introduce Dennis Land, Category Education, Sub-division History, Branch Research, Rank Professor, Mid-Middle." He waved a hand toward the opposite side of the room. "Denny, meet Frank Hodgson, Category Government, Sub-division Bureau of Investigation, Rank Secretary."

In his surprise at seeing Zero Gonzales, Denny had failed to notice the tall man who stood there, looking at him questioningly. He had a strange stance, carrying one shoulder considerably lower than the other. He also had a heavy office pallor and an air of what seemed artificial languor combined with actual weariness.

Denny stuttered through the introduction. Hodgson then seemed to come to some decision he'd been withholding and came forward, hand outstretched. "Welcome aboard," he said easily, almost lazily.

"Aboard what?" Denny said blankly.

Zero chuckled, and plopped himself down on the edge of the smaller of the two desks the room held. He said to Hodgson, "Afraid I can't finish your introduction, sir. I don't know what your caste is. High-Middle? Low-Upper?"

"I don't believe I remember," Hodgson replied, even as he made his way around the larger desk and sank into the chair there. He was completely gray of hair and obviously well beyond the age at which most retired.

Denny was still staring at the oldster. Didn't remember what his caste level was? Why, everyone knew his own caste rating—knew it as well as his own name.

Hodgson looked up at him. "Please have a chair, professor." He smiled softly. "I must admit, it is not every day that one meets a professor of anthropology who is at the same time a young man who has just won through the finals of the national games." He held up a hand to cut Denny short. "Zero explained the circumstances under which you were, ah, sucked into the games. But that you were physically qualified at all astonishes me."

Denny shrugged and found a chair. "My father was quite a student of Etruscan, Greek, and Roman life. Each of those peoples considered physical attainments as important as mental ones. They did not consider a man wise who devoted full effort to his mind, but ignored his body. My father raised me in that tradition. I've possibly made a fetish, by present standards, of keeping myself fit."

Hodgson was nodding pleasantly. "Zero told me of your studies of the Etruscans. A fascinating civilization, so I understand."

"My *former* studies," Denny said sourly. "I have just been given indefinite leave of absence from the University, and my research appropriation has been rescinded."

"I see. As a result of the notoriety you gained by participating in the games, no doubt. Possibly we can do something about that at a later date, professor."

The remark caught Denny by surprise. Do something about his problem? How . . . and why?

Hodgson rubbed his hands together. "Well. I think I shall call you Denny. You seem much too young to carry the heavy title of professor. At any rate, Denny, what do you think of the theory that the Estruscans established trading stations along the Iberian coast, at what is now known as the Costa del Sol of Spain, even before the Phoenicians or Greeks sailed those waters?"

Denny, in spite of the strangeness of the setting, was indignant. "Ridiculous. The Etruscans were competent seamen, but they established ports no farther from Etruria proper than the town of Luna, in what is now Northern Italy. Liguria, to be exact."

Frank Hodgson smiled gently. "Nevertheless, Denny, we plan to send you on an expedition to Southern Spain to investigate the possibility of just such Etruscan trading stations. Zero, here, will be your assistant."

Dennis Land was too appalled to remember tact. He looked from Hodgson to Zero. "I assume you have some espionage or counterespionage game in mind," he said. "I can't imagine why you thought I'd be interested. But whatever the reason, no thank you. I am not interested in cloak and dagger—"

Hodgson interrupted him. "Denny, when you signed up for the games, you volunteered, in case of victory, to remain for one year on call for the West-world—"

"Yes," Denny blurted. "But that's in the unlikely case the World Court rules for a trial of combat. Not for spy games."

"The West-world is now calling, Dennis Land, and, although there is no trial by combat, the situation is equally serious."

"Don't you think you might ask for volunteers?"

"We *are* asking for volunteers, in the old army method of asking for volunteers. You, you, and you." His finger stabbed the air. "Your country's situation has pickled. It needs your services desperately. You are Professor Dennis Land, Etruscanologist, internationally respected in your field—a perfect cover for the mission we depend upon to pull us out of the dill. You also are a perfect physical specimen, with abnormally quick reflexes and superbly trained, or you would never have survived the games. The Bureau hasn't another agent with your qualifications, Denny."

"Hey!" Zero complained. "I survived the games, too. I keep telling you, Frank, you underestimate me."

"I ought to have you demoted, you cloddy. You could have gotten yourself killed in that slaughterhouse."

"I told you I'd make it," Zero laughed.

"Fine," Hodgson replied, "but you aren't a bonafide and recognized historian who might be doing research on the Iberian coast. As an assistant to Professor Land, you'll have some protective coloring. If we sent you alone, someone in that espionage-conscious region would spot you the first week. You know that."

Denny had the impression that the exchange

was at least partially for his benefit, but he was not about to give in to praise or cajolery. He had better things to do than spend time on a sham dig, although he wasn't at that moment quite sure what. He did know that he was not going to be made a tool of one bureaucracy after having been used and booted out by another. "I'm simply not available," he said impatiently.

The elderly bureaucrat swung from side to side in his swivel chair, his face impassive, though Denny had the impression that there might be a certain amusement lurking there. "Listen to my fling before making a decision, Denny."

"I'll listen, but I'm not interested in crossing categories from Education to Government." That was the rub of the matter for Denny. For nothing less would he have risked offending this man.

"That wouldn't be necessary," Hodgson said. "Denny, would you say the world is stable so far as politics and economics are concerned?"

Denny looked from the older man to Zero, then back again. "Why, of course. Things've been stable for decades, ever since the Universal Disarmament Pact and the establishment of the World Court. The re-establishment of the World Court, I suppose I should say."

Hodgson was shaking his head gently. "No. Popular belief to the contrary, the socio-economic system is in a continuous state of flux. This applies not only to us," he half smiled, "but to the Sovworld, the Neut-world and, especially at this time, to Common Europe as well."

Denny felt argumentative, though he didn't know why. "I can't see any changes that have taken place in the West-world in my lifetime. And I can't envision any in the immediate future."

"No?" the other's voice was dry. "Let's use but one example—the gladiatorial meets that both you and our friend Zero, here, just came through." Hodgson made himself more comfortable. "As a historian, you will, of course, see the parallel between the original Roman games and our own."

"The purpose was different," Denny said, vaguely unhappy. "Their games were purely for the entertainment of the mob . . ."

Zero chuckled, but said nothing.

". . . while ours are for selecting the most competent combat men in the West-world, to defend our cause in case the World Court calls for a trial by combat in some international disagreement."

"Yes, that is the official view. But I find it hard to believe that it is yours as well." The bureaucrat was smiling. "Denny, when the Roman empire evolved to the point that the wealth which poured into Rome was so great that its people no longer worked, but existed on free food issued by the government and the bounty of enormously wealthy patricians who bought their votes, it was found that even slobs do not live by food alone. Something else was needed to keep the mob from explosion, from revolting against the frustrating, meaningless lives they led. Aware of it or not, the majority of the populace was indeed frustrated with its utopian existence."

"Bread and circuses," Zero interjected.

"This is hardly news to me," Denny said, irritated.

"Of course not. The parallels in the evolution of

our own society were foreseen by a good many politico-economists decades ago. Automation—the second industrial revolution—provided an abundance of food, clothing, shelter, medical care, education, other necessities, and even luxuries, for all. At the same time, fewer and fewer employees were needed in industry, especially unskilled employees, and they were soon all but eliminated. To keep these unemployed from starving or revolting, the rapidly evolving Welfare State provided unemployment insurance, pensions, relief—a score of different ways to get something for nothing. And slowly the most incompetent members of our society sank to little more than brute level. Trank was devised to keep them happy and off the streets. Telly violence, the final aspects of which could have been predicted when the medium first developed, increased and increased. Anything to keep the mob content."

Hodgson twisted his mouth ruefully. "As a friend of mine once put it, the jerks had at last inherited the earth. And, given safety from reprisal, Denny, the brute will come out in the slob. It's been shown over and over again. One example was the Roman mob and the *ludi*. A more recent example, just in case you're inclined to say that that was two thousand years ago, were the Nazis. Never forget the Nazis. When Hitler gave them a Master Plan to dispose of the Jews, the Poles, the Gypsies, the Slavs, they responded with vigor—not just as individuals, but as a society."

Denny said, "If society hadn't first degraded these people, they wouldn't have had the neuroses that demanded sadism to give them the necessary emotional relief."

"Which people? Are you sure you aren't putting the cart before the horse? There are, I believe, some aspects of history in which you are not as learned as you think!" Hodgson paused, started to say something, then seemed to think better of it. There was a tense silence before he continued.

"And there is more than just the brute in all of us that must be dealt with. The vast majority of the idle population—the mob—must be kept occupied, lest they become aware that they are not living to their fullest potential, and then seek to enlarge their horizons. At any rate, in our own society, the mob's demands are met in more restrained fashion than they were in, say Nazi Germany. The fracases evolved from prize fighting between individuals and teams to fighting between corporations and unions, between union and union over jurisdictional squabbles, between competing corporations. Now our modern equivalent of the mob drools over the violence on their telly sets."

"What's this got to do with changes taking place in the status quo?" Denny asked impatiently. "And what's it got to do with me going to Spain?"

The other nodded. "We're at the point of my example. When you were a lad, Denny, just how big were the gladiatorial meets?"

The question caught Denny by surprise. "Why, I don't even remember . . ."

"Of course not. They're a fairly modern innovation. The fracases got to the point where it took whole divisions to fight one. They were approaching the level of the wars of the Twentieth Century, with a more formal set of rules. The country was being bled white, as Rome was once bled white to support its games. So we had to taper off the fracases, build up a considerably cheaper method of satisfying our mob and of accommodating those members of society who fit the mold of the professional soldier—the man of action, as it were. Plus, there was ever the threat of full-scale wars breaking out of the controlled fracases.

"So, some twenty years ago, there began a rapid shift in the structure of the fracas and the social structure behind it. All of this was encouraged by the governments involved, and we soon arrived at what we have today. Gone are the legions of mercenaries, along with the potential threat of those legions being whipped into shape by one element or another for a private purpose."

"But, the World Court—"

"Was with us before, too. Keep in mind that it is not just the West-world that needs bread and circuses to keep the mob happy and control violence, but the Sov-world, and, to a lesser extent, Common Europe as well. The Sov-world's proletarians, as they call them, also glory in watching telly violence.

"To wrap it up, Denny, the fracases have withered away, their place being taken by gladiatorial combat. Now do you see? In place of wars, we have the smaller-scale violence that the mob lives on. But there is still the potential for full-scale warfare, and—"

The telly screen on his desk lit up, and Denny could see Miss Mikhail's elderly face. She said something obscured by the hush-circuit, and Frank Hodgson replied, "Very well, send her in, please."

When the door opened, the three men came to their feet.

Hodgson said, "Bette, may I present Professor Dennis Land. Denny, this is Bette Yardborough, the third member of your expedition-to-be."

It was a strange introduction, Denny thought. No mention of Category, Sub-Division, Rank, or even caste. The girl, herself, was quite startling. She bore an aura of not only excitement, but of energy. Her handshake was firm and decisive, and she looked into his eyes when she acknowledged the introduction, as though attempting to go beyond them to the inner man. And to say that she was not unattractive would be an understatement. She was probably in the vicinity of thirty, only two or three inches shorter than Denny, athletic-looking, red of hair, disturbingly green of eye, and small of mouth. The mouth, Denny decided, didn't live up to the rest of her, especially when pursed in exasperation, as it was now.

"A pleasure, professor," she said. "I understand that you, as well as this cloddy Zero—"

"I surrender," Zero chirped.

"—participated in that disgusting display of vulgarity last week." Before Denny could answer that, she spun on Frank Hodgson, who sighed and resumed his chair. "Do I understand that you are sending me to be a junior third member of a team, one of whom has never been on an assignment before?"

Hodgson chuckled nervously. "Back off, Bette. I wouldn't put it that way, my dear. On the surface,

Denny will be in command as Professor Land, doing historical research. Zero will be his self-effacing assistant, and you will be his secretary. In practice, you will be working as equals."

"Who will be in command when decisions involving the assignment are to be made?" she demanded.

The bureaucrat said gently, "I suggest you consider yourself as a team and utilize the democratic principle, as disparaged as it is these days."

"Oh, damn! This will be a project," she snapped, sinking abruptly into the chair that Zero was holding for her.

"Will you marry me, Bette?" Zero murmured, leaning close to her.

"Not even if they bounced me to Upper-Upper," she answered.

"All right, all right," Hodgson said. "You'll have time for horseplay later. We have arrived at the point where you'll wish instructions."

Denny had the distinct feeling that he was being railroaded. "I keep telling you I have no desire to play cloak and dagger—in Spain or elsewhere," he announced. He was getting more than a little annoyed at the easy assumption on the part of the BI agents that he had already agreed to join them. The fact that he felt free to exhibit that annoyance spoke volumes for Hodgson's diplomatic skills.

"Fine," Bette said. "I can probably handle this much easier if both of you stay right here and play with your swords and spears."

"Before you came in, Bette, I was proving to Denny that, far from the world being stable, it is in a continual condition of flux," Hodgson said.

"Whether we wish it or not, socio-economic institutions are ever changing." He twisted his mouth wryly. "The best we can do is attempt to direct them somewhat. Bette, you have had some briefing on the situation of interest here, but please bear with me while I fill your counterparts in on the details."

Denny realized that Hodgson was about to drop a bomb into the conversation, and he did just that. "It would seem that the Premier of Europe continues to enjoy the favors of the Goddess of Luck. Just when his weird controlled-demand economy absolutely requires expansion into new markets—and new sources of raw materials—he has found a method whereby he may descend upon profitable areas of the Neut-world without risking retaliation by either the West-world or the Sov-world. Unless, that is, international tempers flare, in which case we can look forward to rapidly escalating global war." He lowered his voice. "Nuclear war."

Zero said, for once no undertone of amusement in his voice, "Either or both of us would *have* to retaliate. If Common Europe could add the Neut-world to her apron strings, she would be in a position to eventually dominate the world. The balance of power would be over."

"Exactly," Hodgson said, nodding. "And the Premier knows it. At this point he isn't motivated by that long-range potential. It is simply that his economy is on the verge of a depression such as hasn't been seen since the middle of the Twentieth Century. Depressions are a thing of the past here, and were never acknowledged in the Sov-world, which had a sort of permanent depression, but Common

Europe didn't take the same path either of us did."

"What's this method you're speaking of?" Bette said, worry in her voice now. "I know that something's up with Common Europe, and that I'm going to be thrown in on it, but that's about it."

"An offbeat research engineer, you might call him, a certain Auguste Bazaine from Belgium, has devised a workable long-range, beam-guided laser, a defensive weapon. Worse, he's stumbled on some obscure and evidently misplaced results of West-world research from the last century—an artificial intelligence program with the capability to handle a comprehensive space- and land-based nuclear defense system. The program—and to label it such is over-simplification—also sports the capability to plan and implement offensive and counter-offensive strikes.

"With this system in place, the Europeans could defy the World Court and world opinion—nuclear weapons would no longer present a threat to them. Conventional warfare already lacks the threat— Common Europe is far overdeveloped on all fronts, and much of its production has gone into military hardware. In any event, both the West-world and the Sov-world, lacking such a defensive weapon, would have to stand to the side while they carved out portions of the Neut-world as desired. By the time we could develop similar technology, we would be faced with a *fait accompli*. If, that is, the world isn't plunged into war first."

He frowned. "They've let us know this much. And I do mean let us know. We figure the information has gone out along the intelligence networks to prepare us for Common Europe's move. And we're sure that Sov-world intelligence has been leaked the same information."

The realization came to Denny slowly. Although the terms used meant little to him, he could appreciate the gravity of the situation. "Then, this is something that would make Common Europe invulnerable?"

"Yes," Hodgson nodded. "It is the first defense against nuclear weapons delivered by missiles or bombers that has the potential to be one hundred percent effective, and it has no little application as an offensive weapon."

He eyed the trio thoughtfully. "The thing is that something has screwed up the Premier's plans, according to our Paris agents. This Auguste Bazaine evidently refuses to communicate with officials of Common Europe. It is the unsupported suspicion of our agents already there that Bazaine alone has the complete know-how for constructing his beam-guided laser and is being temperamental. And, of course, the location of the AI 'entity' is known only to Bazaine."

"Soooo . . .?" Zero prompted.

"So you are to repair immediately to Barcelona. There we have hired a small sailing yacht which you will take down the Spanish coast to Torremolinos, where Bazaine is hiding out. You will stop briefly at Tarragona and Cartagena, as though testing the possibility of Etruscan merchant ports having been established at those points before the arrival of the Greeks or Phoenicians. However, you will get to the Malaga area as quickly as feasible and make contact with Auguste Bazaine."

Frowning, Bette said, "What if he's hiding out? Do we play fox and rabbit, or what? Do you have anyone there doing the necessary groundwork to dig him out? That would take a lot of local manpower."

"That is not exactly the case, although he has hidden himself well and will talk with no one that he doesn't wish to see. He has contacts there, among a certain political clan of neo-socialists, and they are quite capable of covering for him, and willing to use whatever force necessary. He could be rooted out by a squad of commandos, but the Premier knows that Bazaine can't be forced to work with Common Europe and indeed might suicide in the face of capture. The man is temperamental, as I said, and must be handled with care. And *we* certainly do not want to go in with force, except as a last resort. Bazaine would almost certainly prefer death to capture by us. The repercussions would be an international incident the likes of which haven't been seen since the fusion bomb fiasco in old Eastern Europe.

"We must, unfortunately, play by the rules."

He paused and looked at Denny. "By delightful coincidence, it would seem that friend Bazaine is an amateur anthropologist, specializing in Phoenicians and Carthaginians."

Zero said, "All right. So we get to this mad-scientist type, whose new device could set the whole world off eventually. Then what do we do?"

Hodgson looked at him questioningly. "I hardly expected that question from you, my impetuous Zero. You work off the cuff, of course. If you can simply steal his programs and blueprints, assuming such exist, do so. I wouldn't count on what you find being the only copies, but given Bazaine's knowledge, we can maintain the balance of power. If it proves practical, you might destroy his discovery and his plans. If there are no such plans, perhaps kidnaping might be in order. You will have the yacht, which is large enough for sea voyages, and the crew, competent agents. And if it becomes necessary . . . well, Auguste Bazaine is expendable in this world of ours."

"Oh, great," Zero muttered.

Denny said, "I haven't agreed . . ."

Hodgson looked at him impatiently. "What is the name of your superior in Category Education who had you dismissed, Denny?"

"Updike. Academician Ronald Updike."

"Very well. Upon your return, following successful completion of your assignment, you will be reinstated. Would you like to take over the seat of this academic foe of yours?"

Denny stared at him. "Updike's a Low-Upper."

Hodgson smiled softly. "Somehow," he said, "we'll find a way. Are you in?"

Suddenly Denny realized that he was long past the point of no return. These people were competent. They needed him, but no one was indispensable. If he didn't join them, they would find a way to accomplish the task without him. When they had done so, they might even turn him loose . . . as a Low-Lower?

The next thing he realized was that the adventure of it appealed to him. Or was that appeal simply the survivor in him making the best of the unavoidable? Maybe. And maybe his experiences of the past year had given him a taste for excitement. All Denny knew or cared about was that suddenly he felt free, and ready for anything.

And on another level, the reality and import of this thing was getting to him. Save the world? Why not? He'd give it a shot anyway.

"I'm in."

Hodgson looked relieved. Land had proved unexpectedly difficult. Without his loss of academic standing, he might even have refused. Good thing they had thought of that.

"Very well, then. Miss Mikhail will give you some details, and Zero will see to your equipment. Just tell him what special items you'll need. You'll leave for Barcelona to join your yacht, soonest."

Zero, the lady agent, and Land all stood to go.

Hodgson said, "One other thing. Rumor has it that Yuri Malyshev has been given the same assignment you have. That is, to get to this Bazaine before the Premier makes his peace with him."

"Damn!" Zero hissed.

"Who's Yuri Malyshev?" Denny asked.

Bette said slowly, "The most competent, and certainly the most ruthless hatchetman of the Chrezvychainaya Komissiya."

"What's that?"

Zero grinned sourly. "It's the same as this department, only without the vestigial conscience that BI has. They lost it—or were born without it—about a century and a half ago."

As they filed through the door, Hodgson called out, "I needn't tell you what it would mean for your country if you fail."

☐ CHAPTER FIVE ☐

The three of them spent the next hour with Miss Mikhail, who, Denny decided, was much more than the traditional office receptionist. He wondered in passing what her category, rank, and caste might be, but didn't ask.

The Bureau of Investigation seemed to be the most slipshod organization he had ever seen, but in its lack of what could be called system and discipline, there was an elusive efficiency at work. For instance, Miss Mikhail had already made arrangements on the shuttle for passage to Barcelona, and evidently the yacht they were to use in the supposed exploration of the Iberian coast was already crewed and waiting. On the face of it, Frank Hodgson had not even considered the possibility that Denny would refuse to go.

After the details had been worked out, Zero, grinning, announced that he had some odds and ends to clear up before leaving, and that Denny should not take advantage of his absence to get next to the woman he loved.

Bette feigned indignation. "Overtranked again," she taunted. "Delusions of grandeur."

Zero waved, and was gone. Miss Mikhail followed him, on some errand or another.

Denny regarded Bette. He'd better make his peace with this woman, he decided. He was going to be in close company with her for the next couple of months, and he was not able to sustain the type of running battle that seemed the norm for her and Zero. He wondered what their actual feelings toward each other were.

He nodded after Zero. "Quite a guy," he said, letting the words mean anything.

"Don't get the wrong impression of Jesus Gonzales," Bette replied. "He's the second best agent in this bureau."

"Second? Who do you consider the best man?"

She looked him in the eye. "Me."

"Oh," Denny said. He hadn't quite caught the grammar, but the idea came through. "Why don't we go for a drink somewhere, and discuss this project further?"

She looked at him suspiciously. "I don't suppose you're the amorous kind?"

"Sometimes. But only on occasions other than business," Denny said stiffly.

"All right, let's go. There's a bar in B-12 corridor that makes the best Far Out Coolers in Greater Washington."

Denny let her lead the way for a moment, then caught up.

The bar proved to be a good five minutes' walk away. Denny kept his silence as they walked, and Bette didn't seem inclined to speak either. As expected, it turned out to be an autobar, and they found a table easily enough at this time of day.

Before Denny could bring his own credit card forth she had slipped hers into the bar's slot and ordered two Far Out Coolers.

"I sometimes wonder about the elimination of coinage and paper money," she said, after their drinks had arrived. "For even the tiniest purchase you use your credit card. Can you imagine the number of terminals and computers involved in reading your card and deducting from your account, even, say, the purchase of a single aspirin? Why not have at least minor coins? We used them a lot, for saving and small purchases, when I was growing up."

Denny shrugged. What was this to her? Coins were curiosities for collectors, and the present system worked well enough. Besides, the question had never occurred to him. The use of the universal credit card had been with him all his adult life. "The amount of work involved isn't particularly important," he said, his disinterest obvious. "Besides, the moment you have actual legal tender, it can be lost, stolen, or conned away from you. Each month, my dividends are deposited to my account. Only I can spend them, and on whatever I wish. My rent, my utilities, all those basic expenses are automatically deducted. It works. Why change it?"

She sipped her drink. "It seems to be the slogan of our day: 'Why change it?' Have you thought about the fact that our using credit cards for everything makes it very convenient for Category Security to track the daily activities of any individual?" She sighed. "But back to Zero. It might do your long-term morale good to realize that Frank Hodgson isn't as easygoingly gentle as he just loves to project. When he sends a team out, it's composed of just the elements he thinks are necessary for the job. He's seldom wrong. Zero is unsurpassed as a bureau operative."

"But why pick on me?"

"Hodgson told you. First, your perfect camouflage; second, your proven ability in action. But third, and probably most important of all, as an archaeologist dealing with Bazaine's favorite period, you'll probably open doors to get to him."

He looked at her anew, realizing, as though for the first time, how really pretty she was. Then he said without thinking, "That accounts for Zero and me. How about you?"

Her mouth tightened, but then relaxed and took on an impatient twist. "You might have figured that out for yourself. If I know Frank Hodgson, he decided we needed an extra *in*, in case your fling didn't work."

Denny frowned at her.

She drummed her fingers impatiently. "This Auguste Bazaine has two hobbies: archaeology—and women."

She suddenly smiled—for the first time—and then laughed. "Wait until you see me go into my act," she said. Then added, sober again, "If necessary." She looked at her watch. "I've got an appointment before too long."

Denny's first impression of Bette Yardborough had been one of dismay. He disliked aggressive, domineering females; his taste ran to the serene type. His life had been such that he had found little time to devote to worrying about his sex life and the usual complications involved; he just didn't want to get embroiled in emotional situations. He liked quiet girls, good-looking but not necessarily startling beauties. Get a great beauty on your hands and, sure as hell, sooner or later complications arose. And he preferred uncomplicated relationships. His typical involvement with a woman was limited to a couple of weeks of mutual enjoyment.

She broke into his thoughts. "What was all this about you being dismissed from the University because of participation in the games?"

He gave her a brief rundown of the situation. She had heard Hodgson's promise to have him reinstated, so he didn't have to mention that. She was indignant. "You mean this Lower-Upper curd had you kicked off the faculty for no other reason than that you had been drafted, in spite of yourself, to fight in the games?"

"That's about it," he replied.

"The scum!" she railed. "But it's just what you have to expect. A hereditary aristocrat! Have you ever heard in history of a hereditary aristocrat that was worth last year's credit card? Sure, sure, the first generation slugs its way to the top. He's an outstanding warrior, or possesses an unusually agile mind. Then the second generation comes along, inheriting the old boy's titles, position, and wealth, and he's a second rater. Then the third, raised by his generation, is a molly. By the time you get to the fourth generation, you get the hemophilia of the Romanoffs, the withered arm of the Kaiser, and the chinless wonders of the Hapsburgs. Zen knows what their brains were like!"

Denny was gaping at her. Never in his career

had he heard this open an attack on the caste
system of the West-world—not even as an under-
graduate, that freest of life's periods.

He cleared his throat and said mildly, "There
have been examples of remarkable ability being
handed down from one generation to another. For
instance, Philip of Macedon, a military genius,
and his son, Alexander, an even greater one."

She turned her wrath on him. "Trying to find
excuses for the very cloddies who exploit you, eh?
Anything to maintain the status quo? Don't rock
the boat, something worse might happen to us. So
far as Alexander is concerned, I've often wondered. At a time when the Persian Empire was on
the verge of collapse, depending on Greek mercenaries to defend it, Philip trained the most competent army the world had yet seen, and developed
such top general officers as Parmenion, Nearchus,
and Antipater. Alexander inherited it, and the de-
cadent Persians fell apart before him. But how
much did he really have on the ball? And what
happened to *his* children, this third generation of
Macedonian aristocrats?"

"They had their throats slit," Denny admitted,
with no little chagrin.

Instead of continuing the verbal barrage, she
stood up. "I'm afraid I've got to go. As I understand it, we meet tomorrow at Zero's place, ready
to depart for Barcelona."

"That's right." He came to his feet, too. "Mind
showing me the nearest vacuum-tube pick-up? I'll
have to get back to my place, pack, and make
some arrangements."

"Come along," she said briskly.

Bette Yardborough, Denny decided, could turn the charm on and off like a faucet. He shuddered inwardly at the thought of getting involved with her, even as he hurriedly followed after.

Bette had turned out of the small auto-bar and into the main Octagon corridor beyond, and Denny was forced to jog to catch her. He sped up and caromed off a pedestrian hurrying along on his own business.

"Oops, sorry, friend," Denny blurted. He caught the other, to steady him, then let go and turned to follow Bette.

"*Just* a moment, *friend*," the other rasped.

Denny turned back, in an instant taking in the well-cut material of the other's dress, the air of arrogant indignation.

Uh, oh.

"Have you no regard for your betters? No respect for the color of my shirt?"

Oh. Thus far, Denny had failed to note that. The blue shirt. Symbol of labor. Not only was the other an Upper, but a labor leader as well, the touchiest, most class conscious of them all.

Bette had returned. The charm was suddenly turned on at full blast. "Oh, sir, it's all my fault. Bette Yardborough, Category Government, Subdivision Bureau of Investigation, Rank Special Agent, Upper-Middle. Professor Land here, the hero of the national games, has been given an assignment with our department. I'm afraid we're in such a rush . . ."

He was not even partly placated. Denny could tell from the sheen of his eyes that the other had been doing mescaltranc. It didn't help his disposition.

He was shouting now. "Some examples should be made of you brash young Middles—I assume you're a Middle, though you act more like a slum element of Low-Lower—who make some ridiculous pretension of notoriety and seem to think that automatically runs you up several castes. Let me tell you, young man, bluffing your way through the national games does not put you on a basis where you can brush citizens of Upper caste from your path."

Denny wet his lips. This jerk had a problem, and Denny didn't want to make it his own problem. "No, sir. It was entirely inadvertent. I—"

"The dignity of labor has been forgotten in this benighted country. Let it be known that I'm David Hoffaman the sixth, Mid-Upper, Category Transportation, Rank Labor Leader, and I demand I be treated with the respect due me!"

"Sir, I . . ." Denny began.

"Sir, I am sure . . ." Bette said, smiling her all-but-cringing self-depreciation.

"No, no, you've made it clear how little respect you have for the institutions of the West-world. Let me have your full name, category, and rank." He glared at them. "Out with it, or I call Category Security!"

That was all he needed. This might even result in a reduction in caste to Upper-Lower. With that, he would never aspire to a professorship again, not to speak of an appropriation for historical research.

Without thinking, Denny blurted out, "Dennis Land, Category Education, Subdivision History, Branch Research, Rank Professor, Mid-Middle Caste. Northwest University," he finished, biting his tongue when he realized that he might have gotten away with a lie.

The other, still in a rage, was noting it down. "Professor, indeed. Mid-Middle indeed. A gladiator, I understand. A ruffian, fit only to participate in the games. We'll just investigate these ranks and castes of yours, *professor.*"

Bette said urgently, "But sir, the professor is on a particularly urgent mission for the Bureau . . ." She was all but fawning on the indignant man.

The air fairly crackled with his arrogance, "You're both dismissed!"

They turned and left.

Denny's face was gray. Bette's eyes blazed.

When the horrible little man was out of sight, Denny erupted. "A parasite. Of all the useless members of society, it's a labor leader. We've gotten to the point where not only are the Lowers no longer useful members of society, but neither are the Uppers! We Middles do everything needed to produce the West-world's needs." He was having second thoughts now about how they had handled the situation; it probably would have been better if they had simply moved on, instead of according the man any courtesy at all.

She looked at him, her eyes still blazing resentment. "Do you really mean that?"

"Of course I mean it!"

"All right, then. Come along with me. I told you that I had an appointment."

He frowned, some of his ire leaving him. "Come along to where?"

"You'll see."

Denny shrugged. He did have a little time, and

he had to admit that Bette Yardborough intrigued him.

By routes that only later occurred to him were devious she led him to what was probably a Low-Middle section of town. Low-Middle, barely above the lowest caste. He wondered at her interest in or her acquaintance with such a neighborhood. He seemed to recall that she was Upper-Middle herself, just one level below the exalted position of Upper.

After taking a hovercab out of the city proper, she led him through some labyrinth turns on foot, probably, he decided, to confuse him to the point of not being able to find the place again. They entered a community building, and finally approached a guarded door.

To the man at the door, a somewhat nervous, wizened little type, she said, "Progress!"

"It must be resumed," he responded, speaking as if in ritual. He opened the door.

Bette and Denny entered a room containing some hundred folding chairs, with possibly thirty people occupying them. A speech was going on, and as they found seats, several of the audience glared at the commotion they made.

The speaker, a man somewhere in his fifties, spoke intimately and sincerely, rather than with ardor.

He was saying, "Consider these statistics, citizens. In my youth, the Uppers consisted of nearly two percent of the population, approximately ten million persons. Today, in spite of population growth, they number considerably less than one percent, some four million persons. During that same period, the Middles have grown a bit in percentage, admittedly; but the Lowers are not too far different."

Denny whispered to Bette, "What is all this about?" He felt a certain trepidation.

"Shush," she said. "You'll see." She herself was leaning forward, her eyes shining, obviously anxious to follow the speaker's words.

The speaker continued. ". . . an old, old proverb, fellow citizens. The rich get richer, and the poor get poorer. Speaking percentage-wise, it is still so. The vise is tightening. In the early days of the Welfare State, supposedly anyone, on his own ability, could rise to the ranks of the Uppers. But slowly, slowly, the avenues have been squeezed shut. Now those doors are closed: today *no one has been promoted from the ranks of the Middles for three full years!* The truth is manifest. The Uppers have frozen the rest of us out. *Their* children become Uppers, receive Upper education and privileges, but so far as allowing their despised underlings to ever aspire to their positions of opulence and power, they have closed the gates."

Denny whispered to her, "He can't say that. Security will be down on this gathering like a ton of bricks. We'd better get out of here, Bette."

"Oh, don't be a funker. Sit still. Allow yourself to hear something new for a change. These Sons of Liberty meetings are held all over the country."

"Sons of Liberty?" he said blankly.

One of their neighbors was angrily hissing at them, but Bette said, "Good God, Dennis. Have you been so wrapped up in your ivory tower that you didn't realize there was an active underground in this country?"

Wide-eyed now, Denny listened to the speaker. "All our instincts are against change. Change means upsetting whatever security we have established. Change means unknown problems to face. Besides our instinctive fears of it, all the means of molding public opinion have been utilized from our very births to disparage change. Our children, hardly before they are out of the cradle, learn slogans such as 'You mustn't speak against the government,' and 'What was good enough for daddy is good enough for me.'

"But there comes a time when things as they are become intolerable, when no matter what our instincts, no matter what our deepest training, we are forced to change. Our world, fellow citizens, is in full stagnation. A major percentage of our population, an overwhelming percentage, is either completely unutilized, or doing make-work. Whatever happened to our dreams of conquering space? What foundered all the projects of the late Twentieth Century? Well, one thing that foundered them was that such projectes threatened the status quo. When you start such major developments, you never know where they might end.

"It is something like the old wars. You started a war with definite aims in view, but before it terminated, you might end up with anything. Take World War One. The powers launched into the conflict over issues involving foreign trade, sources of raw material. Germany wanted her place in the sun, equal to France and England, who had launched into colonialism centuries before the Germans got going. But I doubt if any of the powers involved realized that before the war was through, half the crowns of Europe would be rolling in the dust, with nobody to pick them up. And, most frightening of all, the Russian bear had overthrown the old and was embarked on a new and dangerous theory of socio-economics."

Bette whispered to Denny, "Well put!"

The speaker's voice rose in pitch. "Now our present regime, our Upper Uppers in control, wants no startling developments, either political or scientific, which might start a snowball rolling that they could never stop. Thus all that makes any difference is clamped down. Fellow citizens, let us face reality. We must organize to overthrow the Welfare State if man is to resume his march of progress. Certainly, his destiny is not to stagnate, fuzzy with trank pills and spending the greater part of his waking hours staring at telly, and particularly the gladiator games and fracases, which are the most popular programs by far. No, we must organize behind the banner of the new Sons of Liberty and—"

And then there was a scuffling outside, and three shots, followed by a shout from the door. "You're all under arrest! This meeting is under arrest for subversion. Do not resist."

"Oh, Christ, didn't I tell you so?" Denny snarled, jumping to his feet. "Let's get the hell out of here. If we're taken in, we'll be bounced down to Low-Lower!"

As if by magic, a tiny automatic appeared in Bette Yardborough's hand. "Get out how?" she demanded, without a tremor in her voice.

The room was in complete confusion and Category Security men, in uniform and heavily armed, were pouring in from the same door through which Denny and Bette had entered, not fifteen minutes before.

"Come on," he snapped, "there must be at least one rear entrance. Some way to get down to the cellar, or up to the roof. Let's go." He led the way like a quarterback going through a broken field, pushing the members of the audience this way and that as they milled about in panic. In an instant he had dropped the role of a member of the audience listening to a lecturer, and become the quick-reflexed athlete who had won through the nation's final gladiatorial games.

Bette, lithe and silent, was right behind him. He had no doubt whatsoever that she was perfectly competent and more than willing to use the vicious little gun she carried.

There was indeed a rear door. Two of them, in fact. There was no time to debate which one to take. Denny made a snap judgment, thinking absurdly of ladies and tigers as he did so, and pushed through the left one, Bette close on his heels. He wondered if the speaker, and the members of the committee who had been sitting behind him, had managed to escape. If so, he hadn't seen which way they had gone. As Bette closed the door, he scanned the area.

There was a corridor beyond—a long and empty corridor, with another door at the far end.

"Let's go!" he yelled at her over his shoulder.

Just as they reached the far end, the door be-

hind them opened and a voice ordered, "Halt, or I
fire!"

Bette, cool as ice, whirled and flicked two shots
into the woodwork, not two inches above the other's head. The Security man gasped, glanced up at
the near miss, and made a quick retreat, slamming
the door behind him.

Bette made a contemptuous moue. "Funker,"
she muttered. "I should report him."

Denny had the next door open. There was yet
another corridor beyond it, this one lined with a
succession of doors. "Hurry—" he began, looking
back.

But another voice interrupted, pleasantly. "All
right, you two. You're under arrest for subversion.
Drop that gun, sister!"

Bette blurted, "Zero!"

☐ CHAPTER SIX ☐

"Holy jumping frogs!" Zero Gonzales yelped. "What are you two doing here?"

Bette had spun and shot home the bolt in the door behind them. Now she snapped, "If we had time for pleasantries, we might ask you the same thing."

He bit right back at her. "I came along with some of the boys to raid a meeting of subversive crackpots."

Denny said, "Well, we're two of the crackpots."

"Oh, great! Come on," Zero ordered. "Let's get out of here. If they nab you, it'll take a month of interdepartmental Sundays to get you cleared."

"Lead on, lead on, and cut the chatter," Bette told him.

They followed Zero, who had turned and was darting down the corridor. "Throw the gun away," he told her. "These Category Security people are all armed and trigger happy. If one of them spots that he'll zap you for sure."

"Not if I see him first," Bette said grimly. "You just keep leading the way." She held on to the gun.

Even as they ran, Zero rolled his eyes upward in resignation. "Oh, fine. Hodgson is going to love this. Three of his operatives in a gun fight with Category Security agents on a raid. Great!"

They came to a turn in the corridor, with a door immediately beyond. Zero skidded to a halt and held up a hand. His voice was a whisper now. "Listen, I can't be seen. I came along on this raid for laughs."

"Some sense of humor," Bette sniffed.

"And, of course, Security knows I'm along. Anyway, there are two of them on the other side of this door, both armed with handguns." He turned to Denny. "You're going to have to take them alone. They can't be allowed to see me."

Bette proffered the gun, but Zero stopped her. "You can't shoot them, Denny—unless you think that you can't handle it any other way."

Denny considered his options, and what he knew about Category Security men. "O.K.," he said. "Get ready to open the door for me. And do it quickly."

Bette glanced from one to the other. "You said there were two of them, with guns. Are you trying to get Dennis killed?"

"When I flick my hand," Denny ordered, "get the door open fast, and get yourselves out of the way."

Zero had his hand on the knob. "Right."

Bette shifted from one foot to the other, puzzled. "Boys, listen . . ."

Denny, in a half crouch, moved his hand in signal, and Zero jerked the door open, standing back and to the side.

Hesitating on the fraction of a second that it took to scan the scene before him, Denny dashed through, screaming, "*Sut!*" in a Kai yell. Bette watched, eyes wide, as he bounced to a halt before the two startled men who stood there, talking. One carried a gun, held negligently in his right hand. The other's weapon was holstered at his side. Her original idea had been to bring up the rear, ready, if necessary, to bring her own weapon into the fray. It took less than a second to realize that Dennis Land was not going to need any backup.

He had dropped into the *Kokutsu-dachi*, layout position, his left foot forward, toes out and knees slightly bent. Even as the gun-bearing agent began to bring his weapon up, he blurred into action, screaming "Sut!" again. His left hand chopped out to the inner wrist of the other's gun hand, thrust it to the side; his right foot lashed out to the agent's groin. Simultaneously his right hand, pointed spearlike, thrust forward to the man's larynx. The Security operative dropped as though dead.

Before the fallen man touched the floor, Denny whirled and dropped into the *Zenkutsu-dachi*, lunge position, facing the second agent. The man was no coward, no matter how bewildered by the developments of the last two seconds, but those had startled him so that he had been unable to move. He knew better than to try for his weapon now. The screaming madman before him was not going to give him time to get at it.

The Security man had training, but he was no Dennis Land. He tried a quick right snap-kick, which should have connected but didn't. Denny yelled and chopped against the foot with his fist, Okinawa style, thumb side pointed forward. An instant later, he whirled around and hit the other on the left temple with the same fist as he brought his right knee up hard into the other's groin, and his other hand up, knuckles first, to his chin. The agent was already collapsing, but Dennis reversed the fist, knuckles down, and slugged him across the left clavicle.

It hadn't taken five seconds in all

Denny turned to them quickly. "Let's get out of here," he rasped. "The first one will be out for about ten minutes. The second for possibly fifteen."

Bette was staring from him to the two fallen men, and then back again. "What did you do?" she asked.

Zero began to laugh, even as he led the way. He had remained hidden behind the door until the two guards were eliminated. "You'll have to read through Denny's dossier some time," he said. "He holds one of three seventh-degree black belts in the West-world."

"Black belt?" Bette said blankly.

"A karate award," Zero told her, taking her arm to hurry her along. "Karate used to be very popular, but the authorities decided a karate-trained populace was too much like an armed populace. They didn't forbid it, exactly, just discouraged it. People who taught it tended to lose status, and word got around."

"It's been sort of a hobby ever since I was in my teens," Denny said, an element of apology in his voice.

"Some professor," Bette chuckled. "What do you teach, mayhem?"

"I teach history," he said, suddenly defensive.

She was still staring at him strangely as Zero hustled them along. "What was all the screaming about?"

"That's the Kai yell. It's, well, partly psychological, to startle your opponent."

"Well it scared me, and I was on your side."

"And it's part of the karate exercise. It enables you to utilize your full strength."

"Some professor," she repeated.

They had come to a door leading out on the street. Zero opened it, looked up and down. "By pure luck, I parked my hovercar on a side-street, away from the others," he informed them. "Come on, let's go. Look nonchalant. And Bette, ditch that gun before we get on the street."

Bette's small automatic went back into her purse. She composed her face, lit until now with excitement, and they stepped out into the glare of day.

Denny was still breathing deeply from his encounter with the two Security agents, but Zero maintained a running banter as they walked along the street. If any fellow pedestrians turned to look at them, it was for the sake of Bette's good looks, or because of recognition of Denny, rather than because the trio appeared out of place.

At the car, the three crowded into the front seat. Zero powered up, dropped the lift lever, pressed the accelerator, and they were off. As soon as they had moved into the traffic, he began cursing under his breath.

"All right, all right." Bette glared at him. "If you have something to say, say it."

He snarled, "Tomorrow we take off for Common Europe on a top-priority mission. And what do you two do? You get yourself involved with a gang of impractical malcontents who are on the subversive list, and almost get caught."

"Members of all revolutionary organizations are considered impractical malcontents," Bette said tightly, "until they've put over their revolution. Then they're heroic patriots—fathers of their country and what not."

Zero shot a disgusted look at her. "I knew you'd been flirting around with these two-bit do-gooder outfits, but I didn't think you were serious. And what the devil were *you* doing there, Denny? I didn't know you were interested in politics, let alone subversion."

"I went along for the ride," Denny told him.

The dark-complected agent grunted his irritation. "I'm going to drop you two off. We're due to leave in the morning. Think you can stay out of jail until then?"

"'Yes, daddy," Betty said sweetly.

Yuri Malyshev, dressed foppishly as a high-echelon Party member, arrived in Madrid at the landing strip near Mirasierra on the northern outskirts of the Iberian capital, and put on an act of all but feminine impatience at customs examinations. Common Europe's customs inspections of arrivals from the Sov-world were on the thorough side. Not only was every article of his baggage inspected by eye and hand, it was also subjected to X-ray and sonic scanning. The hidden compartment, the secret pocket or chamber, these were things of the past.

For that matter, he thought contemptuously, did they for a moment dream that a real agent, an experienced operative, would be carrying anything incriminating? But, he told himself, it was all a part of the game. The customs officials sternly searched for that which they knew was not there, while Yuri masked his boredom with indignation. He expected this treatment, and they expected his response. It was known who he was, if not why he was here, and the delay was standard operating procedure.

Finally cleared, Malyshev hired a chauffeur-driven hovercar to take him to his destination. It was his first visit to Madrid, and he was mildly surprised at the lack of transport automation. It was evidently true, then, that European economists deliberately made work to keep the potentially unemployed busy. The basic theory, as he had heard it, was that a busy member of the lower class was less prone to make trouble. He shrugged. Perhaps they were right; the Lowers of the Westworld and the overwhelming majority of the Proletarians in his own nation had largely been automated into complete idleness and were a potential volcano.

Maintaining his air of bored disinterest, he gave directions in Spanish, then watched idly as they entered town. They drove down the broad Avenida del Generalisimo Franco, named, he vaguely recalled, after an adventurer who had seized power during the confused early Twentieth Century before Common Europe had amalgamated. This avenue blended into Paseo de La Castellana, and after about a mile they went through a plaza with a statue of Christopher Colon. Several blocks farther, the next plaza—it seemed to be a city of great plazas—contained a huge statue which brought a scowl of attempted memory to his face. He asked the driver, who told him it was the ancient goddess Cibele, or Cybele. They proceeded down Paseo del Prado, and pulled up before the imposing Embassy of the Sov-world. Ordering the driver to wait, Yuri Malyshev disappeared through the portals.

He was not unexpected. A young military attache—a lieutenant, and a Pole by the looks of him, Malyshev decided—took him immediately to an ornate suite of offices. They eventually arrived at a paper-strewn desk behind which sat a beleaguered-looking, heavyset man who had torn open his collar as a concession to Spain's summer weather.

Once through the Embassy portals, Yuri Malyshev had dropped his airs. Now, though in mufti, he half came to attention.

The official behind the desk said, "That will be all, Lieutenant Sobieski. See that I am undisturbed until further notice."

The lieutenant clicked his heels and said, "Yes, Comrade Colonel." He about-faced and was gone.

Yuri announced himself. "Yuri Malyshev, on assignment from . . . from Commissar Kodaly in Budapest."

The other grunted acidly. "Zoltan Korda, you mean, don't you?"

Malyshev said nothing to that. He had learned

the pricelessness of silence on delicate ground early in his career.

The other came to his feet and extended a hand. "I'm Colonel Valentin Dumitrescu. We'll be working together on this Auguste Bazaine matter."

Malyshev shook his head warily. It wasn't going to happen again. "I understood that Comrade Matyas Petofe was head of the Komissiya here in Madrid, colonel. If you'll pardon my saying so, my current assignment is such that I must deal with the highest echelons."

Dumitrescu waved him to a chair, and settled back into his own. "Are you a Party member, colonel?"

"No."

"Neither am I, colonel. Matyas Petofe, of course, is, this post being such an important one. However" —the Roumanian cleared his throat—"his excellency is so taken up in making, um, higher decisions, working on overall policy, that sort of thing, that a great deal of the more mundane matters fall upon my shoulders."

"I see," Malyshev said.

"Yes, indeed," Dumitrescu sighed. "You'd be surprised at the considerable detail work we have here, Colonel Malyshev. By the way, I've heard quite a bit about your activities in the East. Your reputation as a good man in the dill, as the Westerners say, precedes you."

Yuri nodded his appreciation of the flattery.

The Roumanian sighed again. "Holding down a desk job such as this can be wearisome, colonel. Particularly one in Spain, the least progressive region of Common Europe. The Spanish are incredibly naive, politically. Why, do you realize that at a reception the other evening I stood in a discussion in which several of the local politicians, members of the Premier's party, expressed the opinion that Trotsky lives on in Mexico."

Startled, Yuri Malyshev looked at him a long moment before quietly voicing the response, "And will never die."

The other's eyebrows went up. "So. You are one of us."

It needed no answer.

Dumitrescu said, "It has been a long time since my last visit home. How is the movement progressing?"

Malyshev shook his head, traced a finger along his jaw line. "Slowly, my friend. Slowly. But progress it does. Our greatest strength is the growing weakness of the enemy. Not a month past I was shown some statistics on the Party and its decline. Do you realize that Party membership is now less than half what it was twenty years ago? This very poor policy of theirs, allowing only the children of members to become members, is destroying them. Their women are even going through a fad in which they avoid childbirth."

Dumitrescu nodded. "I've heard about that. It's been going on for years. However, we can't wait for them to breed, or rather to fail to breed, themselves out of existence." He suddenly slapped a palm down on the paper-laden desk before him. "They'll ultimately have to be shot out, Comrade Malyshev. They've become parasites on society beyond what the Romanoffs ever were."

Malyshev twisted his mouth. "I've often wondered where the world would be today, had history taken a different path in 1917. Suppose that Kerensky had never been overthrown by the Bolsheviks and his group had formed a government similar to those prevailing in the West at that time."

The Roumanian smiled. "Or suppose the assassin's bullet had never cut Lenin down, and the mad-dog Stalin was never able to take over his position. What then? Or suppose Stalin had failed in his efforts to destroy the Old Bolsheviks, including your ancestor, Vladimir Malyshev. Would they have directed the country in other fashion?

"I suppose what you are suggesting is correct. But there is no turning back history. We must deal with what the past hands down to us and go on from here. Lenin is gone now, Trotsky is gone. So are Stalin, Beria, Brezhnev, Gorbachev, and so many of the rest. What we have to do is press on, taking advantage of what they *did* accomplish. Finish off the Party as it is now, and return to the principles of free men!"

The Roumanian rose suddenly from his chair and approached a sideboard. "I do not want to give the impression that I operate like a sot of a Party member," he said over his shoulder, "drinking in mid-morning. But it has been some time since I've met a fellow member of the underground. I recently acquired a bottle of stone age *Tucia* from Transylvania, and insist that you try a glass with me."

Malyshev came to his feet. "Gladly."

The other filled two small shot glasses.

Malyshev held his toward the Roumanian. "Trotsky lives!"

"And shall never die! Down with the Party!"

They knocked the fiery Roumanian liqueur back over their palates.

Resuming his seat, the Russian agent said thoughtfully, "That brings something to mind. When I was in Zoltan Korda's office in Budapest, he asked me if I had ever heard our passwords. I told him no, of course. But it worries me that he knows of them."

"No underground organization can remain completely undetected. They know we exist. As a matter of fact, I am surprised that, to my knowledge, thus far none of us have been arrested."

Malyshev grunted contempt. "The Party grows inefficient, lazy, and sodden with their drink and this new escapism they've acquired from the West-world."

"New escapism?"

"It's a chemical euphoria agent based on mescaline, I believe. At least they call it mescaltranc in the West-world. The ingredients are evidently quite difficult to come by, so that it's expensive and only Party members can afford its use. It's become quite the fad."

"Everything is fad among the parasites these days. Everything but work. However, even though the Party itself has grown lax, don't underestimate such as Zoltan Korda. He is neither lazy, nor incapable."

Yuri growled, "He's not a Party member, either. I wish he could be recruited to our cause."

"All in good time. Perhaps he will be, one day.

Meanwhile, Comrade—I use the term in the old sense, of course, not as though we were Party members—we must get to the matter of Auguste Bazaine, and the immediate threat he poses to the safety of the world."

Yuri leaned back in his chair. "Yes. Korda told me you might be in possession of some more recent details of the situation. Frankly, it astonishes me. Is the Premier's power so feeble that an individual scientist can defy him?"

The Roumanian scowled unhappily. "It would seem, if my information is correct, that there is conflict among the Premier's closest advisers. He is not, of course, an *absolute* dictator, in the old sense of the word. Though Common Europe is united, it is still composed of a variety of elements, and there is considerable interplay of interests. Elements in what was once Germany often have reason to conflict politically and economically with those of, say, Spain, Italy, or Sweden. And, of course, there are the old traditions. When the Premier recently officiated at the unveiling of the colossal statue to Hermann Goering and the Luftwaffe, there was considerable ill feeling in that area once known as the Netherlands, and particularly Rotterdam, which was leveled in the Second War."

"I realize that there are inner conflicts in Common Europe," Malyshev said impatiently.

"Well, this conflict seems to be more important, from our viewpoint, than most of them. It would seem that our Auguste Bazaine actually wishes to *build* this ultimate defense system of his."

The Russian suddenly stiffened. "*Build* it! Build

weapons and defense systems that could bring the world to its knees, if not to the final confrontation first? Insane! It's against the Universal Disarmament Pact. The International Disarmament Commission wouldn't stand for it, not to speak of the World Court."

The other was nodding. "Yes, yes, I know. But what power does the World Court hold over those who do not choose to accept its limitations and rulings? At any rate, a split has taken place. One faction wishes to back Bazaine, and go into production; the other wishes to abide by the Universal Disarmament Pact to the extent of keeping the plans of the device as a sword over the heads of the rest of the world, but going no further.

"Bazaine, like many of his ilk, is tempermental, and will not be forced in any way to do what he does not consider appropriate, for his own motivations. He has, of course, hidden the program and plans where they cannot be discovered." He grinned briefly. "Otherwise, we or the Europeans or the West-world would have found them by now."

"They're mad!" Malyshev blurted. "This Bazaine is mad."

The other shrugged. "That will be for you to discover. He is evidently sulking in Torremolinos, refusing to reveal his secrets until his demands are met. The situation is, of course, delicate, and we must be subtle; Bazaine has quite an army of supporters here—*las comunistas*, as it turns out. They're a holdover from pre-amalgamation days, and hold no love for Sov-world politics."

He cleared his throat. "But in the way of useful information, our Auguste Bazaine does not seem averse to relaxation, being known to have an eye both for a good vintage and a well-filled bikini."

Malyshev chopped out a short laugh. "They should have sent someone better equipped than I, in that case. They sent the wrong . . . uh, man."

The Roumanian scowled, not being long on humor. "Well. Let us get down to details."

☐ CHAPTER SEVEN ☐

They stayed half a day in Barcelona. From the shuttle strip, they made their way immediately to the port area and the Paseo de Colon. If Frank Hodgson's scheme was going to work at all, they had to get down to Torremolinos as soon as possible, which wasn't nearly as soon as it should have been.

Their basic problem was to get to Auguste Bazaine at all. It was to be assumed that the man was no fool. Even if he were, the European Premier's counterespionage was not to be minimized. Common Europe would have no intention of allowing a man as important as Auguste Bazaine to be approached by West-world agents.

They had, then, to use some of their precious time building up their protective covering. They had to convincingly be Professor Dennis Land, noted Etruscanologist, and his party, on research into the question of early Etruscan penetration of the Iberian peninsula. Otherwise, they would have moved immediately to Torremolinos. As it was, they could only pray that the Premier and Bazaine didn't make their peace before they got there.

The yacht wasn't conspicuously large. It was crewed by three men, each a BI agent, or at least a trusted employee. Whatever their level of affiliation with the agency, they acted completely in character. Supposedly, they were citizens of Common Europe, employed on a charter boat. Two of them spoke, or pretended to speak, only broken English. Throughout the period Professor Land and his two assistants were aboard the yacht, *La Carmencita*, none of the crew spoke on any subject other than the working of the yacht.

For that matter, the small craft's skipper, a Miguel Bienvenida, was almost as taciturn. When the three of them came down the narrow gangplank of *La Carmencita*, he greeted them, supervised the loading of their luggage, and, when the porters had gone, led them into the salon.

Captain Bienvenida was very brief. He offered them a *fundador*, then made his speech. "My instructions are to captain this yacht. We are to sail along the coast to Torremolinos, making a stop or two along the way. I have no instructions beyond those other than that, in an emergency, my men and I are to cooperate completely and follow your orders, whatever they may be. I am told that the operation is Priority One. I suggest you tell me no more than is necessary, *por favor*."

Denny started to say something, but Zero anticipated him. He merely said, "Very sensible, captain. I understand you have some equipment for us."

"*Sí*," he nodded. "I have a suitcase to turn over to you. I have no idea what it contains." He grimaced in amusement. "Books, perhaps."

He was a small man—typically Catalonian, typically a sailor—his eyes narrowed from long squinting into the glare of the Mediterranean, that brightest of seas, his skin like mahogany from long exposure. He would do, and more than do, obviously. Denny wondered how the other had come into the service of Frank Hodgson, then shrugged it away. He doubted he would ever learn.

The yacht was supposedly a sailing craft, but it contained powerful inboard engines. They left the dock and departed the harbor of Barcelona at a neat clip.

Zero retired to the depths of the vessel to check the contents of the suitcase Bienvenida had been entrusted with. Denny and Bette stood at the rail, watching the city disappear, brooding castle crowning the heights above it.

"Holy Zen! That's beautiful," Bette murmured.

Denny was looking at her, thinking, *so are you, girl*. But he did not voice the thought. Instead, he said, "Zen is the science of meditation or deep concentration, not an individual. It originated in India as the Dhyana school founded by legendary Boddhidarma. Why do people use the word as though Zen was a god or a prophet or something?"

"Always the history professor!" She laughed. "Haven't you noticed, Dennis, that, its priests and strongest adherents to the contrary, a religion invariably evolves, continually changes? Take Buddha. Siddhartha Gautama actually lived and taught a not overly complicated philosophy; but after a few centuries his followers had made a god of Gautama, which undoubtedly would have horrified him. Or take Joshua of Nazareth, who taught

meekness and the brotherhood of man to the poor
on the seashores and in the hills. Look what his
image changed to in a few centuries."

"Now who's being the history professor?"

She looked at him quizzically. "You're an odd
one, Dennis Land. Are you really a professor?"

He shrugged. "Why not?"

"Now, looking at you, listening to you, I could
believe it. You're mild, quiet—perhaps even gentle. It just doesn't jibe with being a gladiator, or
with holding a . . . what did Zero call it? A karate
black belt."

Denny looked back to the receding shoreline.
"I'm afraid I chose my hobbies poorly," he said
bitterly. "If I had my way, right this moment I'd
be back at the University, up to my ears in the
past."

She said nothing, continued to look at him
questioningly.

"I made the mistake of deciding that most histories did a poor job of describing ancient warfare,
ancient weapons, gladiatorial combat and such,
because it was a field about which they knew
nothing. So I spent my off hours learning about
violence first-hand. I figured on showing up the
experts."

Bette put a hand on his arm, moved closer to
him. "Between your accomplishments as a scholar,
and a . . . a man of violence, I would assume you
have little time for women, Dennis Land."

Was she playing with him? Denny scowled. "I'm
no eunuch."

She laughed again, and withdrew her hand. "After seeing you dispatch those two trained Security

lads, I'm sure you're not, Dennis." She turned abruptly to go below.

He looked after her. Did she *want* him to be confused? Was he supposed to follow her? He spent a long minute trying to understand just what was happening here. Certainly, Bette was among the most appealing women he'd ever met—so innately appealing that she had changed his personal definition of the word. But why this game of tag? If she wanted his interest, why didn't she just leave the charm turned on, give him a signal that she was indeed serious? Why was she putting him through this on-again, off-again stuff?

He stared out over the dark waters, wondering at women and their relationships and thought processes. He had always been a little backward where the opposite sex was concerned—it took, it seemed, almost a direct invitation from a woman before he was sure of himself, and he ruefully admired men who could simply move on the slightest cue, or no cue at all, self-confident and assured. Of course, what was it that his last lover had told him, on the eve before he left for the national games? Yes, she'd said, "A woman wants to be wanted, Denny— why do you think we make men do all the work?"

He marveled at how it never changed. Old novels, films, and other works of fiction all followed the same pattern when it came to love—the man chases the woman, until *she* catches *him*. He laughed out loud at the thought.

Still, he couldn't bring himself to believe that this alluring woman found him attractive. What if it was all in his own mind, if he had been reading her actions and words wrong? Would she be offended at his forwardness? And, would it cause problems with Zero, affect the mission?

Wait a while, he told himself. He moved away from the rail, studied the ship's rigging for a few moments, then strolled to the yacht's small bridge. Captain Bienvenida was at the wheel. He looked up and said, "There's a copy of *El Pueblo* on the chart table. It's the largest of the Madrid papers. Has an article about your expedition on the second page."

Denny looked at it blankly. "I don't read Spanish. What does it say?"

"That you're looking for evidence the Etruscans spotted trading stations along here, before the Phoenicians. The Spanish archaeologists are quite indignant."

"So am I," Denny sniffed. "What chance is there this will be seen in Torremolinos?"

"The paper's nationally distributed."

Just what he had always wanted. An international reputation as an incompetent crank. Denny frowned and studied the chart. "Our first stop is Tarragona," he said. "I'll want to take a quick look at the ancient walls there, especially the megalithic ones. There's some argument that they're pre-Roman Iberian. If so, there's a remote chance that they go back to even before Phoenician times. I'll need some data with which to argue, when we reach Torremolinos. Figure a day and a half there."

After a few more minutes of idle chatting with Bienvenida, Denny returned to the outer deck, his mind filled with thoughts of what was to come and what might be.

*   *   *

They stopped briefly at Tarragona, which was a bust, and again at Cartagena, where there were even fewer remains of antiquity. Had the expedition been a serious one, Denny would have been in despair. On the fifth day, they pulled into Malaga.

Making contact with Auguste Bazaine proved easier than they had feared. Word had gone ahead of them that the crank Etruscanologist Professor Land was also the fabulous Denny Land, one of the eight survivors of the West-world national games. Ranking matadors, usually the idols of the expatriate capital, took a back seat. *La Carmencita* was met at the dock with invitations for Professor Land and his party to half a dozen cocktail parties, dinner parties, and just plain brawls.

Denny frowned unhappily, took the stack of them down to the small lounge and tossed them to Bette. "We seem to be invited everywhere except to Auguste Bazaine's," he said. "I suppose that would be asking *too* much. I don't recognize the names of any of these people at all. Do you?"

As they glanced through the invitations, Zero came in from the bridge. "Just picked up a scrambler message from the chief," he announced. "Do you have an invite from a Bill Daly there?"

"William Daly," Bette said. "Supposedly a cocktail party, but it doesn't start till seven."

"The chief says to accept it. You two will have to attend."

"How about you?" Denny said. "You're more up on this sinister slinking stuff than I am. You ought to be there. What's our program, anyway? What good does it do to go to this party?"

"Hold it, hold it," Zero told him. "How would I

know? You play it by ear. I suspect that this Bill Daly is Hodgson's man in Torremolinos. BI is almost sure to have an agent here. Half the big shots of Common Europe, and quite a few of the Sov-world, either retire here or come down periodically to throw their wingdings. Did you ever visit a sin city?"

"No," Denny said.

Zero clapped his hands to his head and made a mock gesture of tearing his hair out. "Where have you been all your life? No, don't answer that— you've been cloistered! Anyway, this is one. No holds barred. Anything from absinthe to hashish to the oldest profession, either sex or both."

Bette said, "I still think you ought to go, Zero. As Dennis says, he's a tyro."

Zero smiled grimly. "Not until we find whether Yuri Malyshev is around. He'd spot me. Until we know what the Sov-world agents are up to, I'd better do my snooping around at night, and on the sly."

"How do we recognize this Yuri cloddy when we see him?" Denny said.

"He has a faint scar down the side of his cheek, all the way from his temple to the point of his chin," Zero replied. "I ought to know, I gave it to him. But don't underestimate Yuri Malyshev. He's no cloddy. He's deceptively easygoing, even gives with an air of being slow moving. Just remember, he's the most dangerous agent Korda has at his command. That's why he's here."

"Who the devil's Korda?"

"Zoltan Korda, the actual head of the Chrezvychainaya Komissiya."

"He's only the front man, of course. The Party member who holds the title is Ferencz Kodalay. But Korda does the work. He's a good man—speaking of an enemy, of course."

"I give up," Denny sighed. "It'd take years for me to get into this game to the point where I knew what was going on. Very well, Bette and I will attend this party without you."

Torremolinos lay eight miles to the south of Malaga, on the road to Gibraltar. Malaga—once Phoenician, once Carthaginian, once Roman, once Visigoth, once Moorish—was the largest city on the Costa del Sol. Torremolinos, its resort neighbor, was the most notorious. Since the middle of the Twentieth Century, when the town first emerged as an artist-writer's colony, it had grown and boomed several times over.

There seemed to be something in the very atmosphere that attracted the offbeat, the hedonist, the expatriate, the misfit, the seeker of illicit joys. And to Torremolinos swarmed the well-heeled steel barons from the Ruhr, oil sheiks from the Neutworld, high-ranking Party members from the Sovworld, expatriates from the West-world, wealthy refugees from all points on the globe, bearers of long forgotten European titles, and, of course, their hangers-on. It was Saturnalia on a year-round basis—Bacchanalia every day of the week.

Bette and Denny took a hovercab from Malaga to the resort town, Denny noting again the use of such common labor as porters and an actual human driver. Common Europe, or at least this section of it, had far to go to achieve the degree of emancipation from drudgery that the West-world enjoyed. He wondered if it was deliberate policy on the part of the authoritarian government, and decided it must be. This set him to wondering whether the same policy might not be superior in his own country, working on the assumption that anything was preferable to having the overwhelming majority of your citizenry spending their time bug-eyeing telly shows and sucking on trank pills to achieve happiness. Just how, Denny wondered, had things come to such a pass for the country that had once thought of itself as a beacon for the world?

Bette pointed out a large nightspot they were passing. "*New* Pogo's?" she said wryly to the driver. "Where's Old Pogo's?"

He seemed to find nothing amusing in the name. "There was an original *Pogo's*, way back. Before the Little War. You wanted to go to Big Bill Daly's place? It's up here."

Denny said, "You seem to know him. We've never met. What's he like?"

"The town's oldest resident," the driver said, as though that explained everything.

They pulled up before a monstrous villa, constructed in the old Andalusian style with elements of the Moorish. The party, evidently, was already going on.

Denny slid his credit card into the slot on the cab's meter, then held the door open for Bette. Bette, in her role as his secretary, had seen fit to minimize nature's gifts, and was garbed rather plainly. This almost disguised her extraordinary looks . . . but no quite.

As they mounted the wide steps to a huge terrace where the party was in progress, Denny commented, "I thought you were the second weapon in our arsenal. You know, the Jezebel fling you were giving me. Do you really think you're going to get Bazaine's attention in that outfit?"

"We'll use the second weapon after the first has failed, you cloddy," Bette smiled.

Their host awaited them at the top of the stairs. He was a huge, white-haired man, perhaps in his seventies, but straight and obviously firm. He had a bull of a voice and a hail-fellow-well-met joviality.

He either knew, or guessed, Denny's identity. As he pumped the newcomer's hand, he roared out, "The fighting professor! Dennis Land, the only gladiator in the history of the arena educated beyond basic literacy!" He threw back his head and his laughter boomed across the terrace.

"May I present my secretary, Bette Yardborough?" Denny said, his awkwardness obvious.

Daly shook hands while eyeing her closely. He obviously saw through her demure clothing, and brought his voice down to a shout. "Always the same," he proclaimed, amusement still evident in his voice. "It'll never end—a man's system of picking a secretary!"

An autobar of a model farther advanced than Denny had ever seen rolled toward them from the direction of the house, and their host pressed drinks into their hands. For a moment, there were no guests in their vicinity; Daly moved to a nearby corner, urging them to follow with his eyes.

Denny looked around as they moved closer to the entrance. There were perhaps fifty people present, all dressed rather formally, even trendily. Women in topless or low-cut gowns, men in dark vests, tieless. It seemed to be an eclectic mixture, by age and apparent nationality, and Denny noticed that there were more than a few unattached women. Everyone had a drink, and all were engaged in animated conversation, in small groups or couples.

Bette and Denny followed Daly to an alcove next to a fountain that stylistically represented four entwined lovers.

"Your drinks are sangria, very weak," he was speaking softly now. "You can safely drink it. Bazaine's here. So is Andre Condrieu. I was able to get Bazaine here because you were coming, and he wants to argue with you, but I couldn't keep Condrieu away. He undoubtedly has a couple of agents around, too."

"Who's Condrieu?" Denny asked.

Daly shot a quick, suspicious look at him. "The chief said—"

Bette's sharp whisper cut him off. "The Premier's right-hand man. Some say he's the power, certainly the brains, behind the throne."

"Tough as *nails*," Daly added. "Bad."

Denny pretended to take a sip of the sangria, and nodded approvingly. "Is Yuri Malyshev here?"

"Never heard of him." He frowned in sudden thought. "Oh, yes, I have. Sov-world counterespionage. I wouldn't know him. But there are some Party members present. They're as welcome at these binges as anyone else. It would have been conspicuous if I hadn't invited the usuals."

"Malyshev wouldn't be a usual."

"Some brought guests."

Bette said, "He's supposed to have a scar on his face."

"I haven't spotted him."

Daly suddenly wheeled, his voice booming again, as a newcomer approached them. The other bore a champagne glass, half empty, and walked with a nonchalant air. "Augie!" Daly saluted him. "Here he is—the famed Fighting Professor. Tear into him!"

He turned to Denny and Bette. "You two'll have to excuse me. I'll leave you in the capable hands of Dr. Auguste Bazaine, down from Brussels. Augie's a scientist or something, aren't you, Augie? But all right once he's got a few absinthe frappes in him."

Bazaine, evidently enough of an exhibitionist to wear old-fashioned spectacles in the way of an affectation, glared at Denny. "I came to this *soiree*, sir, simply to take a good look at you."

Denny blinked at him. "I'm flattered. But . . ."

"You shouldn't be! Damn nonsense, Etruscans preceding the Phoenicians to Spain. Nonsense." He turned his eyes to Bette, looked her up and down. "Ah, my dear."

Daly, still playing the role of half-drenched host, had turned away and was booming at still more guests. Denny said, "Uh, Dr. Bazaine, was it? May I present my secretary, Bette Yardborough?"

The Belgian held her hand, rather than shaking it, as though he didn't have much intention of giving it up. However, he continued to glare his indignation at Denny.

"I agree with you," Denny nodded. "Nonsense."

Bazaine seemed taken aback. "But the article in *El Pueblo* indicated . . ."

A tall, thin man, standard glass in hand, had strolled up behind Bazaine. Face impassive, he listened quietly to their conversation. Denny felt a rush of recognition when he looked at the man, and decided that he must have been on telly— some telly newscast.

He turned his attention back to the feisty Belgian scientist. "As usual with newspaper accounts, their facts were inaccurate. Are you interested in the early trading outposts that the more easternly civilizations planted here in Spain?"

Auguste Bazaine was obviously put out that Professor Land did not recognize his name. He sputtered, "I have done several papers on that subject, sir."

Denny snapped his fingers as though in memory. He was enjoying this masquerade. "Auguste Bazaine, University of Liege. I recall your study on the Carthaginians in Tingis; Tangier as it is called now. Intriguing, Dr. Bazaine." Denny turned to the man behind Bazaine. "You are also interested in Mediterranean anthropology, sir?"

The impassive one took a sip of his drink and spoke, his speech slurred by a heavy French accent. "I am interested in anything that interests Monsieur Bazaine, Professor Land."

"Professor Land, Monsieur Andre Condrieu," Bazaine snapped. "Miss Yardborough, Monsieur Condrieu. *Zut!* Condrieu, cannot you leave me for a moment? I begin to feel wedded to you!"

"Professor Land's purpose in Southern Spain

fascinates me, Dr. Bazaine. Everyone I meet seems to think his expedition nonsense."

Denny pretended to be offended. "It's those damned news reports! I'll be the laughingstock of my colleagues."

The French Security chief looked at him with raised eyebrows.

Denny said, "Obviously, the Etruscans—" he turned to Bazaine "—I am dealing, of course, with the city of Volterra, and her part of Populonia, right across from Elba and its iron mines."

The Belgian nodded grumpily. "Their outstanding maritime city-state, of course."

Denny looked back at Condrieu, who obviously was already out of his depth and irritated. "Obviously the Etruscans did not precede the Phoenicians, nor even the Greeks, to Spain. In fact, there is considerable cause to suspect that the Etruscan culture itself *came* from Phoenician, and certainly Greek, backgrounds. I contend that the—"

Bette broke in suddenly. "Zen!" she said, taking hold of Condrieu's arm. "This is all I hear, day and night. I thought we were coming to a *party*. Monsieur, could I entice you to acquire some champagne for me, and then to show me about this charming house a bit?"

"Zut! Yes!" Bazaine snapped. "Leave me to my pleasures for a moment, Condrieu."

Denny merely glanced at Bette. "Very well, my dear, I am sure you are in good hands." Then, ignoring her and her frowning drafted escort, he returned to his original conversation. "I contend that the Etruscans formed several—at least three—trading posts along the Iberian coast, and possibly right here in the vicinity of Malaga, contemporaneously with the Greek and Carthaginian settlements."

"At what date?" Bazaine rapped.

"I would say approximately 540 B.C. At the same time the Phocaean Greeks were colonizing what is now Marseille."

"Hmmm . . ." Bazaine murmured, scowling his doubt.

Denny's mind was racing. This was going impossibly well, but he wasn't sure what to do with the situation. They were at a party, a drunken party at that. It was an ideal situation for talking confidentially with the Belgian scientist, but what now?

Bazaine was saying, not so dogmatically now, "I assume you have some evidence beyond mere speculation. Certainly it is *possible* that Etruscan trading ships—"

Denny slipped his hand into a side pocket and pulled out an inch-high bronze, highly patinaed and obviously that of a warrior of antiquity. He held it out to the other. Bazaine set his drink on the stone ledge next to them, the better to examine the artifact. He squinted in the dim glow of the setting sun.

"Where did you acquire it?" the Belgian hissed.

"From a peasant in a small town near Tarragona. Salou, to be exact," Dennis lied. The little statue was from his own tiny museum; he had brought it against just this possibility.

"It's a fake!" Bazaine declared.

Denny shrugged, as though unhappy about the question of the authenticity of the tiny bronze himself. "If so, a fake *Etruscan* piece. And while I might entertain the possibility that a peasant of Tarragona might fake some Roman, Greek, or even Carthaginian art object to sell to tourists, I would not expect him to have access to Etruscan objects to copy."

The Belgian was suddenly decisive. "A microscope would soon solve the question of whether or not your peasant was taking advantage of your gullibility."

"Admittedly. And as soon as I have returned to my University I will . . ."

"I have a microscope right here in Torremolinos," Bazaine declared.

Denny's heart was racing now, but his exterior was calm. "Well . . ." he dragged out ". . . the party tonight, of course. Perhaps tomorrow?"

Bazaine waved a hand impatiently. "Tomorrow I return to Paris with Monsieur Condrieu. I suggest we repair to my villa and dig into this matter right now. I fear you have been, ah, *taken*, as you Americans put it."

"I trust not," Denny said stiffly, wondering now if perhaps his prize possession was indeed a fake. At the same time, he was frantically trying to figure out how he might find Bette to let her know that he was leaving with Bazaine. Or should he even do that? Condrieu might tag along.

"Very well, then. Let us go." Bazaine glanced around. "We'll have to slip out through the kitchens. Condrieu's agents won't let me go to the loo without escort."

Denny followed him. This was, he kept telling himself, going almost too well. His first night in

Torremolinos and here he was, alone with the Belgian. He had no doubt whatsoever that if he could get Bazaine off to himself, he could either talk the other into coming out to the yacht, perhaps on the pretense of showing him still other supposed Etruscan antiquities, or, if not, get the controversial scientist to the yacht by force. With Bazaine in their hands, by whatever circumstances, the expedition Hodgson had sent them on was a success.

And now the goal was all the more urgent, with Bazaine apparently back in the hands of the Europeans.

As Denny followed him down a back staircase, Auguste Bazaine said over his shoulder, "I have a small hovercar. We can take that."

Denny rubbed a nervous hand across his mouth. He wondered again where Bette was, and how she would take his disappearance. Well, she was a trained agent and obviously capable of taking care of herself. If he could get the Belgian back to the yacht, Zero and he could worry about Bette later.

After a quick trip through several rooms, they hurried through a darkened kitchen and down a slippery stone staircase, emerging into a parking lot immediately behind the Daly villa.

The lot was crowded with a variety of ground- and hover-vehicles, visible only as dim bulks in the waning light. Bazaine was saying something that Denny didn't hear. What he did hear was the crunching of feet on gravel behind him.

Even as he whirled he felt the blow and knew

its nature. He had taken a chop to the top of his spinal column. His last thought, before all turned black, was that he would know whether it was fatal if he awakened.

☐ CHAPTER EIGHT ☐

When the darkness washed away, Denny found himself on his back, looking up into the face of a stranger. It was a hard, positive face, a heavy scar across one eyebrow and one ear strangely twisted, as if it had been partially ripped away, then partially repaired.

There was a buzzing in Denny's head that he didn't like, and the face before him swam in and out of focus.

A voice said, "You're awake, eh? Good. Zero!"

So. Zero was here. At least he wasn't in the hands of the enemy. But *where* was he? Not on *La Carmencita*—this was no ship's bunk he was sprawled on.

The stranger's face disappeared, to be replaced by that of Zero Gonzales. Zero scowled down at him, but there was relief in his expression, as well. "I won't ask you how you feel," he said. "You look like hell, so I imagine you feel the same. I'll make this brief. Bette saw you heading for the back of the villa with Bazaine. She followed and found you on the ground, out cold. She and Daly managed to get you into a cab, pretending you were drenched."

Zero's face grew hard. "Where's Bazaine, Denny?" he demanded.

Denny shook his head, irritated. Zero was all business—not his usual act.

"I don't know. How long have I been out?"

"Almost twenty-four hours. We couldn't risk getting a doctor. There would have been too many questions. You're sure you have no idea where Bazaine is?"

The stranger's face entered his scope of vision again. "No clue at all? Any indication of who got him? This is important, Land."

"I . . . don't know what you're talking about. And who're you?"

Zero said, "Denny, this is Joseph Mauser—one of our best men. There've been some new developments. Frank sent Joe out with new instructions, but this tears it."

"*What* tears it?" Denny said, struggling to sit up. His ears still rang a bit, but his vision was clearing.

"Take it easy, boy," the older man said. "You're still wobbly. Somebody's got Auguste Bazaine. Nobody seems to know who."

Denny's brain was functioning now. A clear memory of the events leading up to the ambush flooded his mind. "Condrieu's got him," he said bitterly. "He had agents all over Daly's place. They slugged me and grabbed Bazaine."

Mauser and Zero were both shaking their heads.

"No," Mauser said. "It's unlikely, at the very least. Bazaine was one of their own people. They didn't need to kidnap him, right in their own territory. Besides, they'd come to an agreement and Bazaine was returning to Paris with Condrieu. It doesn't make sense that the Common Europe agents would have him.

"By the way, when Bette let us know about your being attacked, we took a chance and went up to Bazaine's villa and ransacked it. We were too late, someone had anticipated us."

"This Yuri Malyshev, or whatever his name is?"

Mauser shrugged heavy shoulders. "Possible, though we haven't been able to dig up any intelligence that he's operating around here. And he normally operates in the open."

Denny wondered where he had seen the grizzled older man before. Somewhere . . . it came back to him. "You're Major Joe Mauser," he stated. "Didn't you used to fight in the fracases as a mercenary, under Cogswell?"

Mauser frowned at him. "A long time ago."

"Joe's in Category Government now," Zero chimed in. "Bureau of Investigation, Rank, Assistant to the Secretary. Caste, Low-Upper." He twisted his mouth characteristically. "Is that right, Joe?"

Denny shot a look of surprise at the former mercenary.

"Yes, but don't let it bother you, Land. I was born a Mid-Lower, and came up the hard way." He lowered himself into one of the room's heavy chairs and looked at Denny. "Are you clear enough to assimilate some developments?"

"I feel like I've got a nest of wasps in my bonnet, but otherwise, I suppose so. What developments?"

Zero chuckled.

"Plenty of developments," Mauser told him. "The world's standing on its head. The World Court has been tossed three cases at once. The West-world has accused Common Europe of planning to build particle beam weapons, thus defying the Universal Disarmament Pact. We're demanding that Auguste Bazaine be handed over to a world body and his discoveries suppressed. At the same time—and a bit incongruously, if you ask me—we've charged the Sov-world with abducting Bazaine and attempting to secure his device from him with the intent of building it and thus defying the Universal Disarmament Pact."

"To cut it short," Zero grumbled. "What it boils down to is both of them have filed countercharges of the same thing against the West-world, and against each other."

Denny stared at them. "You mean everybody is accusing everybody else of having kidnaped Bazaine?"

"That's right," Mauser sighed. "Part of it's propaganda, but there are some thinly veiled threats being tossed around."

"Well, obviously, somebody's lying." Denny began to feel a premonition, a sinking feeling. "Look, what's going to happen?"

Mauser came to his feet and walked over to the window to stare out at nothing. "Isn't it obvious?"

"The World Court will rule for a trial by combat?"

"Probably," Mauser said, his voice low.

"And . . . ?"

"And you and I and one of the other funkers who sneaked through the national games will be nominated to represent the West-world," Zero said, sarcasm heavy in his voice.

Mauser turned, and Denny noticed a nervous tic at the side of his mouth; the man obviously wasn't liking this. "Willard Gatling," he said, "the commissioner of our Bureau, doesn't like tossing this into your laps, because your cover is obviously blown. You can imagine what that looks like." He sighed. "But you two are in it already. You know the issues involved; it's possible that during the preparations for the trial, or immediately afterward, or whenever, you might have an opportunity to pick up some information we can use. So, you're still on duty for the BI. And, if nothing else, you've got a fair chance of winning through and defeating the other teams . . ."

"Teams?" Denny said.

"It looks as though they're going to judge it a three-way fight. Nine men will go into the arena—three of ours, three from Common Europe, three from the Sov-world. That surviving side, even if it's down to one man, wins and will undoubtedly demand that Bazaine be turned over to them. The demand, of course, will either be met or the world will be in flames the next day. The World Court has never been defied. Let's hope this won't be the first time."

Mauser smiled grimly and added, "Naturally, *our* side must win—either in the trial or before."

There wasn't much else to say at that point. Zero filled Denny in on their location—a small villa immediately to the north of Malaga, which Daly kept for potential emergencies. He informed Denny that their group was to remain here, under the continuing cover of Denny's research, until further called upon.

With that, Zero and Mauser left, with a promise to return within a couple of hours. Since their cover was no longer needed, they decided that it would be safe to bring in a doctor to examine Denny.

Dennis Land, late a professor, late a national hero and intelligence operative, stared up at the ceiling.

Until further called upon.

What, in the name of all that made sense, was he, Dennis Land, doing here? Control of his life seemed to have slipped entirely from his hands.

First, there had been the Upper who had insisted upon his participating in the national meets, under the threat of seeing him dropped in caste if he refused.

Then the horror of the meets themselves. For the greater part of his life he had played at fighting with the weapons of yesteryear, but never to the point of drawing blood, other than accidentally. It had been fun, educational, and recreational. It had given him material for his volume on ancient arms. He had no real professional or fan interest in the gladiatorial meets, or in international relations and political intrigue. These were things apart from his personal reality. He was wrapped up in his anthropological and historic studies and cared for little else.

Yes, it had started with the Upper who was president of Denny's club. But through a miracle he had survived the games. And to what end? Only to have Academician Updike dismiss him from the position he had won through his own abilities and hard work, his scholarship and research. Updike! Another pretentious Upper.

Possibly Bette, indignant Bette, in revolt against the caste system and stagnation of the West-world, was right. What real use were the Uppers?

But even that hadn't been the end of authority controlling his life. Frank Hodgson had seen fit to draft him into the services of his cloak and dagger bureau, as though Denny had no choice in the matter. Perhaps Zero Gonzales found stimulation in this work, but there was not enough in it for Denny. As fun and challenging as it had become, he had had his fill of it. At this point, only a feeling of duty to his country, so recently developed, kept him from getting up and walking out the door.

And now this. There were implications here that he did not like. Denny was under no illusions. He could easily have died under the attack he had taken at Bill Daly's house. Any additional force behind the blow would have ended it for him. Someone had spared him, for unknown reasons. To frame him, perhaps?

But still he was not to be left alone. This Joe Mauser, yet another Upper, had appeared and given him marching orders he had no desire to take. He was to represent the West-world in a trial by combat—a combat to the death, to resolve a problem that threatened world peace.

Was there no out for him anywhere, short of death? Was this caste-dominated world to use him until it killed him? He rolled over on his side and stared blankly at the tiled wall. Every third tile, he noted, bore a scene from the career of Don Quixote—Don Quixote tilting with the windmills; Don Quixote killing the sheep; Don Quixote riding along in his armor, followed by the faithful Sanchez.

Dennis Land slept.

The institution in its origin went back to legend, perhaps myth.

When Tullus Hostilius, the third rex of Rome, was at sword's point with Alba, it was decided between the Romans and Albans that it was foolish for large numbers of men to be killed in combat between the two evenly matched cities. Instead, it was decided that each side would choose three champions who would fight, and the side that prevailed would be declared the victor and the defeated city must surrender to its foe.

Three members of the Horatian gens were selected by the Romans. The Albans sent three from their Curiatian gens. In the fight it at first seemed that the Curiatii warriors were bound to win, since they quickly killed two of the Horatii and then teamed up on the third.

Surprisingly, the Horatian turned and fled. The Albans, sure of an easy victory, took up the pursuit. However, so the story went, the Curiatii had not gone unharmed in the fight—each was wounded in varying degree. Soon, the stronger of the Curiatii pulled ahead of his kinsmen and the weakest trailed far behind. It was then that the surviving Horatian turned and, taking them on as they came, killed them—one, two, three. Thus was won the conflict and the war. Rome assimilated Alba into her already expanding domain.

History often repeats itself. Sometimes it is tragedy, sometimes a farce. The perversity of the Universe tends toward a maximum.

Regardless of what motivated the reges of Rome and Alba to so decide their differences, trial by combat was pure necessity in the world of the Twenty-first Century. War in its old sense had long since been deemed untenable by the powers behind the powers. The Universal Disarmament Pact had declared that no weapons post-1900 were to be utilized, or even possessed by the armies, police forces, or other armed elements of the world powers. They were not even to be manufactured, nor were there to be plants capable of manufacturing such.

So it was that the great powers, and the small, had solemnly gathered at Geneva after the Little War of 1998 to repower the World Court, giving it strength never before known to an international body. And so it was that when disagreements between rival powers could not be reconciled in peace, trial by combat was recalled as a pressure release. Thus far, no power had dared, in the face of world opinion, to defy the rules of such trial.

However, few were so foolish as to believe that an unresolved international conflict would not bring back all of those weapons forsaken at the treaty table. The know-how of their construction was possessed by all. And, while a war might begin with conventional weapons, there could be no doubt that each side would take such measures as it could to assure victory. And once again the factories would start spewing forth their high-tech weapons, defenses, and counterweapons.

Thus, the supreme importance of trial by combat.

On this occasion, for the first time, the combat was three-way—West-world, Common Europe, Sov-world. Only the Neut-world stood on the sidelines.

Three champions were chosen from each power. The combat was to take place in the traditional glade of trees, covering an area of three hectares—not quite eight acres. Each contestant got to choose his own weapon—knife, sword, or spear of any design, any historic period.

The position of Joe Mauser, the old pro, in all of this was not an enviable one. As advisor, he was at once coach, drill sergeant, and more. He would have far rather participated himself, but he held no illusions. Twenty years ago, yes, he would have taken his stand as one of the three—and proudly, for he had never been one to shirk his duty to his country, or to himself, despite his distaste for his chosen vocation. But the dealing of death is a young man's game, as Mauser well knew, and one does not become an old pro in the game of death by having illusions.

He knew that there was not a lot that he could advise them on. As a seasoned mercenary of the old school, his was a go-to-hell way of fighting that these men could not hope to emulate. They had been trained in a far more sophisticated and formal manner than he. Things that he might have taught them could get them killed, fighting against similarly trained men. Besides, there was no time.

Joe Mauser advised the three, and supervised a rigorous training regimen in a private compound outside Geneva during the weeks leading up to the trial. He knew he was preparing them for death as much as he was girding them for battle, but it could be no other way. Warriors marched into battle, prepared to win and prepared to die—a matter of duty, of doing what had to be done. Men like Joe Mauser, the lucky ones who had stood between the horror of war and their homelands and survived, could but watch, and advise, and hope.

☐ CHAPTER NINE ☐

Joe Mauser worked with the three until the very moment they entered the combat site. He put them on a spartan training program, supervised their food and exercise, brought in a dozen experts highly skilled in the various weapons available under the rules. Mauser was tough on them, but he asked from them nothing that was impossible; he trained right alongside them, subjecting himself to the same discipline and restrictions that he demanded of the team.

But Alex Cameron, at least, chafed against the regimen.

As a professional corporate mercenary—a gladiator for hire—the burly Cameron was well aware of the position he occupied, just previous to this world-awaited battle royal. Had he been allowed to go out on the town, he would have been the toast of Geneva, the focal point of a thousand women anxious to please him, a thousand men desirous of buying him drinks, offering him wealth in exchange for endorsements of products or ghostwritten stories of his supposed career.

But Mauser would not allow that. His team was

going to go into that forest at the keen edge of fitness, with every possible advantage.

Mauser made it plain to the three that the chances of any of them surviving were remote. In one of the earliest planning sessions, he summarized his strategy. "You three know combat. Each of you fought your way to the top in the national games. Statistically, that's an impossible accomplishment.

"Fighting as a team, rather than as individuals, will give you some edge, some additional probability of surviving. But your first task—and your duty—is to survive. Keep that foremost in mind. Don't be heroic at the risk of not surviving. If it is a matter of coming to the aid of one of your fellows at the risk of your own life, abandon him. One or more of you *has* to survive, to be the last man on his feet. You know what happens if this trial by combat is lost.

"It is your duty—to yourself and to your homeland—to walk out of that forest alive. Nothing less will do."

When the names of the opponent teams were released, he put a score of top Bureau men to work seeking out their backgrounds, digging into their dossiers.

He went over each man, individually, with his team. For some, those who had participated in televised combat, he had videotapes. These he ran over and over again at the end of each day's training.

"Now get this lad, on the left. His name is Janos Horthy, a Hungarian. This is a deal he fought in Prague two years ago. He's a top swordsman, and will undoubtedly choose a sword as his weapon."

"He's good," Zero agreed.

"They're all good," Mauser told him flatly. "You're meeting the top combat men in the world. But watch this Horthy. Watch this bit of business where he drops to one knee and gets under his opponent's guard. There! See? He's the cute type. He has quite a bag of tricks."

He loaded another tape. "This isn't a combat scene. It's a shot taken by one of our agents from quite a distance, but I want you to remember this man's face."

It was a shot showing a uniformed Russian climbing out of a car and then entering what was obviously a government building. Zero chuckled. "Well! It's good old Yuri."

Mauser looked at him. "That's right, you've had some dealings with Yuri Malyshev, haven't you? But you, Denny and Alex, note this man. He's probably the single most dangerous opponent you're going to run into in the grove. The others are trained fighting men, but this one combines that with brains. Look out for tricks. Not just cute combat tricks like you'll get from Horthy, but brain tricks. Don't underestimate Yuri Malyshev. Until he's stretched out dead before you, give him top priority. And then kill him again, because he's most likely shamming."

Zero laughed. "I double that."

Alex Cameron grumbled at him, "You're going to be laughing right up until the split second one of these clowns sticks his spear in your gizzard."

Zero looked at Cameron. "I hope so," he said smugly.

Cameron ignored the remark. "If it's O.K. with you, I'll take a boar spear. It can be used either for throwing or as a hand weapon. If we operate as a team, one of us has got to have a spear. Otherwise those curds on the other teams with spears could stand back and knock us off from a distance."

It made sense, from a strategic standpoint, and it fit Cameron's style; Denny recalled that he had been a Retiarius on the final day of the games. Denny nodded. "I'm best with a gladius. I'll handle the close-in work." The gladius was the conventional Roman short sword, with a twenty-inch blade.

"O.K. by me," Zero grinned. "I'll take a rapier. Some of those Common Europe boys are up on their fencing. That short sword might do well enough in close quarters, but some quick-stepping hotshot with a tuck or a bilbo could stand back and cut you to ribbons."

Mauser said worriedly, "A rapier's on the light side, isn't it, Zero?"

Zero nodded. "Deliberately so. It's all in the point with a rapier. You don't hack a man down with it, you puncture him neatly."

"Most of my own experience has been with sabers," Mauser admitted.

Alex Cameron stood and stretched. "There's no way of knowing for sure what the others are choosing?"

"No," Mauser told him. "Not at this point, but I'll work on it. As you know, the scenario calls for you to go in from different entrances, as teams, and hunt each other out. You'll be observed, both from above, and via cameras spotted throughout the woods." His lips tightened slightly when he came to this aspect of it. "There are always the telly lenses. Most of the world will be tuned in to this fracas. But I hardly need to tell you that."

He took a breath and shook the expression of disgust from his face. "You go in at dawn," he continued, "and the scrap continues until one side or another has cut down all opposition. In the unlikely event that a victory hasn't been achieved by sundown, all survivors will leave the trial area, to return the next morning."

Mauser regarded each of them in turn. "If you cop a disabling wound, the medics won't get to you until the fight is over, or until sundown. You'll have to get by as best you can."

"Right!" Cameron hissed. "They don't want to take any chances of a man turning funker and trying to call it quits."

Zero chuckled dryly. "It's going to be quite a party. This is worse than the final day of the national games. At least that only lasted for an hour or so, and anyone left alive got immediate care."

They remained quiet, each immersed in his own thoughts, until Cameron said, "And what do we get out of this, assuming we get out at all?"

Mauser looked at him. "Needless to say, you'll be top man in your field. Probably bounced at least one caste, issued enough Variable stock to keep you in luxury the rest of your life. And, of course, you'll be a celebrity that every fracas buff will drool over."

Cameron seemed to find that satisfying.

"All of which," Denny said evenly, "I desire about as much as I do a galloping case of leprosy."

* * *

They had left Bette Yardborough in Southern Spain to seek out clues as to the location of Auguste Bazaine, or the identity of his abductors. She showed up in Geneva the night before the trial with little to report.

They held a small banquet, rather early in the evening. Mauser wanted them to get at least eight hours of deep sleep.

The feast turned out to be rather grim, despite its light moments. They ate well, but not too heavily, and toasted one another and the Goddess Fortune in fruit juice.

After the toast, Alex Cameron scowled down into his glass and grumbled, "If I get through tomorrow, this stuff here is the weakest liquid that's ever going to go over my tonsils for the rest of my life. From then on, it's going to have a proof content."

They tried to avoid discussing tomorrow, but Mauser couldn't refrain from worrying the subject that was on everyone's mind. "Look," he said, in the middle of the entree, "there is one thing I forgot to mention, although it's obvious. The other teams have been going through the same thing we have for the past week. Keep in mind that they've undoubtedly got tapes of your appearances in the games back home. If you have any favorite tricks, remember that they know them. That particularly applies to you, Alex—they've probably got films and tapes of you going back for years."

Cameron laughed. "I've got a few tricks left, a few that might surprise even you," he said grimly.

"Fine," Mauser said, his eyes piercing, "but

remember that you are a team. Any one of you can lose this fracas by trying to play the hero."

Cameron started to say something, then looked away.

"It's almost a sure bet that any one of you here won't walk out of that glade tomorrow," Mauser said, "but—"

Bette, who had been remarkably quiet during the evening, came to her feet. "Joe, please . . ." she began, then turned and left the room.

Denny stood, too, and tossed his napkin to the table. "Pardon me," he said, and followed her.

"Hey," Zero called, "don't go making time with my woman, Denny. Not if you figure on leaning on my ample shoulders tomorrow."

Denny found her on the terrace, looking out over Lake Geneva. The lake was sparkling with pinpoint reflections of lights from yachts and other small craft. Mauser had taken the entire upper floor of the aging but comfortable Des Bergues hotel on the Quai des Bergues to house their party, and the view was superb.

He walked up behind her, stepping heavily so that she wouldn't be startled at his approach. She didn't turn to see who it was, and for a long moment Denny stood there wordlessly, watching her in profile. He knew what she was thinking. At least six men would die tomorrow—possibly eight, and conceivably even all nine. The percentages of either he or Zero surviving were almost nil.

She looked around at the scene below, her face angry. "Look at them!" She made an abrupt gesture with one hand. "Down there in their snug houses, their comfortable villas, their tight, luxurious yachts. And what are they waiting for? To watch you tomorrow, the nine of you slaughtering each other."

Denny said mildly, "I'm afraid it's not just the residents of Geneva. The whole world will be watching tomorrow, Bette. It's one rung higher than solving international disputes by all-out warfare, though. It's taken mankind a long time to get this far."

She tossed her head in rage. "It's not far enough! There is no reason why this has to continue. It would make as much sense just to flip a coin. What is proved by one of your teams of killers finishing off the others? You know damn well that the side that actually has Bazaine could win, and would that make things right? No!"

His grin was wry. "All right, Bette, you've convinced me. Now, if you can convince all the fracas and gladiatorial buffs in the world, and all the governments, we can call tomorrow off and flip a coin. I'm perfectly willing."

She shook her head miserably. "I know I'm being stupid, but there's no *need* for it." She turned to face him, eyes clouded with tears. "There's no need for it, not when it gets so personal."

Denny realized what the reference meant—Zero.

He looked down over the city, thrusting his hands into his pockets. "I'm afraid there is, Bette. The mob needs entertainment, and the alternative is full-scale war. So Zero and I, and the other seven who go into that fracas tomorrow, are providing the circus and, hopefully, avoiding war."

"But that's what I mean. Why have we allowed

society to evolve this way?" she demanded. "It doesn't make sense. The mob has to have bread and circuses, so that it won't tear our system down. But perhaps that system *needs* tearing down."

"Again, you've got my vote."

She seemed not to hear him. "It's not just our West-world, it's the whole world. Bogged down. Whatever happened to the world's dreams? Whatever happened to the noble democracy of the West?"

Zero called from the door, "Hey, Denny—bedtime. We've got a date in the morning, remember?"

Denny turned to look at him, and tried to match the other's humor. "Oh, yeah," he said, as though it had slipped his mind.

As he turned to go, Bette put her arms around him and said, "Good luck, tomorrow, Dennis." She gave him a quick kiss, to which he responded with a vigor that surprised even him. She responded in turn, and it became more than friendly. She pulled him closer . . .

"O.K., you've had your time with her," Zero said, tapping Denny on the shoulder. "Now beat it, while I go into my fling. I just thought up a wager. Bette, I'll bet you a night in Barcelona that I get through tomorrow."

She said something in reply, but Denny failed to catch it. He returned to the banquet room to find Mauser in a state of excitement. One of his agents had managed to ferret out the types of weapons their opponents were going to use. It gave the West-world team a slight edge to know this before entering the fray.

But neither Mauser nor Alex Cameron was par-

ticularly happy about the choice. The whole Sov-
world team had chosen trench knives; the Common
Europe trio, javelins.

They called Zero back in, and the three, with
Mauser presiding, bent over the table, the dessert
and cheese courses forgotten as they talked strategy. The Sovs would probably plan to make their
play in the most heavily wooded areas of the grove;
the Europeans in the most open. The West-world
team, armed with a diversity of weapons, were in
between.

Mauser's facial tic was manifesting itself. "It's
too late to change now," he said. "You've put a lot
of time into training with the arms you selected."

Cameron growled, "I'd stick to my boar spear
anyway."

Zero managed to get out a chuckle. "What am I
going to do with a rapier in a patch of under-
growth, or, for that matter, against javelins at twenty
paces? I was sure those European funkers would
choose swords." He frowned suddenly. "Maybe
they have more on the ball than we thought, and
chose just what we figured they wouldn't, on
purpose."

Denny said slowly, "My short sword is compara-
ble to the trench knives, except that it has no
brass knucks built into the hilt. But we're sure as
hell going to have to avoid those spearmen."

Jesus Zero Gonzales went down to death in the
first brutal rush.

In the earliest light of dawn, they entered the
grove from the North gate, knowing that the Sovs

were coming in from the East, and the Common Europe team from the West.

Although not permitted to enter the fenced-in grove prior to the combat, they had pored over aerial photos of the hectares of wooded land, knowing full well that their opponents would be doing the same. As a result, they had a comprehensive feel for the land's layout. The most densely wooded area was almost exactly in the middle; the most open, at the far south.

Mauser followed them to the gate at dawn with final words of advice and encouragement. "Work as a team, lads. Alex, I've got the feeling you were considering going to ground—taking a defensive stand and forcing the others to come to you. Once you're through that gate, you're on your own, of course, but my advice is that you stick together."

Alex Cameron mumbled something and nodded.

Mauser shook hands with each of them in turn. "Good luck. Survive, for the West-world . . . and for yourselves."

"Let's go," Alex growled.

The strategy of all three teams seemed obvious. If one team could avoid early combat with either of the others, the enemies might decimate one another, thus handing victory to the trio that had avoided initial battles. If the Sovs could find themselves a strong defensive position in the thickets, and simply remain there until Denny and his group and the Common Europe group champions had done each other in, they would be able to emerge later and finish off any survivors. So, obviously, was the same situation confronting the other teams. He who fought first might well never fight again.

They advanced in a single file, Amerindian style, with Cameron and his short, heavy boar spear in the lead. Zero, naked rapier in hand, brought up the rear.

As soon as they had entered the shelter of the trees, Zero called for a conference. "We're in no danger, yet. They're doing the same thing we are, trying to figure out a way to lie low until the others have bumped each other off."

Denny said, "If there were only two teams, the thing to do would be to go after the enemy as soon as possible. This way, everyone's avoiding everyone else." Even as he spoke, he instinctively kept watch against possible attack. This early in the day the small woods was still dark. He made out a telly lens sunk into a hole of a tree, poorly camouflaged.

Obviously, there would be cameras spotted throughout the grove, so located that there could be no place where combat could evolve without being covered for the benefit of the fracas buffs, and for the representatives of the World Court and the governments involved.

"Well, one thing's obvious," Cameron sourly announced. "The Sovs are going to head for the center area, and the others for the south. So where do we go?" He eyed his teammates for a moment, then cleared his throat before continuing. "There is one thing Mauser said that we might reconsider."

"What's that?" Zero asked.

Alex hefted his heavy spear. "Whether or not we ought to separate. Both of the other teams are going to do what Mauser figured we ought to do—fight as a team. Maybe we'd beat them if we didn't."

"And maybe we'd fool ourselves," Zero told him. "Operating alone would be the end, if one of the other teams ran into just one of us. How long do you think you'd last with that pigsticker of yours against three javelin men, or, for that matter, against three Sovs with trench knives?"

"I can take care of myself," Alex said, eyes narrowed.

"If you couldn't, you wouldn't be here," Zero said. "But you can take care of yourself better with support. This isn't just another one-on-one combat in the arena. The whole West-world's depending on us to see that Bazaine's gadget doesn't get into the hands of either the Sov-world or Common Europe."

"All right, all right, you can save the speech, curd," Cameron snarled. "I know what we're here for. Just remember that I'm—"

It was then that the Sovs rushed them.

How they had managed to get this close before being detected wasn't too much of mystery. In a way, the West-world champions had allowed it to happen.

The Sov team's strategy came to him, even as they clashed. Malyshev, who was probably in charge, had anticipated the thinking of Denny and his companions. They would expect the Sovs, with their close quarters weapons, to head for the heaviest underbrush, where such equipment as javelins and swords would be handicapped. They would expect the Sovs to head for the thickets and go to ground, making it necessary for the others to come in after them.

Which was exactly what Malyshev didn't do.

Instead, he had entered from the East gate, and then set off on the double for the North gate to come to grips with the West-world team immediately. Given a surprise ambush, and a quick victory, Malyshev and his men would have not only their own trench knives for in-fighting, but the weapons of Denny, Zero, and Alex, as well. It was a desperate move, but a clever one. Even as he swung to meet the attack, Joe Mauser's warning came back to him. *Don't underestimate Yuri Malyshev. Look out for tricks—brain tricks, not just cute combat tricks like you'll get from Janos Horthy.*

The Sovs had crept as near as possible while Zero and Alex argued, and while Denny's attention was diverted by the argument, and then rushed.

Denny swung his short sword, the famed two-edged, sharp-pointed Roman gladius which had once conquered the world. He could hear Alex yelling a warning, and the Sov trio was on them.

Zero Gonzales was the nearest to the enemy, his back turned. He whirled, his long-bladed rapier coming up to the defense. Denny had time to see the flicker of light on the edge of a trench knife, to hear Zero's grunt of pain, and that was all. Then there was time for nothing but the fray. Thrusts, counterthrusts, kicks, and elbow blows against the dancing, fast-moving opponent before him.

The knife the other bore was almost as large as Denny's sword. It had the advantage of being a double weapon—brass knucks and a dagger—but the disadvantage of having a triangular blade. Denny had no fear of the outcome of his part of the fight, if his remaining companion could hold out. His knowledge of his weapon, and its superior quality of having a cutting edge, gave him all the advantage he needed. His opponent was good, but not good enough.

Alex, at least, seemed to be carrying his end of the fight. His bull-like roars echoed through the forest, and his knife-bearing opponent was having his work cut out for him, avoiding the professional gladiator's lunges.

Denny sidestepped to avoid a rush, sidestepped again, stepped quickly forward and jabbed. The sword point pierced the other's chest, and sliced upward in a ragged gash.

At the same instant, Denny felt himself struck from behind. Struck, then struck again, lightning fast. He spun, his sword slashing desperately, but the burly Sov who had attacked him bounded back. Denny leaped forward in immediate offensive, tripped over a root, tried to recover, tripped again, and was down on one knee.

He attempted to struggle to his feet. A second was an eternity, and could not be afforded an opponent. He felt the cruel ripping edge of the brass knucks crush into his face and all became a dim haze for him. He could hear Alex roaring in the background, while someone else screamed in pain. Then the haze went black.

He couldn't have been unconscious for more than a moment—seconds at the very most. He opened his eyes, but only to slits. If the Sovs had prevailed and noticed signs of life in him, they would be quick to finish him off.

But the only figure he could make out still standing bore the uniform of the West-world. He opened his eyes wider, and began struggling to stand. It was Alex Cameron, his back to a tree, holding his boar spear in both hands like a pike. His eyes darted about, as though he feared further attack.

Denny finally lurched to his feet and tried to take stock of himself. He was bleeding from several wounds and his face felt crushed. One eye seemed completely blind, but that might only be blood.

Cameron stared at him. "I thought you were dead."

"Where are they?"

Alex Cameron gestured with his head at Denny's first opponent. "One's dead. Two took off, back into the woods. One's wounded. They took Zero's sword, but couldn't get past my spear. They gave up."

"Zero . . ." Denny said.

The professional gladiator gestured again with his head.

Zero was sprawled on the ground. Denny hobbled over to him, trying to wipe the blood from his blinded eye.

He dropped to his knees next to Zero. The other had taken a half dozen or more knife thrusts in his belly and chest. In the past year, he had seen enough men in their last moments of life to know death when he saw it, even though Zero's eyes flickered open.

Zero grinned at him. That . . . curd, Yuri . . . got even for that scar I gave him in Japan . . . eh?"

"Easy," Denny muttered. "I'll get some bandages . . ."

Zero had closed his eyes again. Now he re-opened them. Blood trickled from the side of his mouth. "Listen . . . Denny, tell Bette . . ."

"Yes . . ."

But that was all. Zero stared at him with lifeless eyes.

Denny stayed there for a long moment, on his knees, his face naked of expression. So, this was how it was, he thought. There was no justice in it, but when had the world fostered justice? Justice was what you made it, or as little as you allowed it to be.

He got back to his feet with no little difficulty. He was going to have to take care of his wounds. As yet, he didn't know how bad they were.

Cameron was standing, watching him closely. He held Denny's Roman gladius in one hand, his own boar spear in the other.

Denny took a deep breath and silently prayed that this wasn't what it appeared to be. "Better let me have my sword. The Sovs might come back, or, for that matter, the Europeans could show up at any second."

Cameron shook his head, slowly but definitely.

"What's the matter?" Denny demanded.

"With this spear *and* your sword, I'll be able to make out," Cameron replied. "I didn't even get a nick in that fight."

Denny stared at him. "But then, I wouldn't have anything." He didn't get it. There was no way that Cameron could take on all comers, and—then he realized what the man was all about. Cameron was independent—what other sort would become a professional mercenary—and he had an ego that went beyond overconfidence. Evidently, Denny surmised, his winning through the national games had convinced Cameron that he was invincible. He wanted the glory of winning it all.

"Sorry, professor," Cameron muttered. "That's the way the ball bounces. You've had it, anyway. If we ran into a fight right now, you'd be more trouble to me than you're worth. As it is, I'll get by."

He eyed Denny smugly, as if daring him to make a rush. Denny took a step toward him.

Cameron pressed himself against the tree, gripping his weapons tighter. "You know what Mauser said. If it's a matter of coming to the aid of one of the others, at the risk of your own life, abandon him. I'm afraid that's it, Professor."

Denny smiled at the irony of Cameron twisting the advice that he had scorned to his own benefit. He considered rushing Cameron anyway, perhaps catching him off balance. The odds were against it, but . . .

He shrugged; he would not be seen turning against his teammate while in the fracas, and he hoped that Cameron felt the same. And he was certain the fool would—and could, at this point—kill him in defense. There was no point in attacking him now, just let both of them survive—then there would be a reckoning.

Cameron stepped toward him, then turned on

his heel and went off, walking in a half crouch and peering to the right and left.

Denny shook his head to clear it. Not six feet away, a telly lens gleamed dispassionately at him. He spat at it.

They had brought a minimum of equipment with them, deciding that the added maneuverability achieved by disposing of weight was more desirable than food or water, but each had a very small first-aid packet. Denny fished his out of his clothes, and then, overcoming his distaste of touching his friend's body, found Zero's kit.

He made his way over to the fallen Sov combatant and found that he carried a small canteen. He took it up. At least it would be full, this early in the day. He had hoped for water, but it contained vodka, or some other ultra-strong spirits. Denny took one swallow, used the rest with his handkerchief to swab out the cuts about his face, and to cleanse his other wounds. The alcohol burned, but Denny gritted his teeth and poured it liberally over the cuts that he could reach.

His wounds were bad enough, but not as bad as he had first thought. He would live, for a time, at least. Perhaps the vodka was better than water would have been, at that. At least it was a good cleansing agent.

He used up all the bandages in the two first-aid kits, then approached the fallen Sov again. It had come to him that he hadn't seen a trench knife in Alex Cameron's possession, before the other had deserted him. Maybe it was somewhere about the corpse.

But it wasn't. Evidently Yuri Malyshev and his surviving partner had taken it along with them. That would mean they possessed three trench knives and a rapier.

As yet, there had been no sign of the three javelin men of Common Europe. Probably they were to the south, but probably not. In the same manner in which the Sov-world team had done the unexpected, perhaps the Premier's champions would attempt some surprising strategy.

His best strategy would be to move from this vicinity. The sounds of the fighting and Cameron's shouts would have drawn the attention of the Europeans. Very likely they would make for the spot, figuring that the West-world and Sov-world teams would have largely eliminated each other. Well, they would be right. He stumbled along a narrow path, realizing that the more sensible procedure would be to avoid paths and stick to the most heavily wooded sections of the battleground. But it was all he could do to keep on the path. He found himself wishing that he had taken another slug of that vodka, instead of using it all for washing.

For a time, he railed in his mind against Alex Cameron. The funker, the curd! He'd not only deserted a teammate, but had stolen his weapon as well.

But then he realized that the other may have been correct, however selfish his motives might be. Their job was to win this trial by combat for the West-world. Nothing else made any difference. There were no gentlemen in this bloodbath, and no honorable rules of the game.

However, Zero wouldn't have done it. Nor would he, Dennis Land, have done it to Zero or Cameron.

Professor, the other had called him, just before the desertion. *Professor*. Had he detected a contemptuous tone there? The contempt of the slog for one who has made a mark of achievement in the world of intellect?

What difference did it make, what motivated Alex Cameron? The fact was . . .

Denny mentally kicked himself. He'd been letting his mind wander, instead of watching for his enemies—and there were five of them still in the woods, so far as he knew.

He shook his head. Now he regretted taking that slug of spirits, no matter how good it had seemed at the time. It had merely intensified his thirst, which was now raging.

The thin trail he was following ended abruptly in a small clearing, which Denny stumbled into before catching sight of who stood there.

It was Yuri Malyshev—alone, but armed with spear, rapier, and two trench knives.

☐ CHAPTER TEN ☐

The Russian took in Denny's obvious physical condition. He said, slowly, "So, Professor Land, we finally meet."

Denny attempted to wet his lips, found his mouth drained of moisture. He dropped into the cat stance, balancing on the balls of his feet, body loose, arms ready to block or strike. He waited.

The Russian made no move in response. "I, too, am familiar with karate, Professor." He pulled out one of the trench knives from his belt, flicked it up into the air and caught it by the blade.

It suddenly occurred to Denny that the trench knives the Sovs had chosen were capable of being utilized as throwing knives.

The Russian agent was deceptively fast, considering his size. He made his cast in a blur of speed and, for a brief second, Dennis Land's only thought was one of resignation. He made a futile attempt at ducking, dropping to the ground, and rolling. The knife whizzed by his head before he had started his move.

Then, immediately behind him, he heard the tinkle of breaking glass.

Malyshev said, "Unless I'm mistaken, that's the only telly lens capable of spotting us, at this particular location. And the area is shaded from the cameramen in the choppers."

Denny could only stare at him.

Malyshev said, "I want to know just one thing. Who has Auguste Bazaine?"

Denny shook his head, completely befuddled. "You have him. You and your men got him from me in Torremolinos."

But now it was Malyshev who was shaking his head. "No. I observed developments from a distance, through binoculars. You and Dr. Bazaine entered the parking lot behind William Daly's villa. Then two men attacked you and left you unconscious. With the help of still a third man, they hustled Bazaine into a waiting car. Moments later, your agent Yardborough came up to your assistance."

Denny nodded assent. "What difference does it make? The Europeans have him, then."

"The difference is this," the Russian said. "You were not killed."

Denny felt a small flash of anger at the implied accusation, similar to what he had felt when Zero had confronted him on his awakening at the villa in Spain.

Malyshev continued. "Neither the West-world nor the Sov-world wishes to unbalance the present international situation. In this regard we are in agreement. But Common Europe wishes to expand into the Neut-world for markets and raw materials, and Bazaine is the key to their plans. For some reason I can't understand, they've kidnaped their own man. Possibly their leaders be-

came impatient with Bazaine's temperamental
sulking, and they have him under duress, possibly
torture."

He eyed Denny speculatively. "Despite the fact
that you were left alive by the attack—possibly an
error, possibly not—I believe that you were not in
league with Bazaine's kidnappers. Thus, our interests at present coincide."

Denny was beginning to get a glimmering of
why the other had thus far failed to dispatch him,
and why he had broken the telly lens. "What is
the standing of the trial by combat, thus far?" he
asked carefully, his eyes on Malyshev's hands.

Seeing that the American was beginning to follow him, the Russian nodded. "You and I are the
only survivors of either of our teams."

"Alex Cameron?"

"Went down with a javelin in his guts. He took
his opponent with him." Malyshev hefted his spear.
"That's where I got this."

"Then two Common Europe men remain."

"And two of us," Malyshev said simply.

There came back to him all that he had heard of
Yuri Malyshev these past weeks. Bette saying, *The
most competent and certainly the most ruthless
hatchetman of the Chrezvychainaya Komissiya.* Zero
saying, *Don't underestimate Yuri Malyshev. He's
no cloddy. He's deceptively easygoing, even gives
with an air of being slow moving. Just remember,
he's possibly the most dangerous agent Korda
has at his command.* Joe Mauser saying, *Look out
for tricks . . . he's probably the single most dangerous opponent you're going to run into in that
grove.*

Denny said, "I don't trust you."

The Russian laughed, a short choppy sound. "I don't blame you, Professor Land. However, you have no alternative. It would be easy enough for me to finish you off now. But the fact is, our interests coincide. As you might say, we're in the dill, Professor Land. We cooperate, or we go down."

"You're at least as highly skilled as the Common Europe fighters. Why don't you simply finish me, like you say, and then take your chances with them?"

"Because the world can't afford such chances, Professor. And it would be taking a chance, I assure you. I am told that I am good, and I believe that, but there is always the unexpected. Either the Sov-world or the West-world has got to get Bazaine and suppress his discovery. I would naturally rather it be the Sov-world. But if not, I'm confident that your nation isn't going to upset the balance of power."

Denny said slowly, "This is supposedly a three-way fight to the finish. By the rules of the game, we're not allowed to cooperate . . ."

Yuri Malyshev laughed again. "I assure you, Professor, like most in Soviet government service, I am a student and admirer of Niccolo Machiavelli."

"What happens if and when we eliminate the others?"

The Sov-world agent ran a finger down the side of his face, tracing out a scar—the scar, Denny remembered, that Zero claimed to have put there. In turn, the Russian had killed the irrepressible American, not half an hour past. Yes, it came back to Denny now. It had been Yuri Malyshev who had killed Zero Gonzales.

Malyshev said slowly, "We could then fight it out between us."

Denny grunted in contempt. "You're in better shape than I am. You want to let me live just long enough to help pull your chestnuts out of the fire, and then finish me."

The Russian was nodding. "True. Obviously that isn't a fair alternative. What would you suggest?"

In spite of himself, Denny felt drawn into this scheme. If nothing else, it meant at least immediate survival. He said, "It must be something that allows both of us to live."

"All right," the Russian said decisively. "The rules of the match are that we fight until only one or more of the same team are still on their feet. We will endeavor to eliminate the common enemy, then we will sham a fight between us. One of us will go down, in supposed defeat. The other will then be the winner of the trial by combat, and the medics will dash in to save the wounded."

"Fine. But which one of us shams defeat and allows the other to be proclaimed the winner?"

They stared at each other.

Stalemate.

The Russian agent's face worked. Finally, he said, "You can be the winner, with the understanding that, following the fight, you and Joseph Mauser will meet with me and Zoltan Korda, my immediate superior, and iron out our difficulties behind the scenes, on an equal basis.

"Does that convince you of my sincerity, Professor Land?"

*He's probably the single most dangerous man
you're going to run into in that grove . . . Look
out for tricks, brain tricks.* Why not just rush him
now and get it over with? Denny thought. Certainly, if the Russian was planning on dispatching
Denny once he'd outlived his usefulness, he couldn't
be killed any deader now than later. And there
was just a chance that he might overcome Malyshev.

And then what? Take on the two Common Europe fighters, in his condition? No, he would rather
see the Sov-world get Bazaine, if necessary, than
Common Europe.

"All right," he said. "You're on. We cooperate.
Now, let's divide up those weapons."

But the Russian was considering him. "You're
more badly wounded than I thought, Professor
Land."

"I can still operate," Denny said defensively.

"But not well enough. Do you have neo-amphe-
tamines?"

"No," Denny shook his head. "They're against
the rules of the trial."

Malyshev's face lit up with amusement. He un-
screwed the bottom of his remaining trench knife;
three white pills fell into his hand. He offered
them to Denny. "You'd better take all three. They'll
bring you to a peak of efficiency for possibly half
an hour, but then you'll collapse. A half hour
should be enough."

Denny took the pills, looked from them to his
new ally. "These could be poison."

The Russian chopped out his sarcastic laugh.

Denny took them into his mouth. They had a
bitter taste, and he had trouble getting them down,

his mouth and throat dry as they were. They had no immediate effect; he still felt desperately weak.

"Now, how do we divide the weapons?" he demanded.

The Russian considered. "We have two trench knives, a spear, and this fencing sword. I suggest that we each take a trench knife."

Denny said, "I've been training with a sword. Not a rapier, but still a sword. I suggest I take that."

"Very well." Malyshev handed over the knife, along with Zero's rapier. He went to the destroyed telly lens and recovered the second trench knife. Denny noted, with some surprise, that the Russian deliberately turned his back.

"How are we going to explain what's happened here?"

Malyshev shrugged. "I'll simply tell them that I threw my trench knife at you and missed, breaking the telly lens. Then you rushed me. I stumbled and you grabbed a sword and trench knife and ran off into the brush before I could throw my javelin at you. Good enough?"

"Good enough," Denny replied. He hefted the sword. He felt a sudden strength coursing through his veins. The pills. The rapier felt light, after his short sword.

Malyshev frowned in thought. "We're going to have to get going. Already we've been here, off lens, for a suspiciously long time. The Europeans are probably in some defensive position. They've lost a man, and witnessed two of the deaths on our teams, but for all they know, they still have four enemies to face. We'll have to seek them out."

"Right," Denny said. "Suppose I head east, and then north. You head south, and then west. The first one to spot them waits for the other to reach the area. When we join combat, we first take them on. If and when we finish them, if we both survive, we turn on each other. I clobber you with, say, the trench knife, and you pretend to be knocked unconscious."

"Very well." The Russian turned and disappeared into the trees to the south.

Denny looked after him for a moment, then turned on his own heel, retraced his movements along the path for a hundred feet or so, and then turned south. He still did not trust Malyshev all the way, despite the Sov-world agent's apparent altruism. Denny had had some bitter lessons in trust. He might well be signing his own death warrant if he gave the Sov-world fighter too much knowledge.

His strength had returned completely.

He made his way carefully. With the trees this thick, javelins posed no real threat, but he knew that the Europeans now had Cameron's short boar spear, handy as it was for the close-in work, his own Roman short sword, and one trench knife—a sizable arsenal. They had quite an edge on him and Malyshev.

Denny made his way carefully, all senses alert. He wondered at the efficiency of the drug the other had given him. Give the Sov-world credit for development of such. When it came to the devices of espionage-counterespionage, they had them in profusion.

He spotted the two nervous Common Europe fighters before they spotted him, and slipped behind a tree to devise a strategy. They were in what amounted to a meadow, at least as near to a meadow as existed in the wooded area. They were standing back to back.

Malyshev was right. These two had no idea how many opponents still remained.

And then Denny made out what he was looking for—a slight stir of movement in the thicker woods to the far side of the clearing. It could only be his reluctant ally. He had to admire the Russian's woodsmanship. They had done a superlative job of sneaking up and ambushing Denny and his team, in the earliest moments of the fight. Now here was Malyshev, snaking through the trees, invisible. Had Denny not known what he was looking for, and where to look, he would never have detected the Russian.

Now, the problem was to cooperate with Malyshev, but in such a way that the millions watching would never suspect. Given such suspicion, the fat would be in the fire.

A whisper of sound made Denny glance upward. There was a hovercraft not fifty feet above them. He could make out the excited telly operators, zeroing in on every aspect of the rapidly developing situation below. The ground lenses were tracking them automatically. This trial by combat was covered as though by blankets. Not a motion would be missed.

One of the European men glanced upward, too. Would the presence of the hovercraft tip him off that the enemy was near?

Denny had to make his play. According to Malyshev, the drug he had taken would give him half an hour of top performance. He couldn't afford to waste that time; he must not collapse until the action was over. And he had to hit them before the element of surprise was lost. He cursed the hovercraft and the overeager lensmen.

He came to a decision. He darted forward from his hidden vantage point behind the tree to another, as though attempting to get nearer to the Common Europe duo without them seeing him.

But his movement, as he had intended, was spotted. The Europeans both turned in his direction, javelins ready. They had seen him, but didn't know whether he was accompanied. He pretended he didn't realize they had made him out, and hustled forward to the shelter of another tree.

He had their full attention now, at least for a second or two.

But these fighters were neither inexperienced nor fools. It struck one, almost immediately, that Denny's movements might be a distraction or feint. He turned to check behind him.

Too late, Yuri Malyshev, javelin in hurling position, was already on his feet, dashing toward them. His lips were pulled back over his white teeth in a grimace of physical exertion. He came within casting distance, threw, then fell to the ground and rolled.

The spear caught the second of the two in the shoulder, throwing him back and to the ground. The other, unbelievingly quick of reflex, made his own cast, and missed the rolling Russian by inches. Malyshev bounced to his feet and wrenched the other's javelin from the sod. The point was broken. He threw it aside, pulled his trench knife from his belt, and came in low, in a knife fighter's crouch.

Denny took all of this in as he ran forward, rapier in his right hand, the trench knife held as one would hold a poinard, in his left.

The Common Europe champion whirled, dismay in his face. His eyes darted to the javelin of his fallen comrade, but there was obviously no time. He pulled from his belt the Roman short sword, which had originally come into the grove in Denny's hands, and backed rapidly, seeking a refuge where he could meet his opponents one at a time.

They rolled in as if they had rehearsed their moves a dozen times. Denny feinted, his rapier, considerably longer than the other's short sword, flicking in and all about the hapless fighter. The other, desperate, chopped and chopped again at the fencing blade. By wild luck, he succeeded in breaking the rapier an inch from the hilt.

Denny dropped the useless weapon and bore in with the trench knife.

But Malyshev reached the hapless combatant before Denny. Malyshev's triangular blade stabbed deep into their opponent's back and the man screamed his agony . . . stabbed again, and the other fell even as he attempted to meet his second assailant.

Denny plunged forward, jumping over the body of the fallen warrior. He gripped the trench knife in his fist and bore down on Malyshev.

The Russian darted toward him—reflex, Denny

hoped—then stepped slightly to one side. Denny
followed the motion and swung, connecting against
Malyshev's temple, and the other dropped as though
poleaxed.

Denny scooped up the Roman short sword,
dropped a moment earlier by the last European.
His eyes darted about the clearing. All were down,
except him. The one Malyshev had speared was
thrashing out his death throes, twenty feet away.
The second was already dead; undoubtedly one of
the Russian's knife thrusts had hit his heart.

Denny looked down at Yuri Malyshev, unconscious but still breathing heavily.

The point of the short sword hovered over the
Russian agent's unprotected throat. No one else
could testify to the deal the two had made. If he
finished the man off, the trial by combat was won,
won by the West-world with no tags.

Besides, this was the man who had killed Zero
Gonzales. ·

Dennis Land shook his head, and tossed the
sword aside. He spread his arms, palms up.

A voice boomed from the chopper over the grove.
"All of your opponents are felled, Dennis Land.
Make your way to any of the four gates. You need
only to walk out, on your own two feet, to be
declared winner."

The nearest gate would be the West Gate,
through which the Common Europe team had
originally entered. Denny began to stride in that
direction. It could be no more than a hundred feet
or so.

It was then that the effects of the drug began to
wear off. Malyshev had warned him. Half an hour,

and he would collapse. He set his face in grim determination and stumbled forward.

He considered attempting to run. No, already his eyes were clouding. A sudden suspicion hit him. Had the Russian, in truth, poisoned him? Did the drug offer a final burst of energy before delivering death? No. No, that couldn't be it. The Sovs had obviously brought those pills into the grove for themselves.

His legs were buckling. He could make out the high wire fence which surrounded the fighting grove. It was a few short yards away. But where was the gate? He had to get through the gate on his own feet. If he failed, if none of the combatants were able to leave the grove unassisted, the whole trial was a draw and must be fought over again.

Fought again! He suppressed a cry of pure anguish.

His eyes were dimming. His legs were as water.

He could make out the gate now, farther down the fence. Perhaps thirty feet, no more.

But thirty feet were as though thirty miles to Dennis Land. The black flooded in, and he stumbled forward, came to his knees, and then pitched onto his face, unconscious.

☐ CHAPTER ELEVEN ☐

From a thousand miles away, he could hear a voice calling him. "Dennis . . . Dennis . . ."

Couldn't they leave him alone? All he wished was to be left alone now. Left alone to die. At least, at the very least, left to sleep.

"Dennis! Dennis . . ." and then something else that he couldn't make out, did not wish to make out.

Where was he? All was black. He was desperately weak. He wished only rest.

"Dennis . . . you've got to . . ."

He knew the voice, now. It was Bette Yardborough, though she was far away. Bette. There was something he had to tell her. Something Zero had told him to tell her—or had he? Zero was dead, wasn't he? He seemed to remember that Zero was dead.

"Dennis! You've got to get up. You've got to make it."

She was nearer. Almost as if she was next to him. But that couldn't be. Noncombatants weren't allowed in the grove. Didn't she know she wasn't allowed in the grove?

He forced one eye open.

Bette stood on the other side of the wire-mesh fence, not a dozen feet away. There seemed to be others behind her, but he had trouble enough making her out.

There was a sob in her voice as she called his name.

He shook his head. He could make out the gate now, mere yards away. A multitude of people stood on the other side, but he could see none of them as individuals.

All right. All right.

He struggled to his hands and knees and began to crawl, slowly, so slowly. From time to time he fell, and all went black again. But the persistent voice, Bette's voice with its tears, was always there, nagging him on. Wasn't there something he had to tell Bette? He couldn't remember.

Just feet from the gate now. For some reason he had to get through the gate. Then he would be allowed to . . . then he was allowed to die. But first the gate. First the gate, and then one other thing. He couldn't remember the other thing, but he had to remember it.

Another voice came through to him. No tears in this one. A shouting voice. A voice of command. He dimly recognized it as the voice of Joe Mauser, shouting at him in a voice of commanding thunder. Joe Mauser . . .

"ON YOUR FEET, DENNY! ON YOUR FEET! YOU SLOB! YOU BASTARD! ON YOUR FEET! YOU'VE GOT TO COME THROUGH ON YOUR FEET!"

Slob? He felt the faintest twinge of indignation.

He had fought, hadn't he? He had fought the good fight. He and Zero and, yes, even Cameron.

Then it came back to him, the other thing he had to do. First he had to get through the gate, then he had to talk to Mauser, before anybody else got to him. Especially before any medics got to him. And that was the trouble. There'd be medics galore on the other side of the gate.

Medics who would know what had enabled him to win the fight.

He pushed hard at the ground, came to his knees, and stared longingly at the gate before him. Joe Mauser was there on the other side. Bette, too. He staggered to his feet, and tottered from side to side like a child taking its first steps. Then, after taking what seemed to be only two or three steps, he fell into Joe Mauser's arms.

He whispered, even as he felt the haze descending again, "Joe . . . listen . . ."

The other was lowering him to the ground. "Yes . . .?"

Mauser undoubtedly thought his faint words the mutterings of a man in delirium. But he had to get through. "Joe . . ." he croaked, "listen . . . I mustn't be . . . allowed to be examined by any medics . . . except . . . ours . . ."

And just before he fell into unconsciousness again, he felt Mauser's arms tighten. Joe Mauser was no cloddy. He would come through. Relief washed over him, and he succumbed to the darkness.

When consciousness returned, he was in bed. A hospital bed. It was getting to be a habit. He'd spent more time in bed recovering from injuries, these past three months, than he ever had in his whole life. A doctor, Joe Mauser, and Bette Yardborough were in the room.

Evidently he was in better shape than he would have expected. His hard time there at the gate was due largely to the effects of the drug he'd taken. It had given him the energy, all right, but when it wore off, he had paid. He assumed that he was up to his eyebrows in stimulants now, which probably explained the clarity and strength he felt.

Mauser was looking down at him, poker-faced. He said, "I think you'd survive Armageddon, Denny."

Denny eyed Mauser warily. "Any one else get through alive?" he asked.

"Yuri Malyshev. I knew he would survive. As soon as you got through the gate, the medics charged in, but the only one with any signs of life was Malyshev. Funny thing was, except for a slight concussion you gave him when you slugged him with that trench knife, he was untouched. It was nip and tuck, you winning."

"I know," Denny told him. He looked at the doctor, and then at Bette Yardborough. He said, "I want to talk to you alone, Mauser."

The doctor shrugged and left the room. Bette frowned at him, unbelievingly.

"You, too, Bette," Denny told her.

She looked at Mauser, who made a motion with his head. Bette turned and followed the doctor.

Mauser looked around the room. "Why didn't you want any medics except ours to work on you?"

"By any remote possibility could this room be bugged?"

"No. We're in the West-world embassy. But beyond that I had the boys go over this room to the point where an ant couldn't be hidden in it." He leaned forward. "Why no medics except ours, Denny?"

"Because I was full of some kind of amphetamine. They could have detected it and declared the fight null and void. I couldn't take that chance."

Mauser's tic pulled the side of his mouth. "Your team didn't take any pep pills into the battle. Where did you get them?"

"From Yuri Malyshev."

Mauser was nodding. "When you met him earlier? When he shattered the telly lens, throwing that knife at you?"

"He didn't miss his target," Denny said quietly.

"No, I can see he didn't. I was following it, of course, on the monitors set up outside. I'd given you up. A few minutes later, you came on screen again, in another area of the grove, armed with rapier and trench knife. How are you supposed to have gotten them?"

"The story will be that I hold a karate black belt. I rushed him and wrested the knife and rapier away and escaped before he could get me with his spear."

Mauser was still nodding. His eyes were slits now, but his mind was obviously racing ahead, faster than Denny's revelations were coming. "So he gave you drugs and weapons. What did you give him in exchange?"

"We made a deal. Teamed up against the Europeans."

"So I suspected. You and Zero were more subtle about your deal in the games. But then you finished Malyshev when the Europeans were eliminated."

Denny shook his head, considered asking Mauser how he knew about the games, then discarded the thought. "No. He took a dive. That was part of the deal."

"And now what?" Was that contempt in Mauser's voice?

Denny said evenly, "Now we get together with Malyshev and his boss, and decide what to do about Bazaine."

With a sudden, violent motion, Joe Mauser slammed his fist into the wall above Denny's head. The room resounded with the noise. "Damn!" he snarled. "But we *had* them."

Denny shook his head. "You told me to survive. Very well, I survived—the only way possible."

"I *warned* you against Malyshev and his double dealings!"

Denny's voice was still even. "He played the game right down to the finish, Mauser. He stuck to the arrangements we made. There was no double dealing."

Colonel Yuri Malyshev was on the carpet.

He was in full uniform now, an inconspicuous flesh-colored bandage on the upper portion of the left side of his face. He wore only one of his decorations, the Hero's Award. Any third-rate Party lout of upper rank in either the military or in civil government could cover his chest with medals and ribbons until he looked like a fruit salad. But when one wore the Victorian Cross, the Congressional

Medal of Honor, *Pour le Merits*, or the Hero's Award for distinction in combat, other decorations faded into nothingness, as far as prestige was concerned. And at this moment Colonel Malyshev could use prestige. He was on trial for his life.

He stood at attention, eyes full ahead, and listened to Ferencz Kodaly ranting. Ferencz Kodaly, Minister of the Chrezvychainaya Komissiya, said to be Number One's favorite drinking companion, said to wield more arbitrary power than any other person in the Sov-world save Number One. Forencz Kodaly, one of the few left who needed neither court nor judge when it came to trials—and executions.

A bit to the rear and to one side of the commissar sat Zoltan Korda, who had originally assigned Yuri Malyshev to find Auguste Bazaine, and by whatever methods prevent him from turning his device over to Common European representatives. His eyes bored into the colonel's but he said nothing, dared to say nothing so long as his superior was speaking.

Kodaly was roaring, "I watched it all, you understand, *Colonel* Malyshev. Watched it from beginning to end. Never have I seen such sloppy handling of a major assignment. I tell you now, *Colonel*, Number One is incensed. Given an adroit handling of this from your position of trust, we would have been in possession of Bazaine and his discovery. You and you only, Colonel Malyshev, have prevented our success."

There was something the matter with the other's eyes, Malyshev decided. The man was either so enraged that he had lost control of himself, or was on some narcotic. What was the name of the current fad from the West-world that the Party members were following? Mescaltranc, they called it. In the West, only the Uppers could afford it; in the Sov-world, only Party members. Yes, the commissar was quite probably high.

"I watched your mishandling, Colonel Malyshev, from the stupidity of choosing trench knives, rather than some good traditional Russian weapon such as the yataghan . . ."

Malyshev cringed. He could just picture himself going into combat with such experts as Gonzales, armed with one of those clumsy, curved yataghans. Besides, unless he was mistaken, the weapon was Turkish in origin, rather than Russian.

". . . through your ridiculous attempted ambush of the West-world team. True, I can only guess what happened when the telly lens was broken and somehow, *somehow*, Colonel Malyshev, you allowed the wounded Dennis Land to overcome you to the point of wresting two of your weapons away. Then, the final error, when victory was in your grasp. When you had eliminated the remaining Common Europe men, you allowed the all-but-dead American to knock you unconscious and hence win the trial by combat. You are a fool, Colonel Malyshev, and an insult to the uniform you wear!"

"Yes, Comrade Commissar."

"Silence!" he commanded. "Were it only me, I would have you executed in the manner you deserve. Happily for you, Colonel Malyshev, it seems that my assistant believes that you may still be of some value to the fatherland."

He glanced at Zoltan Korda and Korda spoke

up. "The international press would undoubtedly take notice of the disappearance of the colonel, Comrade Kodaly. After all, he did survive the trial, the only one besides Dennis Land. On top of that, he personally eliminated three of the contestants, giving him a larger score than anyone else. The international press is treating him as a celebrity, in spite of the fact that, by a trick of fate, Dennis Land was able to deal the colonel the blow that felled him at the trial's crucial point."

Kodaly glared at his assistant. "Very well, Zoltan. I'll leave details to you. Needless to say, this matter is not at an end until we have Bazaine or his plans—preferably both. Number One is following this matter closely, Zoltan. I need not remind you that heads will roll if it is not wound up in success."

Zoltan Korda was nodding placatingly. "The better half of the ministry's agents are working on it, Comrade Commissar."

The other stood suddenly erect. "I have an appointment, an entertainment, with some of my equal numbers from Common Europe and the West-world. Geneva is swarming with representatives of the Bureau of Investigation, and the *Ministere de Surete*, from the highest ranks to"—he looked contemptuously at Colonel Yuri Malyshev, who still stood at rigid attention—"cows undeserving of being called intelligence agents."

He turned and marched out of the room.

Korda pursed his lips and studied his underling. Malyshev remained at attention.

Finally Korda said, "All right, relax. Take a chair. You could use a drink, I suppose. Here." He approached the desk just deserted by Ferencz

Kodaly and fumbled in the drawers. "Yes, it was sure to be here." He emerged with a half-empty bottle of barack, and looked at the label. He pursed his lips again. appreciatively this time. "Laid down by Neanderthals, undoubtedly." He brought forth a glass and poured a generous portion. He handed it to Malyshev.

Malyshev downed the potent apricot spirits in one gulp. Korda refilled his glass.

Korda brought forth cigarettes, lit one for himself, offered one to his underling. There was no ashtray on the table; evidently, the commissar didn't smoke. Malyshev declined.

Korda said conversationally, "Why didn't you tell him what really happened?"

Malyshev looked at him. "He wasn't thinking very deeply, if you'll pardon my referring to the commissar in such a manner. I figured he would have me shot, if I told him everything. I don't know how I escaped, as it is. He seemed all but rabid."

Korda nodded pleasantly. "If the truth be known, I had a hard time arguing him out of it. Kodaly doesn't often become involved in the detail work of this ministry. I suspect that Number One had a few disparaging things to say to him." He leaned back in the chair and fixed Malyshev with his gaze. "What *did* happen?"

Malyshev told him, leaving out no details.

"You mean you could have killed this Dennis Land, there where he confronted you, weaponless?"

"Easily."

"And that final scene. You could have eliminated him there, too?"

"Possibly. Probably. By that time he was strong with the energy drug. But I probably could have eliminated him. However, we had made a pact."

Korda lit a fresh cigarette off the butt of the one he was smoking, his eyes registering surprise. "I am amazed that you honored it, considering your reputation, Yuri, and that of the ministry for which you work."

Malyshev said, "Land could have broken the pact, too. He could have finished me off, there at the end when I was unconscious. That would have solved everything for the West-world. He didn't."

"I see," Korda said. "Espionage-counterespionage has evolved to the point where there is honor between rival agents." There was irony in his voice. "Or honor between warriors?"

Malyshev said nothing, but held his gaze level with the other's.

His chief said, "Then perhaps Bazaine isn't as lost to us as the commissar was led to believe."

"No. The agreement is that you and I meet with Professor Land and his superior on the scene, Major Joseph Mauser. We are to decide on an equal basis what to do with Auguste Bazaine, as soon as the Europeans turn him over."

"If you had told the commissar all this, don't you think he might have been somewhat less enraged?"

Malyshev chuckled. "I do not doubt that he would, as I said, have me shot. It's the only way he can save face, at this point. And, I am afraid, comrade—that is, *sir*—that I am getting to the point where I don't always . . . trust the decisions of Party members. Undoubtedly, I am mistaken."

"Undoubtedly," Korda said dryly. "Very well, colonel. You and I shall attend this meeting with Land and Mauser. We'll decide later just how to report to the commissar."

They met in the suite that Mauser had taken in the Des Bergues hotel. The teams of experts Mauser had whipped together to advise and teach his trio of West-world champions were now gone, as were Jesus Gonzales and Alex Cameron for that matter, and the suite echoed emptily to the presence of Mauser, Denny, and Bette. Indeed, Bette herself had withdrawn into silence and remained largely in her room, obviously aware of the fact that something was going on to which she wasn't privy, and resenting that fact; her clearance, after all, superseded Denny's.

Mauser had agreed with Denny that the fewer persons who were aware of the collaboration between West-world and Sov-world, the better. The art of truth serum and hypnosis was far too advanced for secrets to be kept, given physical possession of the keeper by an inquisitive opponent.

At the appointed hour, Korda and Malyshev arrived, in full uniform and with an air of professional politeness. Colonel Yuri Malyshev made the introductions with stiff formality.

He clicked his heels, bowed from the waist in the style the Sov-world military had adapted from the Hungarians. "I believe you gentlemen both know me," he said to Joe Mauser and Dennis Land. "Colonel Yuri Malyshev. And may I present my superior, Comrade Zoltan Korda of the Chrezvychainaya Komissiya. Sir, Joseph Mauser, Category Government, Branch Bureau of Investigation, Rank Assistant to the Secretary, Caste Low-Upper. And Dennis Land, Category Education, Sub-division History, Rank Professor, Caste Mid-Middle."

Korda shook hands formally. "Not Comrade. I am not a Party member."

They found chairs. Mauser offered drinks, which were refused.

Denny examined the Hungarian and the Russian. Zoltan Korda, of whom he had heard only in passing, was a small, intense man with an air of competence. Yuri Malyshev seemed strangely different from the man he had met in the grove—quiet, withdrawn. How had Zero once typed him—easygoing? It was hardly the man who only a few days before had handled the drama in the grove as though he were the director.

Joe Mauser opened the conversation carefully. "As I understand it, Professor Land's victory was not entirely his own."

Korda said, "An understatement, Major Mauser."

"I am no longer in the Category Military," Mauser responded, irritation obvious in his tone of voice. "I might point out that, had he wished, Dennis Land could have finished Colonel Malyshev there at the last when the colonel was unconscious."

Korda nodded. "Or, for that matter, the colonel could have finished Land, when he met him unarmed."

"Perhaps. However, Dennis Land holds the karate black belt, which would make his being temporarily weaponless not quite so important."

"So does Colonel Malyshev, do you not, colonel?"

"Seventh Dan black belt, taken in Okinawa," Malyshev said.

"I trust the javelin, trench knives, and sword with which the colonel was equipped would have been decisive." Korda paused. "We are sparring with words, gentlemen. Colonel, will you tell us as exactly as possible the pact you made with Dennis Land?"

The Russian agent shifted slightly in his chair, crossing his legs. He looked at Denny and said, "The initiative was mine. I broke the only telly lens which covered the area and then suggested that Land and I unite to eliminate the Common Europe combatants. My original idea was that after such elimination we fight it out. He demurred on the grounds that he was wounded, and I strong, and insisted it be done in such manner that we both survive. This dictated that one of us must feign defeat. Since he didn't trust me, I volunteered to pretend to be knocked unconscious. The agreement was that, following his being awarded the victory, we would meet and decide what to do with Auguste Bazaine and his discoveries, once he has been delivered to either side."

Mauser looked at Denny. "Professor Land?"

"That was the agreement. I see no way in which we can renege at this time."

Mauser cleared his throat. "Did it occur to any of you that Professor Land, no matter what the situation he was confronted with in the grove, was in no position to pledge anyone's word but his own? Or do you suffer under the illusion that *I*, ranking no higher than assistant to the secretary of the commissioner of the Bureau of Investigation, can make decisions usually in the hands of the Octagon and White House?"

"This problem is not of our making," Korda said. He ground his cigarette roughly in the ashtray at his side, without looking. "We entered into the agreement in good faith. We, through the colonel, have lived up to every aspect of the pact. Dennis Land would not be alive today, had it not been for the initiative the colonel took."

"The *initiative?*" Mauser snorted. "He broke practically every rule pertaining to trial by combat."

"And in so doing," the Sov espionage official said, "accomplished the end that both the Sov-world and West-world desired." He lit a fresh cigarette.

"Not quite," Mauser replied grimly.

Denny had been listening to Mauser's words with growing anger. Now he said, "I made the agreement with Yuri Malyshev. I'll live up to it. So will our government."

Mauser looked at him, anger flashing in his eyes. "You presume to speak for me?"

Denny said flatly, "If the government fails to back me in this, then I'll take the matter to the international press."

Joe Mauser half came to his feet, hands balled into fists.

At that moment, Bette entered and said, "Sir, an important message."

Mauser glared at her. "I thought I made it clear that this meeting was not to be interrupted."

Bette said nothing, but her green eyes flashed. It was obvious that an operative of her experience wouldn't intrude in the face of definite instructions with something of minor importance.

Mauser said, "Very well, let me have it."

She crossed the room and handed him a folded note. He muttered apologies to the others and read it. His face went blank. He looked at Bette and said, "That will be all."

After she had gone, Mauser looked at Zoltan Korda. "The World Court ruled that Auguste Bazaine be turned over to the West-world, with the recommendation that he be placed under the supervision of an international body and his experiments suppressed."

Korda's eyes were piercing. Obviously something had developed. "So we heard on the news, before we left the embassy to come here. Is that all?"

Mauser frowned, indicating the paper Bette had given him. "Common Europe denies having Bazaine."

Korda dropped his lighted cigarette on his pants. Even as he flipped the spark and ash off his clothing, he snapped, "They lie!"

"The Premier has offered to submit to truth serum and hypnosis and be put to the question by representatives of the World Court, as well as by representatives of the West-world and Sov-world."

Both Zoltan Korda and Yuri Malyshev showed obvious surprise. Looking at them, Denny could not believe they were acting. Unless his every intuition was far astray, these two were as dumbfounded as he was.

Then, in Joe Mauser's face he suddenly caught a

gleam that should not have been there, but it disappeared as quickly as it had come.

Mauser stood, and so did the others. There seemed nothing more to say now. Nothing that could make a real difference, anyway.

Zoltan Korda said, "If the Premier has made such an offer, we can be sure that the result will be negative. In short, Common Europe doesn't have this madman Bazaine."

Malyshev had said very little this evening. He spoke now. "The Premier has set the precedent. If the world is not to be plunged into war, Number One and the President of the West-world are going to have to follow that precedent. They, too, are going to have to submit to the question."

There was no reply to Malyshev's declaration, and this seemed to signal an end to the meeting. With no small talk, and sparse farewells, Korda and Malyshev took their leave.

When the two Sov-world agents had left the room, Denny faced Joe Mauser. After a long moment, he said, "You know where Bazaine is, don't you?"

"Don't be ridiculous," Mauser said.

☐ CHAPTER TWELVE ☐

Yuri Malyshev proved to be a prophet. For a few days, recriminations flew. Then the European Premier submitted to questioning, as promised. Not only were representatives present from the World Court, the Sov-world, and the West-world, but the Neut-world as well. Half a dozen different systems of questioning, including drugs, were used on a man not known for control of temper, but on this occasion, Common Europe's strong man proved more than docile.

Did he know where Auguste Bazaine was at present?

"Non."

Was Bazaine in the hands of Common Europe?

"Non."

Were any papers dealing with the particle beam-laser weapon in the hands of Common Europe?

"Non."

Was Auguste Bazaine still alive?

"Je ne sais pas."

Did the Premier suspect that Bazaine was in the hands of either the Sov-world or the West-world?

"Oui."

Which?

"*Je ne sais pas.*"

There was more. And, although each group worded the questions differently, that was the substance of it.

International temperatures rose. Rumors ran riot about both the West-world and Sov-world secretly scaling up for nuclear production. Inspection teams, a thousand strong, put a quick end to the whispers, but charges and countercharges continued to fly.

Number One gained a propaganda victory by being the first to offer himself for questioning by anyone interested. He submitted himself to the same indignities as had the European leader, and with the same results. He was followed by Seymour Gatling, Category Government, Sub-division Executive, Rank President, Caste Upper-Upper. Again, the results were the same.

Finally, inevitably, the world's eyes turned, with cold accusal, to the Neut-world.

It came to the minds of all concerned that the Neut-world had the most interest in the development of Bazaine's beam-guided laser. Given such a weapon, Common Europe would have felt itself free to carve out what it would from a militarily weak Neut-world. If anyone was interested in removing Auguste Bazaine from the scene, it was the Neut-world. What could be more obvious?

One by one, the leaders of the loosely allied Neut-world nations submitted to the question. And the answers were ever the same. No one knew where the offbeat Belgian scientist was, whether he was still alive, or where his secrets, his papers, and the AI entity were.

With the questioning of the Neut-world leaders, the pressure slowly eased, and the world sank back into a spirit of black mystery. Bazaine had disappeared into nothingness, but the threat and its repercussions did not quite disappear.

Dennis Land followed most of this on the telly newscasts. He had ceased to be an active participant in the world's most secret affairs.

Not that he minded, or so he told himself.

Denny and his cohorts were returned to the West-world by regular shuttle from Geneva. Bette Yardborough and Zero's body were on the same plane, though Joe Mauser had either gone on ahead, or was winding up some last-minute affairs that kept him in Switzerland. The fact was that Denny had seen very little of Mauser since the confrontation with Malyshev and Korda at the hotel. He had wondered, once or twice, if the older man was deliberately avoiding him, but that seemed to make little sense.

There was something wrong with Bette, too. Since he had asked her to leave the hospital room so that he could report alone to Mauser, she had been standoffish. Or, he reasoned, perhaps the relationship between the redhead and Zero Gonzales had been even deeper than Denny suspected, and she was mourning a lost love. Mourning Zero, and perhaps subconsciously resenting the fact that Denny had survived. If such was her trend of thought, Denny felt it just as well that she didn't know the story behind his survival.

After his arrival in Greater Washington, Dennis Land, "The Fighting Professor," had to submit to the adulations of the mob. He was continually followed by camera-toting reporters. He found himself the guest of honor at a score of banquets, at which he was rarely aware of the identity of the sponsor. He was interviewed by gladiator and fracas buff magazines in endless and repetitive fashion. And always, there were the fans. For weeks after his return, he never wanted for companionship, although there were times when he wished for nothing more than a few hours alone. But he was obligated to remain in the capital for debriefing and presentation to the President and others.

He tried to relax and enjoy it, but there had been precious little excitement in his life until he had been caught up in the national games. He had, indeed, led a rather sheltered existence. Consequently, he found this new fame uncomfortable. It was more than a little disappointing, as well. The level of attention he received was that accorded to a national hero, which Denny knew he was. But, dammit, he didn't *feel* like a hero; he just felt like himself, embarrassed at the whole thing, and unable to get a handle on how he was supposed to act. After a few days, he *was* able to relax and enjoy it, by pretending that he was at a role-playing resort, and that this was all a part of the act.

Eventually, he made it clear that he would never appear in an arena again. After so much of this, he stopped cooperating altogether in the manner in which national heroes were expected to cooperate. This cut short his days of acclaim. In the modern world, the mob wanted excitement *all* of the time, and without a willingness to play the hero, Professor Dennis Land wasn't exciting.

Before it ended, though, he was presented to Seymour Gatling at the White House, was decorated and informed he had been bounced a caste to Upper-Middle. The news media came out in force for that, but Denny had no illusions about the West-world leader's attitude toward all of this; the propaganda value was immense.

He was mildly surprised that the President of the West-world differed little from most other Uppers he had known during his career. And when he thought about it, he realized that Seymour Gatling was the only Upper-Upper he had ever met. Contrary to his publicity photographs and occasional newscasts, the President seemed a rather vague man. Pleasant enough, in a politician's way, but rather vague and ineffective. The little speech he had given was a prepared text, and Denny suspected the other had first seen it only minutes before the reading.

Preceding the ceremony, a select group gathered for cocktails with the President, and for a few moments Denny found himself alone with one of the most powerful men in the world. Gatling had asked the standard questions which Denny, by now, could answer by rote. How did it feel to survive the last day of the national games? How did it feel to enter that grove, knowing that nine of the best fighters in the world were going in and that it might be that none would leave alive? To Denny's answers, Seymour Gatling inevitably uttered, "Extraordinary," but in a detached rather than enthusiastic manner.

But one thing remained with Denny, and was to come back to him later. Gatling had said, almost petulantly, "I suppose you know, Professor, that you're to be run up a caste level, to Upper-Middle. Frankly, I was in favor of making it a double jump, one of the few in history. Extraordinary—a jump right from Mid-Middle to Low-Upper. However, my advisors were against it. There hasn't been anyone jumped to Upper in years. The precedent might cause problems; we can't let every Tom, Dick, and Harry become an Upper, or what's the use of having a caste system at all? Sorry, old chap. I was rather keen about it."

The really important meeting, with Frank Hodgson at the Octagon, came later.

In a way, it duplicated their first meeting, except that it was Joe Mauser who was present, rather than Zero Gonzales.

When he entered the Bureau's monstrous reception hall, he was met as before by a nattily attired stereotype who introduced himself and conducted Denny to Hodgson's office. For a moment Denny thought it was the same agent who had met him before, but then decided not. It was just that all those in their late twenties who worked in the Octagon seemed to look, dress, and talk alike. He'd heard somewhere that they all wore the exact same type of shoe, so that one operative might recognize another in an undercover situation, but he'd never remembered to check the validity of that rumor.

His guide opened the door leading to the ante-room, stood aside for Denny to enter. Miss Mikhail looked up from her desk as she had before, her features birdlike.

"Good afternoon, Professor Land," she said brightly. "Mr. Hodgson is expecting you. Go right in."

Denny went in, and found Frank Hodgson with Joe Mauser; the two were obviously waiting for him. After handshakes and the usual formal greetings, the older man studied him.

He said, "Well, Denny. We come now to the payoff, eh?"

"The payoff?"

"Have you forgotten? The last time you were in this office, you were on the verge of despair. You had been placed on indefinite leave of absence from the University. Your appropriation for research had been rescinded. I promised you that if your mission was successful we'd take measures to reverse those decisions. Very well. In spite of the fact that the mission wasn't exactly a success, we have done just that. You may return to the University tomorrow, or whenever you wish."

The implications took a few moments to sink in. When Denny realized that the man meant what he was saying, that the BI was indeed going to deliver what had been promised, he felt a fleeting joy, followed by confusion.

"What about Updike?" he asked. He glanced from Hodgson to Joe Mauser, who sat to one side, and then back again. There was a strange feeling in the room, one that he couldn't quite identify. Or was it his imagination?

"Academician Updike has been, um, kicked upstairs, as we used to say when I was a youngster. He has been promoted to head of one of the smaller universities in Peru. You are to take over his department. It will, of course, mean additional Variable stock to add to your portfolio."

Denny shifted in his chair. "I'm a research man, not a university politician. I don't want to be head of a department." He should have felt—months ago, he *would* have felt—elated about all this. Somehow, he wasn't.

The older man chuckled. "Denny, you have much to learn about bureaucracy. You will have a group of assistants to do the donkey work. Continue your research. Your position as head of the history department will, I believe, enable you to ask for appropriations of almost any magnitude, and to call upon as many underlings as you wish to perform the more tedious tasks connected with managing the department. You might even establish a department of Etruscanology. My dear professor, your Utopia has been reached. Don't you realize it?" He punctuated the question with a sweeping gesture.

Hodgson's voice and expression conveyed utmost sincerity, but Denny knew that it was a formality. Denny could sense a feeling of . . . sarcasm? No, it was more irony—irony, and a lack of respect for Dennis Land.

Denny shot another look at Mauser, who, other than greeting him when he entered, had said nothing thus far. Mauser's face was expressionless, but somehow Denny felt humor emanating from his former mentor.

There was, he knew, something wrong about the whole deal. He wondered at the ease with which he had been handed it all, and he wondered even more at his growing distaste for the situation. Certainly he wanted this, had often dreamed of heading his department at the university, of wielding the kind of power that would enable him to pursue his research to the fullest extent. But now, with that dream realized, it felt wrong; it was like his fame as a gladiator—something was missing, it wasn't *him*.

And ironically, though he felt that he had earned this, it was not of the priority that it once was. There were other, more pressing matters in his life.

He looked the BI chief in the eye. "Look here, I must sound mad, but I'm willing to work on with the Bureau until my present assignment is cleared up."

"What present assignment?" Frank Hodgson asked, glancing at Mauser.

Denny had the feeling that Hodgson was being deliberately obtuse. "Finding Auguste Bazaine," he replied.

"Yes. Of course. Well, your part in all of this is finished. Obviously, you are not a regular agent; you haven't the training. Even if you had, your present notoriety is such that we couldn't use you. Everybody in the world knows the face of Dennis Land, and of all things, a Bureau operative must have anonymity. Thank you, Denny, but we really can't use your services further."

Now he knew what was happening—they were stonewalling him. He was locked out. He had fumbled the assignment given him, had not carried it out as these men had intended, and this was their way of dealing with it.

He knew full well that, with Mauser aware of what had happened with Malyshev in the glade, he could have been tried and executed for treason. But for some reason, as in the past, he was being spared.

But that was not compensation enough for the disappointment he now felt. Hadn't he done his job? Hadn't he tried to move matters to a point where his country could benefit? Certainly he had! And now they were shutting him out of it. He was being set aside and paid off, like Updike.

He wasn't going to take it without a fight. Perhaps if he put all of his cards on the table? "Listen," Denny said, "Zero Gonzales and I were friends. We were sent on an assignment together, and while working on it, Zero was killed. Something happened to throw the wheels off the whole thing; I don't pretend to understand it all. But Zero's dead, and I'm not happy about what's happened, although I do stand by the decisions I made. I get the feeling that Zero died to no end. I want to stay with it. Be in on the final scene . . ."

Frank Hodgson drummed his fingers impatiently. "Professor Land, believe me, your ardor is appreciated. But we simply cannot use you. Admittedly, the Bureau will continue to investigate the whereabouts of Auguste Bazaine. Sooner or later, the problem will be solved. I shall personally inform you of the resolution. That's all I can say."

Denny came to his feet. "I'm being given the brushoff."

Mauser smiled but said nothing.

"I'm being paid off to shut up."

"Shut up about what?" Hodgson demanded. "Do you know something we don't?"

Frustration and anger were building in Dennis Land, but he held the feelings in check. He *felt* something. But there was no substance. He felt what? Suspicion was all. Suspicion, and the impression that all wasn't being done for the cause Zero Gonzales had died for. A lid had been lowered by someone, somewhere.

He turned to go, face drawn. His hand was on the doorknob when Joe Mauser said, "Goodbye, Dennis."

He hesitated only a moment before opening the door and walking out.

Dennis Land had long been aware that it is possible to go through a major portion of one's life quietly, though still in comparative happiness, with little interest in the outside world. Living in a rut, knowing it or not. Doing one's work, living out the days in monotony. He could have gone from childhood, through youth to middle age, and then into senility, never leaving the rut of his life.

But then a bomb had dropped. The world he had known and accepted was gone. His existence was so radically changed as to be unrecognizable, and all in a few months' time.

Upon returning to this apartment at the University, he had trouble relating to the place and the personal belongings once so close to him. He stood in the middle of the small room, taking in what should have been so familiar, but which was alien, cold, and hollow. His comm center, the shelves of tapes, books, reference works. His desk and on it his terminal, with a facsimile sheet, half covered, protruding from the printer. A finished manuscript in a box to the left.

He stared at the paper without recognition. "Chapter Six," he read aloud. "The Tarquin Gens and Its Origin." The Tarquin gens? He had to concentrate to recall the topic. The Tarquins had come down to Rome from Tarquinia, an Etruscan city less than fifty miles north. They had supplied the last three reges for the city on the Tiber before the overthrow of Tarquin Superbus and the declaration of the republic.

It finally hit him, the question that had been flirting with his subconscious since his return to Washington. How was he ever to resume the life of a scholar which had once seemed of such importance? How could he remain in the background of world events, now that he had played a part in them?

He crossed the room to his museum, once his pride. He must remember to get the little bronze warrior from his bags and return it to its place— the little Etruscan warrior he had shown Auguste Bazaine.

Bazaine! Where in the world was Bazaine? Had it not been for Yuri Malyshev witnessing the Belgian scientist's kidnaping, Denny would have suspected Bazaine of having gone off on his own to hide from friends as well as foes. But it wasn't that. The man had been abducted, and someone had him.

His thoughts returned to the present. He was

no longer a professional dagger killer, deep in international intrigue. He was once again Professor Dennis Land, Category Education, Branch History, Rank Department Head, Caste Upper-Middle. Yes, he had made Upper-Middle, and all his children, were there to be children, would inherit that high caste rating—only one caste short of being an Upper. He mentally shrugged at the thought. The only Uppers he had ever met who seemed to have anything on the ball were Joe Mauser, and possibly Frank Hodgson, and right now he was miffed at Joe Mauser, though he didn't quite understand why.

He went to the terminal, pulled his credit card from his pocket, and slipped it into the slot. After entering his access code, he said, "Balance check." It was the first time he'd gotten around to doing this since his return. He was surprised at the report. Of course, he had known that his Inalienable basic stock would be upped to coincide with his new caste rating, and he had also been aware of the Variable common shares that had been added to his portfolio as a result of activity for the Bureau of Investigation and as a prize for winning the trial by combat, but he had never totaled it up.

Frank Hodgson was right. He was now in a position to accomplish just about anything he had ever dreamed of. An extended trip to Italy, say, for a year of study and possibly even excavation at the sites of Caere, Volsini, Tarquinia, Sutri, or any of the other Etruscan cities.

Somehow, it didn't excite him.

He looked around the room again. Once it had been home—all the home he wanted. Now it was just a cold, empty, unlived-in room. Well, at least that would make it easier for him to make his move to the larger quarters that would be his as a department head.

Bette Yardborough gave him three weeks before turning up.

He had almost gotten himself back into the rut. It was a simple matter, as Hodgson suggested, for him to delegate his responsibilities to assistants. He could see now how an ass like Ronald Updike could have held down this position. The other's Upper caste rating had guaranteed his progress through school until he had taken that highest of all degrees, Academician, and then guaranteed him the position of department head in one of the largest universities in North America. Then he had simply delegated his work to others more competent than he, but of lesser rank.

Yes, Denny fitted himself into the routine, but not happily. There was still a nagging doubt that prevented him from returning completely to the study of the past. He had an awareness of the world beyond the campus, a world which he had ignored before.

Early in the game, following his return to the University, Denny had to take measures to protect himself from the fracas buffs, the gladiator fans, and those whose professions battened on these— telly reporters, writers for fracas buff magazines, and the like. He had found it necessary to take an unlisted phone number, to keep secret the location of his apartment, and to have his office staff maintain strict guard over his privacy.

Thus it was that when Bette Yardborough stormed through his door, into what was supposedly his sanctum sanctorum, she was followed by a young-ish assistant professor who was wide of eye and white of face, and who was holding his arm as though it were broken.

Denny looked from her to the poor man she had obviously just assaulted, and said, "All right, Cardillo, that will be all . . ."

"My . . . my arm . . ." the other muttered in anguish.

"It isn't fractured," Denny told him with a sigh. "This woman is a professional. She wouldn't un-necessarily break your arm."

"*Unnecessarily?*" the other sputtered, indignant. He blinked at the redhead, obviously wondering how anybody who *looked* that gorgeous could be quite so ruthless.

"All right," Denny told him. "That will be all."

When the assistant had left, Denny came to his feet. "Was it necessary to practice your judo on my staff?"

She was still in a huff. She looked about the office in distaste, located the most comfortable chair in the room, and plunked herself down. "When I became insistent about seeing you, that cloddy had the gall to put his hand on my arm."

Denny had to laugh. He resumed his chair. "Probably thought you were some fracas buff who wanted my autograph, or a souvenir, or some-thing. One overtranked fan got through to this office last week and wanted to give me ten shares of common in return for the sword I used during the trial."

Her voice was brittle. "A big hero, eh? Why didn't you sell it to him?"

Denny looked at her. "Never give a sucker an even break? As a matter of fact, I don't even have it; I understand that it's in some kind of gladiatorial museum in Italy. You understand, I hope, that I wasn't proud of the killing I did during the games. I was forced into the situation, and defended myself, Bette."

Her eyes flashed for a moment. "Oh, let's stop this, Dennis. I didn't come to quarrel."

God, but the girl looked beautiful when she was angry! He had almost forgotten her startling good looks, her projection of excited energy. "Why did you come, Bette?" he asked. "I thought the Bureau was through with me. I got the feeling I'd been dropped for good."

"I'm not with the Bureau anymore."

Denny was shocked. "I thought you were supposed to be one of the top agents."

She was frowning now. "So did I. But about a week ago I was notified that I was being dropped. Frank Hodgson wouldn't even see me. I was given a bonus, and that was that."

"But . . . why?"

"I think that my underground activities become a bit too blatant, even for Hodgson. Obviously, if the Category Security cloddies nab me one of these days, it wouldn't look too good for Commissioner Gatling's Bureau of Investigation."

"You think Frank Hodgson might turn you in?"

She shook her head. "No. No, Frank wouldn't do that. But he also wouldn't fish me out of the dill, if I got into it."

"We seem to have gotten away from the subject. Why did you look me up, Bette? I figured that you'd about written me off your list."

She pursed her lips. "I finally figured that out, believe it or not. The fact that you didn't want anyone present except Mauser there in the embassy hospital really hacked me off. I figured that you were just being a macho jerk, and I didn't like being cut out of BI business. And it did tie in with the fact that you and Mauser later had a meeting with Malyshev and Korda, didn't it?"

Denny said nothing.

Bette said, "You two made some kind of a deal in that grove—you and Malyshev. A deal to combine against the Common Europe team, and then decide the split later on. The wheels came off the deal when it was found that the Europeans didn't have Bazaine."

Denny said, "Even if that were true, I obviously couldn't discuss it with you, Bette."

She shifted her shoulders disinterestedly. "It makes no difference to me now."

"Then why did you come? Not just to talk over old times, I assume."

Her gaze was very level, and cool. "Don't rush me. I'm trying to come to a decision." She glanced around the room. "You might offer an old colleague a drink."

Denny got to his feet with a sigh, and pushed back the shelf of books which hid his auto-bar. He said, "What'll it be, this early in the day?"

"Oh, a puritan, huh? Just for that, I'll make you drink one with me. Make it a rum and soda."

He winced at the combination, but put his credit

card to the screen and dialed her order, along with a John Brown's Body for himself. When the drinks came up, he passed the rum to her and said, "I just figured out the derivation of the name of this concoction. John Brown's Body—the morning after, you feel like you're moldering in your grave."

"Why, Dennis, you made a funny. Stuffy old you." She held up her glass. "What do we drink to?"

"Zero, obviously."

"Yeah, obviously." She took a sip, then said, "Let's talk about you and the fracas. What happened?"

He turned his back to her and stared out the window at the young people crossing the mall and going in and out of buildings. The forever campus scene.

If he couldn't trust her, who could he trust? Besides, she deserved to know what had happened. He said, "Yuri Malyshev's team ambushed us. Zero's rapier was too long to be effective at such short quarters. He should have beat a quick, temporary retreat and let me and Cameron take them on. But that wasn't Zero's style. He took the first rush and held them for the few seconds necessary to allow Cameron and me to get set. If he hadn't done that, Malyshev's play probably would have worked."

"I know. I watched it happen."

Denny turned back to her, his face composed again. Carrying his glass with him, he returned to his chair. "He was quite a man, behind all that inane chatter of his."

"Yes. Ridiculous that persons of his caliber die in the service of madness."

"Here we go again," Denny said.

"Well, isn't it madness? The West-world, the Welfare State. A fraction of a fraction on top—the Uppers. The overwhelming majority, over ninety percent, on the bottom, automated out of active participation in the economy, useless—the Lowers. And to maintain this situation, a strict caste system, all effort devoted to maintaining the status quo. Don't educate the lower castes, they might become restive. Give them bread and circuses instead."

Denny sighed.

"Well?" Her voice was sharp. "Don't you agree with me?"

"As a matter of fact, I do."

"Then why don't you do something about it?"

"I'm a professor of history, not a revolutionary."

She seemed to switch subjects. "Security got Dr. Fitzgerald."

"Who?" He hadn't the vaguest idea of what she was talking about.

"Lawrence Fitzgerald. He was the speaker at the Sons of Liberty meeting I took you to."

"Oh. I don't think you ever mentioned his name. He was grabbed by the Security boys?"

"Undoubtedly. He's dropped from sight. His family and his friends have had no word from or about him. That's the way Category Security operates, supposedly to scare anyone who might sympathize with his ideas."

"I see," Denny replied, wondering why she was telling him this. "Bette, you're going to have to face reality. That Sons of Liberty organization you belong to is bad news."

She nodded, finished her drink, and set the glass down. Her green eyes came back to him.

"They're a bunch of impractical, inept malcontents," he added.

She nodded again.

"As they are now, as individuals and as a group, they'll never overthrow the government of the Uppers."

"I know," she said quietly.

He threw his hands up in an overdone gesture of appeal. "Then why go with them? You're buying trouble. You admit that the reason Hodgson dropped you is the fact that your support of these crackpots might become known, and I think that you have to admit that Security undoubtedly has them set up for a major crackdown."

Bette said, "I realize they're all you've said. Inept, impractical, certainly malcontents. That's where you come in, Dennis."

☐ CHAPTER THIRTEEN ☐

She took it upon herself to get up and approach the auto-bar. "Let me have your credit card," she said. "I don't want to leave a record of my presence here."

Denny handed it to her, still failing to assimilate what she had said.

She dialed two more of the long drinks, handed one to him. He took it and knocked back a stiff jolt. Bette returned to her chair and took up where she had left off, matter-of-factly.

"One reason why the Sons of Liberty are inept and impractical is because there hasn't been a social revolution for a long time; the art of revolution has been lost. Of course, the government of the Welfare State has had its finger in that pie." She sipped at her drink.

"Oh?" Denny prompted.

"They've made it so easy for the Lowers—the majority of our population, remember—to sit back and let things go by. And things aren't much different for the Middles. Even in your own case, Denny, you've never had much incentive for change, right?"

Denny nodded. "But now . . ."

"But now you have nothing to lose, and everything to gain. Unfortunately, we can't arrange for the rug to be pulled out from under every one of the beneficiaries of our Welfare State. They've got it made, and they know it, and I think they'd even fight to keep what they've got."

"And the government—the Uppers—keep it that way."

"Right!" Bette began speaking in the manner of a teacher to her student, unaware that Denny had made a statement of fact, rather than posed a question. "The change began way back in the middle of the Twentieth Century, when the powers-that-be of the time recognized that they had in their hands a way to keep their power, in the same manner as the patricians of ancient Rome."

Bette took a pull at her drink, sizing up how he was taking this, thus far. But Denny was being noncommittal.

"The vast resources of the world's most powerful nation were available to buy the votes, as it were, of the populace. Special interest groups, representing huge blocs of votes, were patronized, granted executive and legislative favor, but that was just the beginning. The real vote-buying, the real selling out of the democracy, began with the subsidizing of poverty."

"What? No one subsidizes poverty—that's a contradiction in terms, Bette. Why, the very existence of the Welfare State is a negation of what you say; the Welfare State eliminates poverty."

She shook her head. "Any economist will tell you that if you want more of something, subsidize it—this is a fundamental economic law. The latter-day patricians of America and their so-called 'Great Society' subsidized poverty to the hilt, *by encouraging those in poverty to make no attempt to better themselves*. All the welfare and unemployment and food-subsidy programs for individuals—all were inflated and abused to the point where they provided a tool to keep the masses down.

"The average man or woman found endless incentive to *not* work, to feed at the public trough. Human nature being what it is, those enjoying subsidized living, even though it might be at sustinence level, were disinclined to push for changes.

"So, there emerged a system which subsidized poverty to its own benefit. But the aristocracy of the time overlooked one thing—the potential time-bomb that the idle masses represented. This nearly proved to be the downfall of the system, but the system adjusted, and out of necessity trank and the fracases developed, the modern-day bread and circuses. Then, there was no incentive for change left. In time, the very subject of social change became a taboo. The *status quo* must not even be considered to be changeable."

Denny became impatient. "What's all this got to do with me, and with what you said a few minutes ago?"

"I was pointing out that the Sons of Liberty are inept and impractical as revolutionists because we've lost the art of putting over a social change. No one has even wanted to rock the boat for such a long time that there are none capable of it. That's where you come in."

"*Where's* where I come in?" he demanded.

"You're the head of the Department of History at the most important university in the West-world. You have access to suppressed knowledge that we need. What you haven't got, you can get, through the governmental libraries in Greater Washington. Nobody monitors the books of a scholar of your attainments." She had twisted her small mouth when she said that. "You're free to read what you will."

What she said was obviously true.

"And what do you need?"

"Books on history—history and social and political structures. True histories and information on the great democratic societies of the world, and information on socialist theory and its weaknesses. We must first show our citizens what was and what can be, and then show them what is wrong with our present society. You can get all of that for us.

"And, face it, you're a hero. That has to be worth something.

"Aside from all that," Bette drilled on, "you're a man of action. We need spark plugs, people who *do* things. People who have ideas and will see them through."

She smiled. "In short, we need you."

So. It had sought him out. He was not to return to the sheltered life, after all. What had gone before—his being dragooned into participation in the national games, Hodgson coercing him to take on an espionage assignment, his appointment without consultation as one of the three West-world champions at the trial by combat—all had been but preliminary to this. He had no doubt about that now.

But did he want this? It was hard to say. A glimmering of what might be, what might come from this, was already in his mind's eye. A return to true democracy, to the status of free men, for the West-world. Yes, that he wanted. And he also felt a need for action—to act against the forces that had so manipulated him. The University life no longer held the appeal he thought it had; he had indeed found, as one Twentieth-century writer had said, that you can't go back again.

"What are your greatest needs?" he said.

She seemed to be operating on the assumption that he was already one of them. Her green eyes were even brighter. She leaned forward. "First, a stronger organization. One that can ensure that men like Dr. Fitzgerald aren't taken by the Security police. And then, some method of getting our message to the people. As it is, ninety-nine people out of a hundred haven't even heard of the Sons of Liberty, not to speak of their program."

He was nodding. "First of all, the cell system."

She scowled. "The what?"

"The cell system. Five persons to a cell, one of whom is the elected leader. The nihilists, back in the Nineteenth Century, were the first to develop it, I believe. I can study up on the details and report. The general idea is that you know no one in the organization but the other four members of your cell. If you're captured, it is possible for you to betray only four people. If you are a police spy, you will learn the identity of only four people."

Bette was dubious. "How does one cell communicate with another? How are instructions passed around? How do you accomplish things that call for more than five people?"

"The leader of each cell knows the leader of four other cells, and gets together with them periodically. This is called a unit. Each unit elects one of its number to be its unit secretary."

Bette was considering it. "And suppose one of these cell leaders is captured, he can betray his fellow four-cell members, plus the members of his unit."

"Each leader carries poison," Denny said. "Bette, have no illusions. This is no child's game. If this overthrow of the Welfare State is to be accomplished, then the chips are down, and there is no picking them up again. The Sons of Liberty can't remain a little debating society where breathless intellectuals meet to deliciously whisper their revolt against the powers that be."

Bette Yardborough flushed.

He went back to describing the cell system. "Each leader of a unit meets with four other leaders of units, periodically. This is called a division. The division elects a leader to be divisional secretary. Divisional secretaries are in touch with the— we'll call it the board of directors—which works on a full-time basis for the organization. They're the writers, newspaper publishers, editors, and speakers for the organization."

Bette said, "But if one of the board of directors is a traitor, or is caught, he's in a position to betray a good many people."

"I didn't say it was foolproof. We might be able to think up some refinements, but the cell system has been successfully utilized by revolutionary groups for at least a couple of centuries."

Bette Yardborough looked down at the tips of her shoes. She said, "I continue to catch myself underestimating you, Denny Land. I came here to recruit you to supply us with hard-to-get publications. Now I begin to suspect that you are going to take over leadership of the organization." She looked up at him. "I don't object."

"A single-person leadership has too many shortcomings," Denny told her. "Eliminate one person, and the whole movement has had it. That was the Achilles heel of the Incas. All Pizarro had to do was capture Atahualpa, the Inca, and the entire nation fell apart. We'd best stick to collective leadership. I'd suggest that you and I try to become members of the board of directors. Since you're already in, and I presume well known, you can start the ball rolling, forming the cell system. When the membership, from bottom to top, has found a board of directors, we'll hold our first executive meeting. By that time, perhaps I will have rooted out some basic techniques for spreading our message."

Revolution. A word of romantic connotations. Paul Revere's breakneck ride from Boston to warn the Minute Men. *The red coats are coming!* Patrick Henry, his face livid, shouting, *I know not what course others may take, but as for me, give me liberty, or give me death!* Thomas Paine, the propagandist without peer, bent over his rickety desk, a half-empty bottle of rum to the left of his ink pot, *These are the times that try men's souls.*

Washington on a white horse, his face impassive as he holds his spyglass to his eye, watching the long lines of beautifully uniformed French, the less natty lines of his Continentals, slowly working forward from position to position, whilst the artillery shatters Yorktown. In the far distance, behind the British lines, the bagpipes skirling, "The World Turned Upside Down."

Perhaps once it had been so.

However, Dennis Land found hard work and tedium rather than romance.

Revolutionists Jefferson, Madison, Paine, and their contemporaries had been of the opinion that given the printing press and an educated population, tyranny would become impossible. An informed people would rise against it.

They could not have foreseen the evolution of mass media—print and electronic.

In Benjamin Franklin's day, so little reading material was available that each man capable of reading read everything he could put hands to—including the so-called "inflammatory" pamphlets of Thomas Paine. But by the Twentieth Century, not to speak of the Twenty-first, when for all practical purposes everyone *could* read, few did. Less than five percent of the population bought books, and they were usually devoted to sex or mayhem—preferably both.

Even those who did read found themselves beset by a situation never dreamed of by the revolutionary forefathers. Each day they found themselves proffered enough reading material to keep them supplied for the balance of the year. Hundreds upon hundreds of magazines, tens of thousands of

books on any and every subject overflowed the
book stores, the newsstands, the magazine shops,
even the supermarkets. And then there was the
electronic media—both visual and print. In self-
defense of one's time, one could only select desperately, quickly. If a title didn't draw instant
attention, a magazine cover spark interest, a head-
line provoke concern, a reader went no further. If
a story failed to have a provocative narrative hook,
it was discarded after the first few paragraphs.

But above all, the average reader refused anything that proved *hard* to read, that moved too
slowly. The top novelists of the Nineteenth Century would have starved to death in the world of
Hemingway, and later, that of Mickey Spillane.
Television, movies, and radio had taught the average citizen to *relax* in seeking his intellectual entertainment. He didn't want to have to concentrate.

Of necessity, Denny's group had to get its message out in hardcopy. The Uppers controlled the
electronic media—video, radio, and computer terminal links. They could not tap into any of these
systems without leaving a direct and damning trail
back to themselves.

So it was that Dennis Land, Bette Yardborough,
and the Sons of Liberty found themselves up against
a wall in communicating with the masses. Whether
or not their message would be received, once
delivered, was another question. They couldn't
even *deliver* it.

Oh, yes. A recruit here. A recruit there. Usually brought in through individual contact. A friend.
A relative. But how often were they able to attract
a convert cold—hand him a leaflet, give him a

pamphlet or a copy of *If This Goes On*, their skimpy newspaper, and step by step bring him around to their meetings and finally have him request membership? Practically never.

It wasn't for lack of effort and expenditure of energy. Neither Dennis Land nor Bette Yardborough had ever done anything lackadaisically. It was no mistake that Denny had become the youngest full professor in the history of his university. No accident that he was so proficient in ancient weapons that he survived the national games. Nor was it an accident that Bette Yardborough had become a top agent in her violent field.

Denny had started by taking advantage of the facilities he controlled at the university. He smuggled some printing equipment out to the organization, and used some on the school grounds, after infiltrating his department with various Sons of Liberty members.

Such equipment as could be safely purchased without suspicion was bought on the open market. Some that couldn't be, came into their possession through raids conducted by Denny and some of the younger membership. Once committed, Denny Land pulled no punches.

But though they ran off leaflets decrying the Welfare State by the hundreds of thousands, pamphlets and newspapers by the tens of thousands, books to the extent they could, they simply were not getting through. By the most desperate means, they couldn't have printed enough leaflets to supply one for every adult in the West-world. And if they could, and if they could have put them into the hands of each adult, they began to suspect what would happen.

The average recipient would have taken it, looked at the head, which read something like, CITIZENS UNITE TO OVERTHROW THE WELFARE STATE, realized it was something hard, and thrown it to the ground.

They simply weren't getting through.

It was seldom these days that Denny Land found time for a moment to himself without some task pressing upon him. The candle was burning at both ends, and beginning to melt in the middle as well. His duties as department head couldn't be completely fobbed off on others, but his work with the Sons of Liberty was all but a constant thing.

Thus it was unusual for him to stop off in a bar. He had work back at the office, and at least two appointments, but his feeling of emptiness was such that on an impulse he turned into a drink dispensary between his office and the book and tapes outlet he sometimes patronized and found himself a table. He wanted a long, cold glass of bock beer—the darker the better and the stronger the better. He slipped his credit card into the table's slot and dialed the heavy brew.

A voice above him said, "Make mine the same, Denny."

He looked up at the other. It was Joe Mauser.

"Sit down," Denny said. "I'm having dark beer."

Mauser slid into the seat across from Denny. "You know, it's hard to get hold of you except at your office or apartment." Joe Mauser looked about the establishment. "You don't seem to show up in public places very often."

"Isn't an office or an apartment where you'd usually find someone?" Denny said. He felt the same irritation against the older man as he had the last time he had seen him. "And I thought you Uppers never came into Middle-caste bars."

"Did you? I thought I'd told you once that I was born a Mid-Lower. I pulled myself up by my bootstraps, Denny, fighting all the way. By the time I reached my goal, I found it didn't mean much to me." He shrugged his heavy shoulders, a fighting man's shoulders. "But I understand that's often the nature of goals."

"Is that supposed to mean something deep? What did you want to see me about, Mauser? And why couldn't it have been my office or apartment?"

The beer had come and Joe Mauser tasted his. For a moment he grinned a small boy's grin. "You want to know something? I brought some of my Lower-caste tastes with me on my crawl upward. Supposedly, I'm in the vintage wine category now, but frankly, I still prefer beer."

Denny didn't respond to the pleasantry, and Joe Mauser became serious again. "I didn't want to go to your office or home because they are most likely under surveillance." When Denny remained silent, he added, "Category Security, of course."

"Not the Bureau of Investigation?" Denny's voice was bitter.

The old-time mercenary was shaking his head. "Subversion is no longer our jurisdiction, Denny. As a matter of fact, even Category Security details few agents to it these days."

Denny's unexplained irritation at Mauser had kept him from realizing, for a moment, the fact that the other was obviously here for a purpose, not to chat. Now he said, "You've had some news on Bazaine?"

"No. The whole matter seems to have bogged down."

"How do you know that the Sov-world or Common Europe hasn't located him?"

Mauser seemed impatient with the subject. "We don't. But we're doing our damnedest to find out if that's the case."

All over again, Denny felt the intuitive suspicion that something was wrong.

He said, "Well, why did you want to see me? What's the big mystery?"

Mauser worked on his beer some more. "No mystery. You didn't react to something I said a moment ago, Denny. The fact that even Category Security has few agents assigned to subversion these days."

The ramifications of that were manifest. Still, Denny played dumb. "Why not?"

"Obviously, because it isn't important."

"Subversion isn't important to a satisfied caste system such as the Welfare State?"

Mauser was shaking his head, as though regretfully. "You see, Denny, nobody is interested. Just a few crackpots, like our hotheaded Bette, and fuzzy-minded Don Quixotes, tilting against the windmills of injustice, such as our Denny." Mauser grinned his rare little-boy grin again. "I'm waxing absolutely poetic."

That room with the tiled walls in Southern Spain

came back to Denny suddenly—the one with the scenes from the Don Quixote story. He brought his thoughts back to the present.

"What did you want to see me about, Mauser?"

The former mercenary took another pull at the bock, then put the glass down, and folded his fingers together on the table. "Denny, to the extent possible, the Bureau tries to take care of its own. From time to time we hear interdepartmental rumors. Sometimes they affect present or former operatives of the Bureau."

"In short," Denny snapped, "the Category Security people are on to Bette and me, and you think we should discontinue our activities. I suspect that Frank Hodgson is worried about adverse publicity if it turns out that two of his former agents are now active in the Sons of Liberty."

Joe Mauser, his hands still folded, looked at them strangely. "Denny, let me tell you something. People usually believe that they have the kind of government they deserve and want, but it's often the opposite. Those controlling the government quite frequently *make* the people believe that they have the government they want, when really the powers-that-be have the kind of government *they* want. Such is the case today."

Denny's puzzlement was obvious. Mauser was sounding almost as if he was on the side of the Sons of Liberty. "But that's the whole problem we face—the government has forced a system on us in such a way that we must accept it."

The other was shaking his head. "No. Lightweights sometimes think that such phenomena as Adolf the Aryan, last century, imposed himself upon the German people by violence and maintained himself there by the same tactics." Mauser was shaking his head. "Forget about it. The Germans didn't fight the war they did opposed to the government that got them into it. Obviously such minorities as the Jews, the gypsies, the Czechs, and the greater portions of the countries they overran were opposed to the Nazis, but not the Germans. The *Herrevolk* were in there pitching for *der Fuhrer* even after the situation had pickled for them.

"An indication of how it might have gone if the German people had been opposed to him was to be seen in Italy. By the time Il Duce had dragged them into the war, the majority of the Italians had become fed up with him. Have you ever heard such soldiers in the history of warfare? Their battle cry was, *I surrender*. They deserted by the regiment every time they could find a bewildered Tommy or G.I. to surrender to. Mussolini's supposed empire simply fell apart. His people didn't want him."

Denny was staring at the other. The man wasn't really repeating anything new. But in the present context it carried some interesting implications.

Mauser went on, "Russia is another example. After the revolution, and during the ensuing power plays and purges and changes, it was expected that the government of the Soviet Union, and later the government of the Soviet Complex, would collapse. Communism was bad, wasn't it? Very well, it would collapse. But it didn't. Why?"

Denny started to speak, but the other held up a hand and continued. "Because in spite of how we allowed our own propaganda to blind us—by the way, you should never believe your own propaganda, it's even more foolish than believing the other man's—the Sov people were misled into believing that their government could give them what they wanted. They *wanted* the government they had. They proved that in the streets of Stalingrad. They were willing to fight and die for it, in their sad confusion."

Denny said, "Who's the professor of history here?"

Mauser closed his mouth and looked at him.

"What's your point?" Denny demanded.

"I'd think it was obvious by now." Joe Mauser came to his feet. He looked down at the younger man. "Denny, the reason more Category Security lads aren't assigned to such outfits as the Sons of Liberty is because they aren't dangerous. Nobody is interested. The Lowers in particular—and they compose more than ninety percent of the population—are satisfied with the government they have." He grunted contempt. "In fact, they'd *fight* for the kind of government they have. They'd fight you and your handful of Sons of Liberty if they thought you might rob them of their Welfare State, their trank pills, their sadistic telly shows, their fracases, and their gladiatorial meets."

Denny rankled. "And why? In the face of the obvious fact that they are being used, manipulated, and forced to support an aristocracy?"

"Because it's easier that way, Denny. Freedom takes work, and freedom demands sacrifice. Even if you were to get your message out to the people, and even if they were to understand it, you would achieve nothing. Like the Russian state of the last century, the people of the Welfare State *want* what they have; they don't want to risk losing their handout."

The old Category Military pro turned on his heel and started off. "Thanks for the drink," he called over his shoulder. "I would have bought back, but my credit card's no good in a Middle-caste establishment."

"Don't mention it," Denny growled after him.

For some reason unknown to Dennis Land, the words of Joe Mauser left him enraged and confused. When they had first met, in Spain, his reaction had been one of liking. Physically strong, ethically honest, ultrafair in personal relations, a man who insisted on doing his work well, Joe Mauser was one you could trust in the dill.

What had happened? Dennis Land didn't know. But the last few times he had seen Joe Mauser, an iron curtain seemed to have fallen between them.

And now this. These words against the West-world. Was he kidding himself? Were Joe Mauser's words the actual truth, and his irritation caused by the fact that he, Denny, knew them to be true but didn't want to accept it?

He decided against returning to the office and made his way toward his apartment, instead. He wanted to think. He wanted to talk to Bette Yardborough, too.

Something important had occurred to him. This revolution was not one that could be incited, not one to swell from a grassroots origin.

This one would have to be forced. He realized

that now. The only way to wrest control of the West-world from its socialist masters would be to eliminate them. He was surprised that he had not thought of this before. Mauser was right, of course. Even if they could get to the populace, it would accomplish nothing.

The problem was in how to convert their small organization to an *active* military group, if any such group could be formed.

The university had assigned a man to keep watch at the door of the apartment house in which Denny now lived. The number of fracas buffs and gladiatorial fans who had pestered him were falling off now, but still, there were some, and Denny didn't want to be bothered. Denny nodded at him absentmindedly as he passed through the building's entrance.

He took the elevator to his upper floor terrace apartment, bending his legs subconsciously to adjust to the acceleration.

The door recognized him and opened at his approach. He was well into the living room before he noticed the intruder confronting him.

"So, we meet again, Professor Land."

For a second, Denny froze.

☐ CHAPTER FOURTEEN ☐

Denny dropped into the *Kiba-dachi*, straddle position, prepared to attack or defend. Even as he moved, his mind worked furiously. Why was Malyshev here, and how had he gotten in?

Yuri Malyshev shook his head. "I come in peace, professor."

For the moment, Denny maintained his karate stance in spite of the fact that the other carried no weapon and showed no signs of belligerence. "How did you get in here?" he demanded.

The Russian agent chopped out his short laugh. "Now really, professor. You know my profession. Do you think it any problem for a Chrezvychainaya Komissiya agent to enter an apartment?" Ignoring the American's posture, so suited to both offense and defense, he seated himself again and crossed his legs.

Denny relaxed. The other turning up in his home like this had taken him aback, and his mind had already been in a turmoil. But in the past six months he had had greater shocks than this one.

He said now, "I was about to dial myself a drink. Would you like one?"

Malyshev nodded. "I would have already ordered one, but I hardly wished to expose my credit card to your auto-bar. Vodka, please, or barack, if it's available."

Denny turned his back to him, went to the bar, and dialed vodka for the Russian, another bock beer for himself. What the hell was the Sov-world agent doing here?

As he took the two-ounce glass, the Russian said, "You know, this system of credit cards is undoubtedly one of the greatest aids to keeping track of one's people that has ever been devised. For everything you purchase, you must submit your credit card. Not only is the sum then subtracted from your balance, but the computers are in a position to monitor your location. A man on the run in the West-world dares buy nothing. Food, drink, medicine. He reveals himself the moment he buys anything."

"It is, however, the ultimate medium of exchange," Denny told him. "Down through history man has had continual difficulty with his medium of exchange. The universal credit card solves all."

He took a chair opposite the Russian. Malyshev, now attired in West-world dress and wearing it as though he had never known uniform or the garb of the Sov-world, was ever the same. He seemed perfectly at rest, without pressure from the world about him. He threw the high-proof spirits back over his palate in the Russian manner of drinking.

Denny said, "My days of adventure seem to be coming back to me today. Fifteen minutes ago I was talking with Joe Mauser."

"Ah, the estimable Joseph Mauser." The Sov

agent's eyes narrowed infinitesimally. "And what did he have to say?"

"What you have to say is more of interest at the moment," Denny responded. "I think you have more in mind than simply exchanging felicitations with a former foe."

"Of course." The Russian espionage operative pursed his lips. "I'll start from the beginning. In view of your profession, undoubtedly a great deal of this won't be new to you, but I'll cover it all, in way of background."

"Go ahead. It won't be the first lecture I've had."

Malyshev nodded his head. "Very well. In the year 1917, professor, a revolution took place in Imperial Russia. Rather, a series of revolutions, since what began as an attempt to overthrow the feudalism of the Romanoffs and establish a capitalist democracy got out of control. For one thing, the new provisional government of the Social Democrat Kerensky had no intention of dropping out of the war, but expected to fight on with the allies. The Germans, of course, wished to see Russia so torn by internal conflict that she would sue for separate peace. With that in mind, German intelligence located Vladimir Ilich Ulyanov, better known by his Party name, Nikolai Lenin, and several of his closest intimates, including Grigori Zinoviev, Karl Radak the journalist, and"—the Russian cleared his throat—"Vladimir Malyshev, my paternal grandfather, twice removed."

Denny Land's eyebrows rose. "I had no idea your ancestor was one of the Old Bolsheviks, though, of course, I was familiar with the name."

There was nothing to say to that. The Russian agent continued. "They had been living in exile in Switzerland. The Germans, to foment trouble, sent them in a sealed car back to Russia—possibly one of the greatest mistakes in history. Trotsky came from New York, Kamenev, Rykov, Bukharin came out of hiding; the Bolsheviks were gathering."

Malyshev grunted contempt. "At this point I should mention that another turned up on the scene—a third-rater, in Party ranks—a certain Josif Vissarianovich Dzugashvilli, better known as Joseph Stalin. He had been in exile in Siberia. Russia was in a state of collapse and the Bolsheviks were a team of the most competent revolutionists the world had ever seen. Within months, they were in power. With the exception of the Paris Commune of 1871, which lasted only a few weeks, it was the first time a socialist movement had ever come to power—and a sad day in the history of this planet."

Denny came to his feet and went to dial them two more drinks. He knew the story of the Russian Revolution, but had never heard it before from the lips of a Sov-world citizen. It was intriguing, especially since what the Russian agent was telling him was to be presumed treason.

Yuri Malyshev took the drink, downed it, and resumed. "It is ridiculous to say that something that occurred in history was fortunate or unfortunate; however, an assassin shot Lenin in 1918 and Lenin never completely recovered, finally dying in 1924. By that time, Stalin was in control of the Party machinery. Trotsky was the first to go. He escaped Russia and for the next ten years kept ahead of Stalin's killers. They caught up with him in Mexico. Zinoviev and Kamenev were tried and shot in August, 1936; Karl Radek was sent to prison in 1937; in March 1938 Rykov and Bukharin were purged. My ancestor was shot the following year. Stalin's version of the Party was now in complete control.

"Lenin, following Marx in his misguided theory, had taught that before socialism could be fully realized the state would wither away. Stalin, to the contrary, strengthened it—incidentally revealing the true nature of those controlling the revolution and the Party. Quite simply, they wished to create a power structure which appeared to benefit the peasants—and thus gain popular support—but which in actuality gave them everything in the way of power and material wealth.

"The Party controlled all. And, of course, as ever, this new aristocracy took measures to better its own condition and to perpetuate itself. Soon it was difficult to get a ranking job, unless you were a Party member. Party members made sure that the very best schools were available only to their children. The children of Party members became Party members with ease; but by the 1990s, it became increasingly difficult for anyone else to join. Eventually, Party membership became hereditary."

Yuri Malyshev looked at Denny ruefully. "I am afraid I am long-winded, as you call it. However, we have arrived at the present. A hereditary aristocracy heads the Sov-world, and resists all efforts to displace it. Beyond their iron grip, denying freedom and democracy to the citizens of the Sov-world, they are incompetent. Their only defense is to maintain the status quo, to resist progress and change.

"But," the Russian looked Denny in the eye, "free men cannot be denied their desires. Needless to say, an underground has evolved, Professor Land."

Denny's eyebrows rose.

"Unfortunately, things have changed considerably since my grandfather, side by side with Lenin and Radek, issued bolshevik newspapers, wrote pamphlets and books that were smuggled into Russia, held secret meetings in the forests of the Ukraine, the hills of the Caucauses, among the fishing boats of Arkangel. Today, all the means of promoting an idea are in the hands of the Party. Telly, motion pictures, radio, newspapers, magazines, all are controlled by the Party. So are all buildings, all lecture halls. Even could an underground locate a printing press on which to turn out material, where would it find a cellar in which to hide it? All property, including real estate, is in control of the Party."

Yuri Malyshev wound it up definitely. "In short, Professor Land, we are in a position similar to that of the Sons of Liberty."

Dammit, did the entire world know that Dennis Land was a revolutionary? He might as well wear a sign advertising the fact. Even more surprising, however, was the fact that a similar underground movement existed in the Sov-world. Most surprising, indeed.

"What has all this got to do with me, Malyshev?"

The Russian traced his finger down the scar line. "We are in the same boat, Professor Land.

You find it impossible to get your message over to your people. We find it impossible in the Sov-world."

"Just what is your message?"

"That the Party must be overthrown! That the country must be given over to the hands of free men—which is to say that the people must rule themselves, by a government of their choice."

"I see. But I repeat my question. What has all this got to do with me?"

"We cooperated once before, professor."

Denny looked at him blankly. "You want to cooperate? How could we possibly cooperate? Given the fact that we have similar problems, there is simply no manner in which we can aid each other."

Malyshev took another deep breath. "Professor, there is only one medium of communication that really counts in the world today. Telly. In your land and mine, most of the population spends the majority of its waking hours gawking at a telly screen. Very well. Our need is to have telly made available to us, so that we can beam our messages into the homes of your Lowers, our Proletarians."

Dennis Land openly laughed at him. "My dear Malyshev, I agree with you *en toto*. That is our need. And believe me, in the West-world, at least, it will continue to be our need. Our category Communications would no more throw open its facilities to the Sons of Liberty than I could walk up the side of that wall." He grunted contempt of the other's apparent naivete.

Malyshev threw his grenade.

"If we were in possession of Auguste Bazaine, we would have a key that opened many doors, Professor Land. To what extent do you think the telly broadcasting stations of the Neut-world would be made available to us, if we were able to deliver Auguste Bazaine to them?"

Denny eyed him, surprised. Finally, he blurted, "But we're *not* in possession of Auguste Bazaine!"

"Bazaine is within fifteen miles of this building."

It all clicked into place. Denny could see the picture now, the whole picture. It was the chance they needed, but . . . he suddenly felt the whole of history descend upon his shoulders. Dare they make the move?

"Assuming that what you say is true, Malyshev, and assuming that we can get Bazaine, we face still more problems. What guarantees can we have that the Neut-world won't toss us out on our ears, that they won't turn everything upside down by making use of Bazaine in some way?

"Besides all of which," he finished, "the two of us can't handle a job like that alone."

The door chime sounded, echoing through the room.

Denny glanced at the door, shook his head, and said, "There. Go through that door. It's the bathroom."

Yuri Malyshev came to his feet. He scooped up his glass in one smooth movement and slipped it into a pocket, smoothed the rumpled pillow of the couch where he had been sitting, and then, seemingly moving with leisure but covering ground with surprising speed, disappeared through the door Denny had indicated.

Denny crossed the room and opened the door.

Bette Yardborough stood there. She stepped in without invitation, closed the door behind her.

Her voice carried an edge of excitement. "Listen, Dennis, do you know who I thought I saw, a little earlier today?"

He said nothing.

"Yuri Malyshev, the Russian. The one you fought in Geneva."

"I know who you mean," Denny said.

"I lost him in the crowd. Do you think I ought to notify Joe Mauser or Frank Hodgson? What in the world's that curd doing in the country? One thing's sure, he's not an accredited Sov-world attache. Our Category Security would never allow him to be accredited. He's got a reputation that . . ."

Yuri Malyshev appeared suddenly behind her and said to Denny, "That was one of our problems, but now we've got our third man."

Bette Yardborough spun, her left hand flicking up the hem of her short skirt, her right hand blurring for a garter holster.

Denny threw both his arms around her. "Hey!" he yelled, wrestling as Bette squirmed and jabbed with her elbows. He snarled at Yuri Malyshev, who stood there, his arms out to both sides, palms forward, in the universal gesture of being defenseless. "Zen! You confounded fool."

Malyshev was chopping out his laughter. He bowed to Bette, formally. "Third operative, I should say. I should have thought of you, Miss Yardborough."

"All right," Bette said, and relaxed. Denny, wincing at the pain in his ribs, released her and she smoothed her clothes. She glowered at Malyshev, then at Denny. She snapped, bitterly, "And what are you flats up to?"

Denny grumbled, making his way toward the auto-bar. "If any more crises come up involving my needing a drink, I'm going to be drenched before the day's out. A John Brown's Body, Bette? Another vodka, Yuri? I'm going to stick to beer."

"Yuri!" Bette snapped. "First names, yet. What in holy hell is going on here?"

Denny returned with the drinks, offered her the tall glass, went over to where Yuri Malyshev had resumed his place on the couch, and handed him a shot glass. The Russian took it and disposed of it as he had those before. Inwardly, Dennis Land shuddered to see the hundred-and-fifty-proof spirit go down so casually.

Denny said, "Sit down, Bette. It would seem that Yuri Malyshev occupies much the same position in the Sov-world as we do here. That is, he's active in an organization that is attempting to overthrow the Party."

"I don't believe it!" she said, still glaring defiantly.

The Russian shrugged. As usual, he was completely at ease.

"I do," Denny said. "Among other things, I trust Yuri Malyshev. And he trusts me."

Denny took a pull at his drink and regarded Bette carefully. "However, you interrupted our conversation at a crucial point. We'll pick it up in a moment. Meanwhile, briefly, Yuri tells me he is the great-great-grandson of Vladimir Malyshev, once the right-hand man of Lenin. He belongs to an organization whose purpose is to overthrow the Party. It has run into the same basic blocks we have here in our efforts against the Uppers. They can't reach the people, because the means of communicating ideas are in the hands of the enemy. Yuri feels that no media except telly makes much difference any more. He contends that in both our countries, telly time must be obtained."

Denny paused to catch his breath, and Bette snorted.

"Yes," Denny nodded. "My own reaction. However, Yuri is of the opinion that if we were in the possession of Auguste Bazaine we could demand of the Neut-world, if no one else, that we be given access to telly stations to beam programs into the Sov-world and West-world."

"If we were in possession of Auguste Bazaine!" Bette's tone was incredulous.

Denny nodded again. "Sit down. Yuri claims Bazaine is within fifteen miles of here."

"Nonsense!"

"Of course. But that's where you interrupted us. Sit down," Denny repeated, and turned his eyes back to the Russian. "You forget that the President, Seymour Gatling, was interrogated under hypnosis and drugs. He had no idea where Bazaine was."

Malyshev's voice was dry. "I'm sure he didn't. It probably would have been more to the point if Joseph Mauser was put to the question, or your Frank Hodgson."

Denny was shaking his head. "No. You're wrong, there. I was with Mauser all along." But then there came back to him that strange moment in the suite in Geneva when he had *felt* that Mauser had suddenly realized where Bazaine must be.

The Russian said, "I was in charge of the Sov-world operation in regard to Bazaine, but at the time he was abducted my team had not as yet joined me and I was alone in Torremolinos. I watched Bazaine's abduction from a distance. But I *know* my people didn't do it." He leaned back and smiled. "Now, tell me, Dennis Land, what happened to your yacht, *La Carmencita*, with its crew of West-world operatives?"

Denny was blank.

Bette said, "What are you getting at?"

"I've been on this assignment since Geneva." Malyshev's tone was suddenly bitter. "In fact, my life supposedly depends upon concluding it successfully—successfully in terms of the Sov-world government's interests. It's been a long trail, and a highly camouflaged one, but I've finally tracked him down. He was brought to the West-world in *La Carmencita*. He is now some fifteen miles from this spot, in what purports to be a mental institution, but which in fact is one of the most secure detention centers of which I've heard." His voice went dryly humorous. "And it is guarded against persons breaking *in*, as well as *out*."

"You're *sure?*" Denny demanded.

"Yes."

"And you propose to rescue him?"

"If that's the term."

Bette said, interest in her tone now, "How? And why did you want to bring Dennis into it? And now me?"

Malyshev's explanation was valid. "I have no underground comrades in this vicinity who could aid me. Time is of the essense, however; we must act immediately, within hours. There may be plans to move or otherwise dispose of Bazaine.

"Professor Land is a highly capable man and his interests coincide with my own, as do yours. We need three persons to do the job." He looked at Denny. "By the way, we'll have to go unarmed. We can't carry anything that has metal. Their detectors are capable of locating the tiniest pocket-knife."

Denny said, "I begin to see why you choose me, Yuri. The hand is my sword, eh?"

"Yes," the Russian said.

"What in the world are you talking about?" Bette frowned at the two of them.

"An old karate saying," Denny told her. "Yuri Malyshev holds a seventh dan black belt. My own is only fifth dan."

They drove in Bette Yardborough's hovercar, and parked it almost a quarter mile from their destination. Yuri Malyshev had chosen the vehicle's hiding place beforehand. He seemed to have done a good deal of preliminary work, judging from the briefing he gave them during the drive.

As they climbed out of the hovercar in the gathering darkness, Denny said, "This is a long distance to have to retreat, when and if we get hold of Bazaine."

"I know," the Russian said. "But any closer and the car might be spotted."

All three carried small-calibered, silenced automatics. They stayed close to the berm of the road. On the two or three occasions that cars approached, they disappeared into the trees that lined the highway.

Bette said, "Too many of the details aren't clear

for me to be happy. Who is it that has Bazaine? From what you say, it's not the government. The president himself doesn't even know Bazaine is in the West-world."

"I don't know," the Russian admitted. "I couldn't get any further than tracking him to this supposed institution. That, and to discover the wing and hall of the building in which he is housed. A bit of judicious and extremely expensive bribery helped me there."

"You mentioned Joe Mauser," Denny said.

"I have seen him enter and leave the place."

A building loomed before them—a gracious building, surrounded by broad sweep of lawn, by carefully spotted gardens, by gentle paths and graveled roads. There was a high wire-mesh fence, somewhat camouflaged by shrubs and ivory, but topped with barbed wire.

Malyshev brought them to a halt and gave them a brief rundown. "It's a former mansion, built by one of your so-called robber barons a century or so ago. Although the staff is rather large, the defenses are mostly mechanical. Not entirely, however."

Denny asked: "Now how do we get through the fence?"

Yuri shook his head. "We don't. It's too well rigged. Nor can we get over or under it. We'll have to go through a gate. There are three of them. The smallest, about a hundred yards down there, has two guards. We'll have to take them. Leave the pistols here. The moment we're on the other side of this fence, any metal on our persons would set off the alarms."

They left their guns at the base of a tree, where they could easily be found again, and crept toward the gate.

Malyshev said, "I assume this is clear. Denny and I handle any opposition we run into. Bette, you bring up the rear. If and when we get Bazaine, you'll have to take care of him. Our hands must be free."

"I know how to handle myself, gentlemen," Bette said grimly. "And I can handle Bazaine, whether he wants to be handled or not."

"I'm sure you can, Miss Yardborough."

The two uniformed guards were not expecting trouble. The gate was open, and they idled against it, chatting. Their guns were holstered, but they were quick-draw holsters, and the men bore an air of competence.

Dennis Land and Yuri Malyshev burst upon them with a speed and aggressiveness that must have been a terrifying shock to both. The two karate practitioners bounded into position immediately before them, both going into the *Zenkutsu-dachi* stance, the rear knee straight, the front knee bent so that the knee cap is directly over the arch of the foot.

The guards were popeyed, but not frozen beyond the point of activity. One jerked at his gun, the other flung himself in the direction of a phone booth which stood to one side.

Breathing "Zen," in a restricted kai yell, Malyshev lunged forward, blocked the gunman's arm off to the left, simultaneously chopped down on the man's clavicle with the edge of his fist. The other's face went gray in pain, and he collapsed when the second blow took him in the temple.

Denny had taken the second guard before that worthy had been able to get the old-fashioned phone off its hook. A judo chop had sent him to his knees. A second blow, delivered with elbow behind the ear, dropped him, unconscious.

Without looking back to see if Bette followed, they scurried across the lawns to the sheltering dimness of the walls of the mansion. Malyshev led. The open stretches of the lawn were a danger—a late stroller in the gardens might well spot them. And it was to be expected that telly cameras and perhaps motion detectors were spotted around the grounds. Malyshev's information and earlier reconnaissance were good, but he could not count on the path he'd planned to be clean.

Pressed against the wall, the Russian took stock of their position. "There's a service entry to the left, possibly a hundred feet. I doubt if anyone will be in the kitchen at this time of night. If so, we'll have to dispose of them. Denny, did you kill your man?"

"No. He should be out for from fifteen minutes to half an hour."

The other grunted. "Possibly twenty minutes for mine. We must think in terms of being out of here in fifteen minutes, maximum. Let's go." Bending almost double, he scurried along the wall, Denny and Bette immediately behind, copying him.

The service door was locked. Bette said, "Here, let me." She brought a plastic hairpin from her hair and knelt before the lock with it. It took a full, agonizing minute before the door swung open.

They passed through, Yuri leading again. Supposedly, he had memorized the layout of the building.

The halls were lit, but only dimly. Obviously, the kitchen and maintenance staff had gone for the night. They hurried down one passage, turned off onto a larger corridor. They stopped for a moment for Malyshev to take stock again. "Down here must be the wing where Bazaine is kept. I don't know what kind of guard they might have over him. We'll have to be ready for anything."

Denny looked up and down the corridor, nervously. "Something's wrong," he muttered. "This place can't be this empty. There ought to be servants, guards, and other . . . inmates."

"No," Yuri whispered. "It's late. Everyone is in bed. We're having excellent luck, thus far."

Bette said, "Well, let's not just stand here and talk about it. We've got to get back to those guards and give them another clip, in about ten minutes."

Malyshev, running lightly in canvas deck shoes, led the way down the corridor, through a heavy door, and into a wing of what were probably sleeping areas, beyond. They sped along this, to a jog in the corridor, and then to the left, to be confronted by a heavy door. The Russian whispered. "His room should be in the hall beyond this."

Denny tried the door. His lips thinned back over his teeth. "Locked!" he whispered.

Bette examined the handle and lock mechanism and her face went wan. "Not this one. Not with a hairpin. It's *really* locked!"

Malyshev's mouth worked. His finger traced down over the scar line, nervously. "There's another way. Back the way we came, and then around. Hurry."

They started back, turned the jog in the corridor, and were faced with another closed door.

It had been open only short moments before.

The three slid to a halt, stared unbelievingly at it.

Bette slipped to her knees, examined the lock. She turned, and her green eyes seemed to gleam. "There's a key in it, from the other side."

Denny spun and looked back in the direction from which they'd come. A cold feeling radiated from the pit of his stomach. "We've been trapped," he grunted. "Back, and see if we can find a window." He began to lead the way.

As they padded down the hall, a door opened. The three of them stopped, then faded against the walls.

Frank Hodgson stepped from a room, fifteen feet down, and said mildly, "I suppose this is enough. Bette, my dear, you were marvelous. Telly lost a wonderful actress in you."

□ CHAPTER FIFTEEN □

Joe Mauser stepped from still another doorway. He held a heavy military revolver in his hand.

Dennis Land, in despair, went into the *Kokutsu-dachi*, layout position, noting from the side of his eyes that Yuri Malyshev had assumed the *Zenkutsu-dachi*, in preparation for an attempt at the former mercenary.

Mauser was shaking his head. "Don't try it," he said conversationally. "I could pop both your knee-caps before you got to me. "I'm too far away, Malyshev."

Bette's face had its usual intense expression when in time of stress. "Now take it easy, boys. Everything is going to be all right."

Denny slowly straightened. He looked at her. "You're in with them," he said. There was disbelief in his voice.

The door that had blocked them only moments ago now opened and four guards entered, all armed, all hard of face and obviously trained men. Probably mercenaries, Denny thought bitterly.

And now, at last, Yuri Malyshev gave up. He relaxed and stood, as Denny already had, and shrugged. He looked at Bette in bitterness, then shrugged again.

He said, "There's an old Russian proverb: When four sit down to talk revolution, three are fools and the fourth a police spy."

Frank Hodgson laughed easily. "I must remember that. Very good." He turned and started down the corridor, in the direction opposite to that in which Auguste Bazaine's quarters were supposed to be. "If you'll just come along," he said over his shoulder.

Dennis Land was looking at Joe Mauser, not over the sinking feeling of ultimate despair.

Mauser said, "It was sort of a curd of a trick." He gestured with his revolver before slipping it back into a shoulder holster beneath his jacket. "Don't worry about this. The only reason I've been holding it was so that one of you lads wouldn't jump into action and hurt somebody with that fancy Oriental fighting of yours."

Denny blinked at him. They were throwing the curves much too fast for him tonight.

"Come along," Mauser said. "You, too, Yuri. We've got a friend of yours in here."

"A friend?" The Russian scowled.

Frank Hodgson led the way down the hall a bit, opened one half of a double door, and entered. Bette, Denny, Malyshev, and Mauser trailed after. The guards remained outside.

The room was evidently a library. It contained large, comfortable leather-covered easy chairs, an auto-bar, several desks and tables. The room had a comfortable Victorian air. ·

At one of the tables sat Zoltan Korda, poring

over some papers before him. He looked up upon their entry. "Ah, the romantics," he said.

Frank Hodgson said, "Everybody find chairs, eh? Might as well be comfortable, we've got a lot of ground to cover. Joe, will you do the honors?"

Bette interrupted, "We got in through the smaller gate. The boys here eliminated the two guards. They'd better be checked."

Joe Mauser went to the door, opened it, and said something to one of the men beyond, then came back and went to the bar. "Name your poison," he said.

Anger was piling up in Dennis Land. He rapped, "What's going on here? You all act as though we're at a party. Bette! How long have you been a traitor?"

She smiled at him. "Never, so far as I know."

"You betrayed us to these . . . these—"

"Not exactly," she said.

"What is that supposed to mean?"

"I could hardly betray you to your own side."

Hodgson spoke gently, almost lazily, as ever. "I'll take over, my dear Bette. Denny, what's been your goal in your Sons of Liberty work?"

"To overthrow the government!" he blurted. There was no hiding it now. "To get the country back on the road to progress!"

The elderly bureaucrat was nodding. "Very well. Suppose I told you that the revolution you're talking about took place five years ago?"

"Have you gone drivel-happy?" Denny looked about the room, as though they'd all gone mad.

During this, Yuri Malyshev had been gaping at Zoltan Korda as though his superior were a ghost.

"What are you doing *here?*" he was finally able to get out.

His superior lit a cigarette. "It would seem obvious, wouldn't it, colonel? You and Professor Land decided to collaborate to accomplish your mutual ends. Why shouldn't Mr. Hodgson and I do the same?"

"Anybody use a drink?" Joe Mauser said from the auto-bar.

"Vodka," Malyshev demanded. "A double vodka."

"Anything," Denny said. He could not comprehend this. It made no sense whatsoever. He turned to Hodgson. "You abducted Bazaine?"

"Not personally," Hodgson said easily. "Things got complicated very quickly, and we had to act on the spur of the moment. With Zoltan Korda's cooperation, we were able to, ah, rescue Auguste Bazaine, and bring him here. You see, we found him a kindred spirit. It developed that our excitable Belgian wanted to build his offensive and defensive weapons systems as a way of upsetting the world's *status quo*, thinking, somewhat in the same manner you and your Sons of Liberty organization have been thinking, that things simply must get moving again, that the race must be stirred to new efforts and be brought out of the rut." Hodgson cleared his throat in wry humor. "We didn't appreciate his methods, and thought it best to bring him here to join our ranks."

Joe Mauser brought the drinks around.

"We owe you two lads an apology," he told them. "We could have done all this less dramatically. I could have just come around to the school and given you the picture, but it's very necessary to keep this retreat of ours secure, and I was interested in seeing how a couple of top operators such as yourselves would make out trying to crack it. You made out too well, for my satisfaction. I'm going to have to strengthen our defenses."

Malyshev said flatly, "You people had Bazaine all during the time the trial by combat was being readied and then fought." His glare went from Korda to Hodgson, then to Mauser.

Mauser shook his head. "I didn't know about it until right at the end, when I suspected the truth."

Korda said, "We had to go through with the trial. Otherwise, the whole world would have suspected the truth, and it's not ready for the truth. Not yet."

Denny closed his eyes and shook his head. "None of this makes sense to me," he said.

Hodgson said sympathetically, "Let's start at the beginning. Denny, you're a historian. When did the British revolution take place that took them from Feudalism to capitalism?"

"Why . . . why, not at one set date. It took place over a period of time, in the Nineteenth Century. Well, actually, part of it as far back as the Eighteenth Century, I suppose."

Hodgson was nodding. "And, in fact, remnants of feudalism continued far into the Twentieth Century—the House of Lords, the royal family, the old pageantry and traditions handed down from the past. But the fact was the real feudalism was no longer the socio-economic system of England. The king or queen was merely a pleasant figurehead, a symbol. The House of Lords was a debating society, without power."

"What in Zen has all this got—"

Hodgson waved him to silence. "The point is that a well-handled revolution can take place so easily, so gently, that many do not realize it has happened. Such, of course, is the desirable way. Denny, the Uppers haven't been in power in the West-world for the last five years or more. They've been eliminated as a factor in the real government."

"Are you insane! The president is an Upper-Upper. The Commissioner of the Bureau of Investigation, your chief, is an Upper-Upper—"

Joe Mauser chuckled.

Denny spun on him.

Mauser said, amused, "You've met Seymour Gatling. Did you really think that ineffective molly was head executive of the West-world?"

Zoltan Korda said to Yuri Malyshev, "Nor has the Party been in power in the Sov-world for some time, Colonel Malyshev."

"Number One—" Malyshev blurted.

"Is a cow," Korda said contemptuously.

Hodgson said, "Let's get back to it—Denny, Colonel Malyshev. In the past, most revolutions were put over by enraged majorities, in mutiny against what they considered a parasitic, oppressive ruling minority. The masses revolted out of desperation. But today there is no desperation in either the West-world or the Sov-world. The third industrial revolution, with its automation and other techniques, has solved the problem of production of abundance. There is no starving lower class."

"Man doesn't live by bread alone," Denny muttered.

Hodgson snorted. "You'd be surprised how many

do, if you mean that man doesn't live by material things alone. The slob element of society needs no spiritual aims to achieve its version of happiness. Bread and circuses will do it. Telly, trank, and the freeloading, self-perpetuating guarantees of the Welfare State will do it. Your slob element is happy with things as they are, Denny.

"One of the things most social critics, from Karl Marx to the latest current sob-sister, overlook is the fact that slobs who know nothing else but living like slobs will defend their way of life. Put slobs who have been trained as such from birth into a brand-new, pristine housing project, complete with conditioned environment, built-in garbage disposal incinerators, walls of ezykleen plastic that won't hold dirt and can't be smeared because nothing will stick . . . and they'll sweat till they find a way of getting that confounded ezykleen" —Hodgson's voice took on an attempt to speak like a Low-Lower—"affen the walls so they can write somethin' when they wanna. They want to live in homey, slobbish surroundings, and will work to achieve it. The slob is not afraid of starvation; he knows that it will always be somebody else that starves, because he knows how to take care of himself, see. He's not afraid of the collapse of civilization, because he knows how to care for himself, awright. He's not afraid of any catastrophe, because it can't affect a man like *him*. An' anyway, if things bust up, by God he'll get some of the things that's been owin' him for a long time anyhow, so he ain't scared. And moreover, he really isn't, and really never will be, because he will learn to be afraid of the future only during the impossible moment that he is in the process of dying."

Zoltan Korda had been nodding his agreement, once or twice chuckling at Hodgson's examples. Now he said, "You make one error, my friend. Don't subscribe to the common conception of Marx as a misguided do-gooder."

He chuckled dryly. "Misguided yes, do-gooder no! Marx was aware of the slob element, and its usefulness in maintaining social structures. He called them the *lumpen* proletariat and was as contemptuous as you, expecting them to line up with the reaction in the time of crisis. A good many people have a hazy picture of both Marx and Engles. They thought of themselves as scientists attempting to apply the scientific method in studying political economy. The question of good or bad didn't enter into it. The terms are nonsense, given the scientific approach. And their 'work' was nonsense."

Hodgson said wryly, "Be that as it may, I am sure that your Karl Marx never dreamed of a time when fully ninety percent of society had become his *lumpen* proletariat."

Denny put in heatedly, "You both seem to forget that these people are products of our present society, they didn't cause it! Take a healthy child out of any of these slob families, or lumpen proletariat families, as you call them, and on the day of his birth switch him with a Mid-Middle child. You'll find that when he grows to the age of twenty, he'll be as intellectual as you, and the Mid-Middle child who was substituted for him will grow up a slob."

Hodgson chuckled. "All right. Let us hope you

are entirely correct, that it is environment that makes the slob, not the genes with which he was born.

"Our problem, however, is not changed. The slob we have always had. But the growth of our modern socio-economic system, the Welfare State, has fertilized his growth, you might say, until he numerically dominates."

The bureaucrat looked at Zoltan Korda. "The proletariat, the slob, will line up with the reaction in time of crisis. He *likes* being a slob, I repeat. He loves doing nothing and receiving his food, clothing, shelter, and medical care for free. It's not the first time this has happened in history. Have you ever read of Tiberius and Cais Gracchus? At roughly the time of the war with Carthage, these two highly intelligent Romans became aware of what was happening to the populus—and were appalled. The very wealthy were taking over the lands and turning the average Roman citizen into a pauper who had to be fed by the State. The Gracchi brothers attempted to initiate changes to turn their fellow citizens back into men. Denny, you're our historian. What was the final destiny of the Gracchi?"

Denny said slowly, "They were killed by a mob. Their opposition promised the Roman proletariat even greater reforms, more free handouts—more bread and bigger circuses, I suppose. And the mob killed the Gracchi."

Hodgson said, "Very well. There is your mistake, Denny. And Bette's. Suppose you had been successful in making your Sons of Liberty strong enough to contest the Welfare State, stand up against the caste system, call for the overthrow of the Uppers? Where do you think the Lowers would have stood in the time of crisis?"

Dennis Land's face was working. "What do you offer as an alternative? What's this nonsense about the revolution having taken place five years ago?"

Hodgson nodded. "The changes we made, and are making, are not easy ones, admittedly. The problem of bringing the concept of a free and democratic society back to reality, and getting the world out of its rut and back on the path to man's destiny—whatever that may be—is a large one. It must be accomplished in the face of opposition from both the slob element, our Lowers, and the degenerated hereditary aristocracy that supposedly heads the country—the Uppers. And it must be accomplished subtly.

"We of the Middle caste, a considerable percentage of whom are not familiar with what is going on, are slowly taking the steps necessary to change our stratified socio-economic system. In the past, the small Upper caste recruited new blood from the other caste levels when a man of outstanding ability turned up, to maintain the strength of the blood line, as it were. We've ended that. No one's been jumped to Upper in more than three years. We'll allow a really capable man to run up his caste level as high as Upper-Middle, but no higher.

"We deliberately see that the inadequate are put into such positions as President, or, a closer example, into such jobs as Commissioner of the Bureau of Investigation. Willard Gatling, my supposed superior, is a cloddy. I am the actual head of the bureau. Increasingly, we encourage the Uppers not to work at all, not even to hold honorary offices. We encourage them to look upon any useful work as below them. They find it easy, convenient, to suck upon their mescaltranc and live in a dream world. Parasites? Perhaps, but in the present world it makes little difference, production being what it is. In short, 'Sweet Dreams, Sweet Princes.'"

"How about the Lowers?" Denny demanded. "The slobs that you are so contemptuous of?"

Hodgson nodded. "That is admittedly our greatest problem. This is the bulk of our population and must be stirred out of the rut. Already, we seek among them those who have basic abilities but are being ruined by their environment, and manipulate matters so that they are thrust into positions of responsibility—and challenge." He paused and eyed Denny carefully. "In much the same manner, in fact, that we manipulated your ousting from the University and, later, your reinstatement and Updike's removal.

"One of our more ambitious steps will begin next week. We're going to revive the civilian space program. To the extent we can, we will let the fracases and gladiatorial meets fall off, and propagandize the glory of man's conquest of space. We'll make heroes of our spacemen, and the scientists and technicians that construct their equipment, and we'll make every effort to downgrade the gladiator and mercenary in the eyes of our youth. We'll build a desire for schooling—"

Denny was shaking his head. "It's not enough. You're moving too slowly."

Hodgson said wryly, "Aside from the need to move in a subtle manner, one of the major reasons for lack of speed is our lack of competent personnel— dedicated, ah, revolutionists to help in the work. Very well, when one is spotted, we recruit him. As we did Dr. Fitzgerald, formerly head of the Sons of Liberty. As we did Bette Yardborough. And now you."

Denny sank back into his chair, his thoughts racing beyond his ability to assimilate them.

Yuri Malyshev had remained quiet, taking in all that was said. Now he looked at Zoltan Korda.

Korda fished in his pockets, brought out a cigarette case. Even as he lit a new one off the old, he said "Our situation is similar, Yuri. We have introduced mescaltranc, to keep the Party members in a happy daze. We have even encouraged the new fad against children, which has swept Party society. Long since we made Party membership hereditary so new and fresh blood would not be introduced. So in our case, it is a matter of 'Sweet Dreams, Sweet Commissars.' "

His eyes burned into those of his subordinate. "And, as you undoubtedly are aware by now, the goal for which we strive is not to return to the program of the Old Bolsheviks. Their program held no merit in the early part of the Twentieth Century, in the backward Russia of that day, and it most certainly holds no meaning whatsoever in the modern Sov-world. No, we face much the same set of problems as the West-world. And I rather suspect that the plan to get the conquest of space into the hearts of the race, once again, is a valid one. I will recommend it upon our return."

Dennis Land was looking from Korda to Hodgson and back. "Then actually, below the surface, there is considerable cooperation between West-world and Sov-world?"

"Considerable," Hodgson told him. "Unfortunately, so traditional is our enmity that we are having to break it to our Lowers, and to their Proletarians, gently and over a period of time."

Denny leaned forward. "Yes, but how about Common Europe? The danger to peace is still there."

The door opened and Andre Condrieu entered. He looked about the room, and the supposed right-hand man of The Gaulle said, "*Mademoiselle, Messieurs,* I am sorry. Is it that I am late to participate in the welcoming of the so-charming Mademoiselle Yardborough and Professor Land and Colonel Malyshev to our ranks?"

Here is an excerpt from the newest novel by Martin Caidin, to be published in September 1986 by Baen Books:

MARTIN CAIDIN

ZOBOA

The senior officer on duty on the flight line of Guantanamo Air Base on the southern coastline of Cuba checked the time, made a notation on his clipboard, and lifted his head as a buzzer affixed to his ear rattled his skull. He turned. They were right on time. Captain Jeff Baumbach moved his hand more by reflex than directed thought to check the .357 Magnum on his hip. He gestured at the armored vehicle slowing at the gate, its every movement covered by heavy automatic cannon.

"Check 'em *all* out!" Baumbach called. Military Police motioned the truck in between heavy barricades until it was secured. They checked the identity passes of every man, went through, atop and beneath the vehicle, finally sent it through the final barricade to the flight line where two machine gun-armed jeeps rolled alongside as escort. The armored truck stopped by an old Convair 440 twin-engined transport with bright lettering on each side of its fuselage. The cargo doors of the transport of ST. THOMAS ORCHARD FARMS opened wide. The crew wore Air Force fatigues and all carried sidearms.

A master sergeant studied the truck and the men. "Move it, move it," he said impatiently. "Load 'em up. We're behind schedule."

Four cases moved with exquisite care from the truck to the loading conveyor to the aircraft. Each case carried the same identifying line but differing serial numbers. It didn't really matter. NUCLEAR WEAPON MARK 62 is enough of a grabber without any silly serial number.

The bombs were loaded and secured with steel cabling and heavy webbing tiedowns, men signed their names and exchanged papers, doors slammed closed, and the right engine of the Convair whined as the pilots brought power to the metal bird. . . .

In central Florida, horses moved through the tall morning-wet grass of a remote field. It is an ordinary scene of an ordinary Florida ranch . . . until the trees and the fences begin to move.

Tractors pulled the trees, tugging with steel cables to move the wheeled dollies from the soft ground. Pickup trucks and jeeps latched on to fence ends and moved slowly to swing the fences at enormous hinges. Within minutes a clear path seven thousand feet from north to south had been created, and the whine of machinery sounded over the staccato beating of equine hooves. Men kept the animals clear of field center, where high grass moved as if by magic to reveal an asphalted airstrip beneath. Still invisible to any eye, powerful jet engines rose from a deep-throated whine to ear-twisting shrieks and the cry of acetylene torches. Shouting male voices diminish to feeble cries in the rising crescendo of power, and workers move hastily aside as the front of a hill disappears into the ground and two jet fighters roll forward slowly, bobbing on their nose gear.

"Sir, they're loading now," the controller tells the lead pilot, knowing the second man also listens. "Are you ready to copy? I have their time hack for takeoff and the stages for their route."

The man in the lead jet fighter responds in flawless Arabic. "Quickly; I copy. And do not speak English again." . . .

"Orchard One, you're clear to the active and clear for takeoff. Over."

Captain Jim Mattson pressed his yoke transmit button. "Ah, roger Gitmo Control. Orchard One clear for the active and rolling takeoff. Over."

"Orchard One, it's all yours. Over."

"Roger that, Gitmo. Orchard One is rolling." Mattson advanced the throttles steadily, his copilot, John Latimer, placing his left hand securely atop the knuckles of his pilot. The convair sped toward the ocean, lifted smoothly and began its long climbing turn over open water. . . .

The horses shied nervously with the relentless howl of the jet fighter engines. Everyone on the field waited for the right words to pass between the controller in his underground bunker on the side of the runway and the two men in the fighter cockpits. A headset in the lead fighter hummed.

"Control here."

"Go ahead."

"Your quarry is in the air. Confirm ready."

The pilots glanced at one another. "Allah One ready."

"Allah Two waits."

"Very good, sirs. Three minutes, sirs." . . .

They came out of the sun, silvery streaks trailing the unsuspecting shape of Orchard One. Their presence remained unknown until the instant a powerful electronic jammer in the rear cockpit of the lead T-33 broadcast its signal to overpower any electronics aboard the Convair. The shriek pierced the eardrums of the Convair's radioman and he ripped off his headset. In the cockpit, Captain John Latimer, flying right seat, mirrored the reaction to the icepick scream in their ears. Instinct brought Captain Jim Mattson's hands to the yoke. But the automatic pilot held true, and the Convair did not wave or tremble. Only the radio and electronics systems had seemingly gone mad. The flight engineer rushed to the cockpit, squeezed Mattson's shoulder, and shouted to him. "Sir! To our left! There!"

They looked out to see the all-black fighter with Arabic lettering on the fuselage and tail. The pilot's face was concealed behind an oxygen mask and goldfilm visor. "Who the hell is that?" Mattson wondered aloud, and in the same breath turned to Latimer. "You all right?"

Latimer sat back, shaking his head to clear the battering echoes in his brain. He nodded. "Yeah, sure; fine. What the hell was that?"

The radioman wailed painfully into the flight deck with them, his face furrowed in pain. "Jamming . . . somehow they're jamming us. They must have, God, I don't know . . . but I can't get out on anything."

They exchanged glances. Not a single word was needed to confirm that they were in deep shit. Nobody shows up in a black T-33 jet fighter with Arabic markings and knocks out all radio frequencies unless they're a nasty crowd with killing on their minds. Mattson instantly became the professional military pilot.

"Emergency beacon?"

"No joy, sir. Blocked."

"Anybody see more than one fighter out—"

The answer came in a hammering vibration that blurred their sight. The Convair yawed sharply to the right as metal exploded far out on the right wing. "There's another one out there, all right!" Latimer shouted. "He just shot the hell out of the wing! He's coming alongside—"

They watched the black fighter slide into perfect formation to their right and just above their mangled wingtip. His dive brake extended. The pilot pointed down with his forefinger and then his landing gear extended.

"Jesus Christ!" Latimer exclaimed. "He's ordered us to land!"

"Screw that," Mattson snarled. "Sparks! Get Patrick Control and tell them we're under attack. We need—"

"Sir, goddamnit! I can't get out on any frequency!"

Glowing tracers lashed the air before the Convair. The T-33 on their left had eased back and above to give them another warning burst. They looked out at the fighter to their right. The pilot tapped his left wrist to signify his watch, then drew a finger across his throat.

SEPTEMBER 1986 • 65588-4 • 448 pp. • $3.50

To order any Baen Book by mail, send the cover price plus 75¢ for first-class postage and handling to: Baen Books, Dept. BA, 260 Fifth Avenue, New York, N.Y. 10001.

Here is an excerpt from Charles Sheffield's newest novel, The Nimrod Hunt, *to be published in August 1986 by Baen Books:*

THE·NIMROD·HUNT

CHARLES SHEFFIELD

They were close to a branch point, where the descending shaft divided to continue as a double descent path. He had not seen that before, or heard of it in any of the records left by Team Alpha. It suggested a system of pathways through Travancore's jungles more complicated than they had realized. Chan looked again at S'greela and Shikari. They were both still engrossed in the Angel's efforts. He strolled slowly down along the sloping tunnel and looked out along each branch in turn.

They were not identical. One continued steadily down towards the surface of Travancore, five kilometers below them. The other was narrower and less steep. It curved off slowly to the left with hardly any gradient at all. If it went on like that the narrow corridor would provide a horizontal roadway through the high forest. Chan took just three or four paces along it. He did not intend to lose sight of the other team members.

After three steps he paused, very confused. There seemed to be something like a dark mist obscuring the more distant parts of the corridor. He shone his light, and there was no answering reflection.

Chan hesitated for a moment, then started to move back up the tunnel. Whatever it was in front of him, he was not about to face it alone. He had weapons with him—but more than those he wanted S'greela's strength, Shikari's mobility, and Angel's cool reasoning powers.

As he turned, he heard a whisper behind him. "Chan!"

He looked back. Something had stepped forward from the middle of the dark tunnel. He froze.

It was Leah.

Even as Chan was about to call out to her, he remembered Mondrian's warning. *Leah was dead.* What he was seeing was an illusion, something created in his mind by Nimrod.

As though to confirm his thought, the figure of Leah drifted *upwards* like a pale ghost. It hung unsupported, a couple of feet above the floor of the tunnel. The shape raised one white arm. "Chan," it said again.

"Leah! Is it you—really you?" Chan fought back the sudden urge to run forward and embrace the hovering form in front of him.

It did not seem to have heard him. Chan saw the dark-haired head move slowly from side to side. "Not now, Chan," said Leah's voice. "It would be too dangerous now. Say goodbye—but love me, Chan. Love is the secret."

Ignoring all common sense, Chan found that he had taken another step along the tunnel. He paused, dizzy and irresolute.

The figure held up both arms urgently. "Not now, Chan. Dangerous."

She waved. The slim form stepped sharply backwards, and was swallowed up at once in the dark cloud. The apparition was gone.

Chan stood motionless, too stunned to move. At last a sudden premonition of great danger conquered his inertia. He turned and began to stagger and stumble back towards the others. A voice inside his head was screaming at him. *"NIMROD. Nimrod is active here. A Morgan Construct can produce delusions within an organic brain—it can change what you see and hear. Get back to the others—NOW!"*

He was suddenly back in the part of the tunnel where he had left the other team members. It was totally deserted.

They were gone! To his horror and dismay, there was no sign of the rest of them. *Where was the team?* Surely they would not have left him behind and gone back up the tunnel without him. Had they fallen victim to Nimrod?

Dizzy with fear, emotion, and unanswerable questions, Chan began to run back up the tunnel, back to the sunlight, back to the doubtful safety of the cetent in the upper vegetation layers. As he did so, the face and form of Leah hovered shimmering before his eyes.

AUGUST 1986 • 65582-6 • 416 pp. • $3.50

To order any Baen Book by mail, send the cover price plus 75¢ to cover first-class postage and handling to: Baen Books, Dept. BA, 260 Fifth Avenue, New York, N.Y. 10001.

Here is an excerpt from Book I of THE KING OF YS, Poul and Karen Anderson's epic new fantasy, coming from Baen Books in December 1986:

THE KING OF YS: ROMA MATER
POUL AND KAREN ANDERSON

The parties met nearer the shaw than the city. They halted a few feet apart. For a space there was stillness, save for the wind.

The man in front was a Gaul, Gratillonius judged. He was huge, would stand a head above the centurion when they were both on the ground, with a breadth of shoulder and thickness of chest that made him look squat. His paunch simply added to the sense of bear strength. His face was broad, ruddy, veins broken in the flattish nose, a scar zigzagging across the brow ridges that shelved small ice-blue eyes. Hair knotted into a queue, beard abristle to the shaggy breast, were brown, and had not been washed for a long while. His loose-fitting shirt and close-fitting breeches were equally soiled. At his hip he kept a knife, and slung across his back was a sword more than a yard in length. A fine golden chain hung around his neck, but what it bore lay hidden beneath the shirt.

"Romans," he rumbled in Osismian. "What the pox brings you mucking around here?"

The centurion replied carefully, as best he was able in the same language: "Greeting. I hight Gaius Valerius Gratillonius, come in peace and good will as the new prefect of Rome in Ys. Fain would I meet with your leaders."

Meanwhile he surveyed those behind. Half a dozen were men of varying ages, in neat and clean versions of the same garb, unarmed. Nearest the Gaul stood one who differed. He was ponderous of body and countenance. Black beard and receding hair were flecked with white, though he did not seem old. He wore a crimson robe patterned with gold thread, a miter of the same stuff, a talisman hanging on his bosom that was in the form of a wheel, cast in precious metal and set with jewels. Rings sparkled on both hands. In his right he bore a staff as high as himself, topped by a silver representation of a boar's head.

The woman numbered three. They were in ankle-length gowns with loose sleeves to the wrists, of rich material and subtle hues, ornately belted at the waist.

The Gaul's voice yanked him from his inspection: "What? You'd strut in out of nowhere and fart your orders at *me*—you who can talk no better than a frog? Go back before I step on the lot of you."

"I think you are drunk," Gratillonius said truthfully.

"Not too full of wine to piss you out, Roman!" the other bawled.

Gratillonius forced coolness upon himself. "Who here is civilized?" he asked in Latin.

The man in the red robe stepped forward. "Sir, we request you to kindly overlook the mood of the King," he responded in the same tongue, accented but fairly fluent. "His vigil ended at dawn today, but these his Queens sent word for us to wait. I formally attended him to and from the Wood, you see. Only in this past hour was I bidden to come."

The man shrugged and smiled. My name is Soren Cartagi, Speaker for Taranis."

The Gaul turned on him, grabbed him by his garment and shook him. "You'd undercut me, plotting in Roman, would you?" he grated. A fist drew back. "Well, I've not forgotten all of it. I know when a scheme's afoot against me. And I know you think Colconor is stupid, but you've a nasty surprise coming to you, potgut!"

The male attendants showed horror. One of the woman hurried forth. "Are you possessed, Colconor?" she demanded. "Soren's person when he speaks for the God is sacred. Let him go ere Taranis blasts you to a cinder!"

The language she used was neither Latin nor Osismian. Melodious, it seemed essentially Celtic, but full of words and constructions Gratillonius had never encountered before. It must be the language of Ys. By listening hard and straining his wits, he got the drift if not the full meaning.

The Gaul released the Speaker, who stumbled back, and rounded on the woman. She stood defiant— tall, lean, her hatchet features haggard but her eyes like great, lustrous pools of darkness. The cowl, fallen down in her hasty movement, revealed a mane of black hair, loosely gathered under a fillet, through the middle of which ran a white streak. Gratillonius sensed implacable hatred as she went on: "Five years have we endured you, Colconor, and weary years they were. If now you'd fain bring your doom on yourself, oh, be very welcome."

Rage reddened him the more. "Ah, so that's your game, Vindilis, my pet?" His own Ysan was easier for Gratillonius to follow, being heavily Osismianized. " 'Twas sweet enough you were this threenight agone, and today. But inwardly—Ah, I should have known. You were ever more man than woman, Vindilis, and hex more than either."

He swung on Gratillonius. "Go, Roman!" he roared. "I am the King! By the iron rod of Taranis, I'll not take Roman orders! Go or stay; but if you stay, 'twill be on the dungheap where I'll toss your carcass!"

Gratillonius fought for self-control. Despite Colconor's behavior, he was dimly surprised at his instant, lightning-sharp hatred for the man. "I have prior orders," he answered, as steadily as he could. To Soren, in Latin: "Sir, can't you stay this madman so we can talk in quiet?"

Colconor understood. "Madman, be I?" he shrieked. "Why, *you* were shit out of your harlot mother's arse, where your donkey father begot you ere they gelded him. Back to your swinesty of a Rome!"

It flared in Gratillonius. His vinestaff was tucked at his saddlebow. He snatched it forth, leaned down, and gave Colconor a cut across the lips. Blood jumped from the wound.

Colconor leaped back and grabbed at his sword. The Ysan men flung themselves around him. Gratillonius heard Soren's resonant voice: "Nay, not here. It must be in the Wood, the Wood." He sounded almost happy. The women stood aside. Vindilis put hands on hips, threw back her head, and laughed aloud.

Eppillus stepped to his centurion's shin, glanced up, and said anxiously, "Looks like a brawl, sir. We can handle it. Give the word, and we'll make sausage meat of that bastard."

Gratillonius shook his head. A presentiment was eldritch upon him. "No," he replied softly. "I think this is something I must do myself, or else lose the respect we'll need in Ys."

Colconor stopped struggling, left the group of men, and spat on the horse. "Well, will you challenge me?" he said. "I'll enjoy letting out your white blood."

"You'd fight me next!" yelled Adminius. He too had been quick in picking up something of the Gallic languages.

Colconor grinned. "Aye, aye. The lot of you. One at a time, though. Your chieftain first. And afterward I've a right to rest between bouts." He stared at the woman. "I'll spend those whiles with you three bitches, and you'll not like it, what I'll make you do." Turning, he swaggered back toward the grove.

Soren approached. "We are deeply sorry about

this," he said in Latin. "Far better that you be received as befits the envoy of Rome." A smile of sorts passed through his beard. "Well, later you shall be. I think Taranis wearies at last of this incarnation of His, and—the King of the Wood has powers, if he chooses to exercise them, beyond those of even a Roman prefect."

"I am to fight Colconor, then?" Gratillonius asked slowly.

Soren nodded. "In the Wood. To the death. On foot, though you may choose your weapons. There is an arsenal at the Lodge."

"I'm well supplied already." Gratillonius felt no fear. He had a task before him which he would carry out, or die; he did not expect to die.

He glanced back at the troubled faces of his men, briefly explained what was happening, and finished: "Keep discipline, boys. But don't worry. We'll still sleep in Ys tonight. Forward march!"...

It was but a few minutes to the site. A slate-flagged courtyard stood open along the road, flanked by three buildings. They were clearly ancient, long and low, of squared timbers and with shingle roofs. The two on the sides were painted black, one a stable, the other a storehouse. The third, at the end, was larger, and blood-red. It had a porch with intricately carven pillars.

In the middle of the court grew a giant oak. From the lowest of its newly leafing branches hung a brazen circular shield and a sledgehammer. Though the shield was much too big and heavy for combat, dents surrounded the boss, which showed a wildly bearded and maned human face. Behind the house, more oaks made a grove about seven hundred feet across and equally deep.

"Behold the Sacred Precinct," Soren intoned. "Dismount, stranger, and ring your challenge." After a moment he added quietly, "We need not lose time waiting for the marines and hounds. Neither of you will flee, nor let his opponent escape."

Gratillonius comprehended. He sprang to earth,

took hold of the hammer, smote the shield with his full strength. It rang, a bass note which sent echoes flying. Mute now, Eppillus gave him his military shield and took his cloak and crest before marshalling the soldiers in a meadow across the road.

Vindilis laid a hand on Gratillonius's arm. Never had he met so intense a gaze, out of such pallor, as from her. In a voice that shook, she whispered, "Avenge us, man. Set us free. Oh, rich shall be your reward."

It came to him, like a chill from the wind that soughed among the oaks, that his coming had been awaited. Yet how could she have known?

To order any Baen Book by mail, send the cover price plus 75 cents for first-class postage and handling to: Baen Books, Dept. B, 260 Fifth Avenue, New York, N.Y. 10001.

WE'RE LOOKING FOR
TROUBLE

Well, feedback, anyway. Baen Books endeavors to publish only the best in science fiction and fantasy—but we need you to tell us whether we're doing it right. Why not let us know? We'll award a Baen Books gift certificate worth $100 (plus a copy of our catalog) to the reader who best tells us what he or she likes about Baen Books—and where we could do better. We reserve the right to quote any or all of you. Contest closes December 31, 1987. All letters should be addressed to Baen Books, 260 Fifth Avenue, New York, N.Y. 10001.

At the same time, ask about the Baen Book Club—buy five books, get another five free! For information, send a self-addressed, stamped envelope. For a copy of our catalog, enclose one dollar as well.